GREENER PASTURES

What Reviewers Say About Aurora Rey's Work

You Again

"*You Again* is a wonderful, feel good, low angst read with beautiful and intelligent characters that will melt your heart, and an enchanting second-chance love story."—*Rainbow Reflections*

Twice Shy

"[A] tender, foodie romance about a pair of middle aged lesbians who find partners in each other and rediscover themselves along the way. ...Rey's cute, occasionally steamy, romance reminds readers of the giddy intensity falling in love brings at any age, even as the characters negotiate the particular complexities of dating in midlife— meeting the children, dealing with exes, and revealing emotional scars. This queer love story is as sweet and light as one of Bake My Day's famous cream puffs."—*Publishers Weekly*

"This book is all the reasons why I love Aurora Rey's writing. It's delicious with a good helping of sexy. It was a nice change to read a book where the women were not in their late 20s–30s..." —*Les Rêveur*

The Last Place You Look

"This book is the perfect book to kick your feet up, relax with a glass of wine and enjoy. I'm a big Aurora Rey fan because her deliciously engaging books feature strong women who fall for sweet butch women. It's a winning recipe."—*Les Rêveur*

"The romance is satisfying and full-bodied, with each character learning how to achieve her own goals and still be part of a couple. A heartwarming story of two lovers learning to move past their fears and commit to a shared future."—*Kirkus Reviews*

"[A] sex-positive, body-positive love story. With its warm atmosphere and sweet characters, *The Last Place You Look* is a fluffy LGBTQ+ romance about finding a second chance at love where you least expect it."—*Foreword Reviews*

Ice on Wheels—*Novella in* Hot Ice

"I liked how Brooke was so attracted to Riley despite the massive grudge she had. No matter how nice or charming Riley was, Brooke was dead set on hating her. A cute enemies to lovers story."—*Bookvark*

The Inn at Netherfield Green

"I really enjoyed this book but that's not surprising because it came from the pen of Aurora Rey. This is the kind of book you read while sitting by a warm fire with a Rosemary Gin and snuggly blanket."
—*Les Rêveur*

"[Aurora Rey] constantly delivers a well-written romance that has just the right blend of humour, engaging characters, chemistry and romance."—*C-Spot Reviews*

Lead Counsel—*Novella in* The Boss of Her

"*Lead Counsel* by Aurora Rey is a short and sweet second chance romance. Not only was this story paced well and a delight to sink into, but there's A++ good swearing in it and has lines like this that made me all swoony because of how beautifully they're crafted."
—*Lesbian Review*

Recipe for Love

"*Recipe for Love* by Aurora Rey is a gorgeous romance that's sure to delight any of the foodies out there. Be sure to keep snacks on hand when you're reading it, though, because this book will make you want to nibble on something!"—*Lesbian Review*

Autumn's Light—*Lambda Literary Award Finalist*

"Aurora Rey has a knack for writing characters you care about and she never gives us the same pairing twice. Each character is always unique and fully fleshed out. Most of her pairings are butch/femme and her diversity in butch rep is so appreciated. This goes to prove the butch characters do not need to be one dimensional, nor do they all need to be rugged. Rey writes romances in which you can happily immerse yourself. They are gentle romances which are character driven."—*Lesbian Review*

"[*Autumn's Light*] was another fun addition to a great series."—Danielle Kimerer, Librarian (Nevins Memorial Library, Massachusetts)

"Aurora Rey has shown a mastery of evoking setting and this is especially evident in her Cape End romances set in Provincetown. I have loved this entire series…"—*Kitty Kat's Book Review Blog*

Spring's Wake

"[A] feel-good romance that would make a perfect beach read. The Provincetown B&B setting is richly painted, feeling both indulgent and cozy."—*RT Book Reviews*

"*Spring's Wake* has shot to number one in my age-gap romance favorites shelf."—*Les Rêveur*

"*Spring's Wake* by Aurora Rey is charming. This is the third story in Aurora Rey's Cape End romance series and every book gets better. Her stories are never the same twice and yet each one has a uniquely *her* flavour. The character work is strong and I find it exciting to see what she comes up with next."—*Lesbian Review*

Summer's Cove

"As expected in a small-town romance, *Summer's Cove* evokes a sunny, light-hearted atmosphere that matches its beach setting. …Emerson's shy pursuit of Darcy is sure to endear readers to her,

though some may be put off during the moments Darcy winds tightly to the point of rigidity. Darcy desires romance yet is unwilling to disrupt her son's life to have it, and you feel for Emerson when she endeavors to show how there's room in her heart for a family."
—*RT Book Reviews*

Crescent City Confidential—*Lambda Literary Award Finalist*

"*Crescent City Confidential* pulled me into the wonderful sights, sounds and smells of New Orleans. I was totally captivated by the city and the story of mystery writer Sam and her growing love for the place and for a certain lady. ...It was slow burning but romantic and sexy too. A mystery thrown into the mix really piqued my interest."
—*Kitty Kat's Book Review Blog*

"*Crescent City Confidential* is a sweet romance with a hint of thriller thrown in for good measure."—*Lesbian Review*

Built to Last

"Rey's frothy contemporary romance brings two women together to restore an ancient farmhouse in Ithaca, N.Y. ...[T]he women totally click in bed, as well as when they're poring over paint chips, and readers will enjoy finding out whether love conquers all."
—*Publishers Weekly*

Winter's Harbor

"This is the story of Lia and Alex and the beautifully romantic and sexy tale of a winter in Provincetown, a seaside holiday haven. A collection of interesting characters, well-fleshed out, as well as a gorgeous setting make for a great read."—*Inked Rainbow Reads*

"One of my all time favourite Lesbian romance novels and probably the most reread book on my Kindle. ...Absolutely love this debut novel by Aurora Rey and couldn't put the book down from the moment the main protagonists meet. *Winter's Harbor* was written beautifully and it was full of heart. Unequivocally 5 stars."—*Les Rêveur*

By the Author

Cape End Romances:

Winter's Harbor

Summer's Cove

Spring's Wake

Autumn's Light

Built to Last

Crescent City Confidential

Lead Counsel (Novella in The Boss of Her)

Recipe for Love: A Farm-to-Table Romance

The Inn at Netherfield Green

Ice on Wheels (Novella in Hot Ice)

The Last Place You Look

Twice Shy

You Again

Follow Her Lead (Novella in Opposites Attract)

A Convenient Arrangement (with Jaime Clevenger)

Love, Accidentally (with Jaime Clevenger)

Greener Pastures

Greener Pastures

by
Aurora Rey

2022

ISBN 13: 978-1-63679-116-6

This Trade Paperback Original Is Published By
Bold Strokes Books, Inc.
P.O. Box 249
Valley Falls, NY 12185

First Edition: April 2022

Credits
Editors: Ashley Tillman and Cindy Cresap
Production Design: Susan Ramundo
Cover Design By Jeanine Henning

Acknowledgments

Several years ago, Sandy Lowe planted the seed for a book in which a hapless femme finds herself taking care of a hobby farm, only to be rescued by a handsome butch with ulterior motives. It took some percolating, but I love the story that grew from that seed and will always be grateful for its planting.

After settling on a cider maker for Rowan's livelihood, I embarked on the requisite research and fell in love with the cider and the proprietors of Eve's Cidery. If you ever have the chance to meet Autumn and Ezra or to sample the gorgeous ciders they produce, I can't recommend either more highly.

And thanks as always to the usual suspects… Ashley and Cindy for the best editing in the world, Jaime and Leigh for beta reading, and everyone at Bold Strokes Books for running one hell of a company. And maybe most importantly, to everyone who reads these stories of mine. I'm so grateful you go on these adventures with me. Thank you from the bottom of my heart.

Dedication

For PN
Again and always

CHAPTER ONE

Rowan pulled into Ernestine's driveway and frowned. The BMW hardtop convertible parked next to Ernestine's Subaru belonged to no one she knew. Or cared to know, for that matter. She considered leaving, but she'd offered to unload several forty-pound bags of feed from Ernestine's car in exchange for a batch of lemon bars. While she wasn't one to leave a friend in a lurch, she also had a serious hankering for lemon bars.

She parked behind Ernestine's car instead of the mystery guest with the hope they were just leaving. She hadn't made it halfway to the back door when a voice she didn't recognize caught her attention.

"Nice chickens. Good chickens." Pause. "No. Bad chickens. That's not nice at all."

Unable to resist, she veered toward the chicken coop. No sign of Ernestine, but she found the owner of the voice. It belonged to a gorgeous woman she was sure she'd never met but who looked vaguely familiar. A woman who had somehow managed to scramble onto the roof of the chicken coop and now appeared to be stranded. "Hello?"

The woman jumped, clearly not expecting company. "Hi."

"You seem to be having a little bit of trouble."

"Whatever would give you that idea?" Her voice had that perky sarcasm thing going, but her eyes held legit panic.

She shouldn't make fun, but seriously, how could she not? "What seems to be the problem?"

The woman huffed. "I was trying to feed them, so I came in looking for a dish and they swarmed me."

"I see." Swarm was a bit of an overstatement. The dozen or so hens clucked with enthusiasm, flapping here and there as they jockeyed for position near their visitor.

The woman regarded her with pleading—and slightly exasperated—eyes. "Please tell me you speak chicken."

She was all about helping a damsel in distress. But something about this woman gave her pause. Maybe it was her attire—sleek black pants and a silky blue blouse with what appeared to be Ernestine's muck boots. And of course it wasn't any chicken coop. It was Ernestine's. The whole thing struck her as fishy. "I'm happy to help, but I'm not sure what exactly you're asking me to do."

The woman let go of the roof ridge but quickly thought better of the move, clasping it again with one hand. She used the free one to gesture frantically at the chickens below. "Can you shoo them or distract them or something so I can get out?"

She wouldn't really leave the woman to her own devices, for the sake of the chickens if nothing else. And rescuing her would hopefully lead to finding out who she was and what she was doing in Ernestine's yard. "I'll be right back."

She headed to the barn, ignoring the indignant questions about where she was going, and returned with a bucket of feed. She made a few tuts and clicks and tossed a handful of seed to the ground. In a matter of seconds, the girls abandoned their investigation of the newcomer and contentedly pecked the ground. The mystery woman moved slowly, as though not entirely trusting the new focus of their attention.

"Just give them a couple feet of space and they'll ignore you."

The woman heeded the advice and then some, skirting the flock as much as the fenced-in area would allow. She opened the gate just enough to squeeze through and latched it behind her. Rowan couldn't help but notice the loveliness of her shape but opted to keep that observation to herself, at least for now. The woman gave a full-body shudder before making eye contact. "Thank you."

It was hard to remain suspicious with a gorgeous smile and a pair of warm brown eyes focused on her. "My pleasure."

The woman stuck out her hand. "I'm Audrey."

The pieces clicked into place. Ernestine's niece—great-niece?—the fancy New York City accountant. The one that was practically her daughter but only visited a few times a year. Interesting. "Rowan."

"Uh…" Clearly, Audrey didn't know her from Adam.

"I'm Ernestine's neighbor."

"Oh. She's mentioned you, but I don't think I ever got your name. It's nice to meet you."

The unreserved enthusiasm in Audrey's voice now went a long way in smoothing over Rowan's first impressions. "Likewise. Are you okay?"

A shadow passed through Audrey's eyes. She opened her mouth but closed it again, as though rethinking what to say. She glanced at the house, then at the chickens behind her, before making eye contact again. "Ernestine had a stroke."

All the playful and flirty thoughts flitting through her mind vanished. In their place, a hollow sensation settled in the pit of her stomach. "Oh, no."

"Yeah."

"Is she okay?"

Again, Audrey seemed to consider what—or perhaps how much—to say. "Well, she made it through surgery. The doctors won't know the extent of the damage until she wakes up."

Rowan's stomach lurched at the possibilities. "Oh, that's awful. What can I do to help?"

"Hmm." Audrey looked her up and down. In any other circumstances, she'd read all sorts of delicious things into it. Now, it compelled her to make a case for herself.

"Ernestine talks about you enough that I know you're a city mouse." That seemed a more generous descriptor than pretty-but-clueless.

"She does?" Audrey's eyes narrowed for the briefest of moments before she closed them and shook her head. "Sorry. Not the point."

"The point is I'm no stranger to farm chores and I'm happy to lend a hand."

Audrey offered a tentative smile. "It's kind of you to offer."

She went for the gentle tease over the hard sell. "I mean, no disrespect, but based on how you fared with the chickens, I'm afraid to leave you alone with the goats."

Audrey blinked a couple of times and Rowan braced herself. But instead of a tirade, Audrey laughed. Like, really laughed. When it took on an almost manic quality, Rowan worried it teetered on the edge of crying. Audrey wiped her eyes, though, and sighed. "Sorry. I've been awake for way too many hours."

She took that to mean Audrey hadn't slept at all the night before. "How about you let me help with morning chores and then lie down for a while? You won't do Ernestine or anyone else any good if you're dead on your feet."

"Yeah."

She was glad to have Audrey concede, if reluctantly. "Great. Do you have a list or are you playing it by ear?"

Audrey pulled a piece of paper from her pocket. "I made a list of everything I could think of to pass the time while she was in surgery. I don't know how to do all of it, but I know it needs to be done."

The thought of Audrey all alone in some hospital waiting room, scribbling down farm chores she had no clue how to do, broke her heart a little. But she had a feeling saying so might snap Audrey's already frayed nerves. "I've helped out here and there. I'm sure, between the two of us, we'll figure it out."

"Thank you." Audrey sniffed, then smiled, seeming to will herself not to cry.

Rowan knew firsthand how that combination of stress and relief and fatigue could trigger a meltdown at the drop of a hat. Since she imagined Audrey wanted that even less than she did, she marched them both into the barn to get started. "So, chickens are all set."

That earned her an unguarded and totally adorable snort of laughter. "Yes."

"All the feed lives in here." Rowan flipped on the light in the small interior room. "Ernestine's fondness for her label maker will work to our advantage."

Audrey let out a sigh and a soft chuckle. "She loves that thing."

"The sheep and the goats get both feed and hay."

"Right." Audrey whipped out her phone and started typing. "Sorry. I'm just going to take notes. I don't trust myself to remember everything in my current state."

"Go right ahead. But I'm more than willing to come back, too. I'm right next door."

Audrey nodded at that but didn't say anything. Not in a dismissive way, exactly. More like her focus was exclusively on the task at hand. They fed the goats and sheep, then the barn cats. She estimated amounts and said as much. Audrey typed more things into her phone.

"They also need fresh water twice a day." She gestured to the hose.

"Right." Type type type.

It took effort not to laugh at Audrey taking notes on such an obvious thing, but at least she was eager to learn. "I can do it, so you don't mess up your nice clothes."

Audrey looked down. Her dark pants were smudged with dust and flecked with tiny pieces of hay. She returned her gaze to Rowan and tipped her head. "Oh, I think that ship has sailed."

It was the first hint that, under the frazzled nerves and uppity exterior, Audrey had a sense of humor. It made her instantly more likeable. Not to mention more attractive. "I was trying to be nice."

"You're being exceedingly nice, and I appreciate it." Audrey grabbed the nozzle end of the hose and dragged it to the trough in the sheep pen. She squeezed the trigger and, of course, nothing happened. She frowned.

"You have to turn it on first."

Audrey cringed. "Right."

The level of Audrey's cluelessness was kind of cute but also concerning. She had no idea how anything worked. Anything. It made Rowan wonder if she even stayed at the house when she visited. She'd gotten that impression from Ernestine, but maybe she'd been mistaken. "I got it."

She turned the old knob. The hose tension changed, but water dripped from the connection, too. She made a mental note to come over with a new rubber washer in the next couple of days. "Okay. You're good to go."

Audrey squeezed the trigger once again. She'd aimed for the trough, but the water came out with such force that at least half of it sprayed back at her. She squealed, sending both Scooby and Shaggy scrambling for the opposite end of their enclosure. "Sorry," she said, clearly to them.

Rowan couldn't suppress the laugh this time. "Here. Let me see."

Audrey handed over the hose like it had attacked her of its own volition. "Be my guest."

She clicked the setting wheel a few notches and pointed out the spray options to Audrey. "That should do it."

Audrey nodded and tried again, more cautiously than before. When the water came out at a reasonable rate, her shoulders relaxed. "Phew. Okay."

They managed to water the garden without incident and by the time they were done, she couldn't decide whether she felt sorry for Audrey or wanted to ask her out.

Audrey pulled out the list and scanned it. "That's everything I came up with."

As if on cue, Ernestine's old beagle mix came loping around the side of the house. "What about Matilda?"

Audrey regarded the dog with affection. "Fed her first thing. That, I know how to do."

Matilda let out a howl, though it was hard to tell whether in agreement or protest.

"What else can I do?"

Audrey looked around. "I think that's it, at least for now. I'm going to try to get a nap in before visiting hours and doing it all again."

The thought of this frazzled woman on the road, even after a nap, seemed like a less than stellar idea. If Rowan remembered correctly—that Audrey lived in New York City—it meant she'd already spent more time driving than sleeping in the last twenty-four hours. "Could I go with you? Offer to do the driving?"

Audrey's eyes narrowed. "Are you trying to be nice or hoping to visit Ernestine?"

She might tease Ernestine about being in it for the baked goods, but the truth of the matter was that Ernestine had become one of her closest friends. Family, almost, even if her own family lived close by. If Ernestine was in the hospital, she absolutely wanted to visit. She offered her most winning smile. "Yes."

She thought maybe Audrey would dismiss her, or at least put up a token protest. But instead, her features softened, making those brown eyes and already pretty face even more beautiful. "That sounds really nice. I'm not sure Ernestine will know you're there, but I'm sure she'd love to see you in theory."

She also wanted to do whatever it took to get that soft smile back on Audrey's lips. "Then it's settled."

"I want to shower and try to sleep a little, but I'm flexible on time."

"Same. How about you call me when you're up and we'll go from there? Give me your number and I'll text you so you have mine." Audrey didn't hesitate before rattling off a series of digits. It made Rowan wonder if she gave out her number often or it came with the territory of being rescued.

"So, I'll call you when I'm ready. Or text. Do you have a preference?" Audrey asked.

"Either is fine."

"Okay, thanks. And thanks for…earlier."

Rowan couldn't help but smile. "My pleasure."

Audrey's smile was almost shy this time. "I'm glad you stopped by when you did."

"Me, too. Oh."

"What?"

"You reminded me of why I stopped by in the first place." She angled her head. "I promised Ernestine I'd unload some heavy bags."

"You did?" Audrey sounded more charmed than surprised, which Rowan appreciated.

Rowan headed to the back of Ernestine's car and popped the hatch. "I trade heavy lifting for baked goods and I'm not ashamed to admit it."

Audrey laughed, a sexy and lovely sound Rowan instantly wanted to hear again. "I appreciate your honesty. Though, I don't have any baked goods to offer you."

"No worries. I'll take a rain check." She winked to make it extra obvious she was kidding and began moving the sacks of feed.

Audrey smirked. "I'll see what I can do."

"You really don't have to." Since Audrey had hefted a bag and followed her, she gestured to where it should go.

Audrey dropped the bag with an oof and wiped her hands on her now even dustier pants. "Seems like the least I can do. Besides, I know my way around a kitchen better than I do a barn."

She liked that Audrey could poke fun at herself, that she wasn't too uptight. And that she didn't seem afraid of a little work. "Well, I'm guessing you could use help over the next few days at least, so maybe we can work something out."

She'd meant it playfully, but Audrey's whole demeanor turned serious. "I am. I am going to need help."

It was as though the reality of her situation—of Ernestine's—only hit her in that moment. Rowan gave her hand a squeeze. "It'll be okay."

"Thank you." Audrey straightened her shoulders and gave a decisive nod. Like she realized she was talking to a virtual stranger more than she believed Rowan's assurances. "I'll call you this afternoon. Maybe between two and three?"

She thought of the work she'd slated for the afternoon, the things she could push off until tomorrow. "Like I said, I'm flexible."

"Okay." Another nod. A smile, too, though this one seemed more guarded than before. "I'll see you soon."

Audrey dragged her suitcase into the house, Matilda dutifully at her heels. She considered a snack, but the pull of a shower and bed proved stronger. It had been a very long, very intense twenty-four hours.

She glanced at her watch on her way upstairs. Just after eleven. This time yesterday, she'd been prepping the annual audit presentation for her biggest client and looking forward to the salmon Caesar salad her assistant had ordered her for lunch. And then her phone rang with a number she didn't recognize, and her world came crashing down.

Okay, maybe crashing down was a bit dramatic, but it felt like that in the moment. The absolute last news in the world she expected was that Aunt Ernestine had suffered a stroke. Because even though Ernestine was eighty-six, she had the energy of a woman half her age. And even though Audrey didn't truly believe it, she wasn't entirely kidding when she said Ernestine would outlive her, her parents, and pretty much everyone else.

The frantic few hours it had taken her to ensure things at work were covered, pack a bag, and get on the road were followed by the endless six hours it had taken to drive to Rochester. Only to find Ernestine still in surgery. She spent an hour badgering nurses and, eventually, a doctor for details. Other than the fact that Ernestine had made it to the hospital, that she'd survived the procedure to break apart the blood clot, there had been little in the way of good news.

She'd finally been allowed to see Ernestine in the wee hours of the morning. She held the hand of the woman who'd been more of a parent to her than her own parents ever were. She studied it, thinking for the first time in her life that it looked frail. The delicate bones and almost translucent skin belonged to an old woman. She'd never, not even in passing, thought of Ernestine as an old woman. When the nurses made it clear they'd bent the rules of the ICU long enough, they gently nudged her to go home, get some rest.

Home.

Such a simple concept but a slippery one, too. She'd never really felt at home in the houses of her childhood. Of course, they'd changed every few years as her parents hopscotched across the country in support of her father's scramble up the corporate ladder.

Ernestine's home in Rochester's Corn Hill neighborhood, where Ernestine lived for the entirety of her thirty-year teaching career, had been the closest thing. Until Ernestine retired and threw her life savings into a twenty-acre hobby farm in the Finger Lakes. Audrey had questioned the decision until she saw the unbridled joy Ernestine found in tilling her vegetable patch and tending her chickens and sheep. Not what she'd choose for her own retirement, not to mention a crap ton of work, but who was she to judge?

Audrey enjoyed visiting the farm, even if it never spoke to her in the way Ernestine's tidy Queen Anne in the city had. But for now, it was home. Home base at least. She had no idea what Ernestine's prognosis was or how long she would need to stay, but there was no chance she'd be back in her apartment in the Upper West Side anytime soon.

She stripped out of her day-old clothes and got halfway to the bathroom before changing her mind. A shower would jolt her out of the grogginess of napping, and it would be nonsensical to take two. She backtracked to the bedroom that was hers when she visited, wondering for the first time if Ernestine ever had guests besides her.

Like Rowan.

Silly. Rowan lived next door, so she obviously had no need for a guest room. But how often did she come over? She knew her way around pretty well. And her concern about Ernestine seemed to go beyond casual acquaintance. If she helped Ernestine even a fraction of the way she came to Audrey's rescue today—in the chicken coop but also with the other chores Audrey really had no idea how to do—she was a good friend as much as a good neighbor.

Not hard on the eyes, either. Between her tall, not quite lanky build and the combo of short blond hair and blue eyes, Rowan could be a model. A dreamy butch model for some kind of rugged, outdoorsy brand. Or a farm supply. Did farm supply companies have models?

Audrey pulled the covers back and climbed into bed, laughing at herself. She'd definitely crossed the line into overtired. She settled in and her body practically sighed with relief. She set her alarm for a couple of hours and closed her eyes. And overtired or not, it was Rowan's playful smile that carried her to sleep.

CHAPTER TWO

Huh? Wha?" Audrey lurched to a seated position. She scanned her surroundings, frantically attempting to get her bearings. Floral wallpaper, patchwork quilt, antique four-poster bed. Right.

It was the middle of the day. She was at Aunt Ernestine's. And Ernestine was in the hospital.

She rubbed her gritty eyes and ran her fingers through her hair a few times before reaching for her phone. Before she could unlock the screen, the alarm went off. Nice to know her internal clock worked even in such wonky circumstances. She shut the alarm off and checked her notifications. Several dozen work emails but nothing else.

Good. That was good. At this point, no news was good news.

She tossed the covers aside and padded to the bathroom. She'd just finished soaking her hair when she realized she forgot her toiletry bag. After squinting at her options, she shook her head and laughed. Ernestine wasn't a traditionalist, but she fell squarely in the camp of if it ain't broke, don't fix it. She squirted a blob of Alberto VO5 into her hand and worked her hair into a lather. She had no doubt of the frizz she'd fight later, but it didn't smell half bad.

Wrapped in one of Ernestine's fluffy, buttercup yellow towels, she studied her reflection while brushing her teeth. Less of a mess than before her nap, but that wasn't saying much. The dark smudges under her eyes made her already pale countenance almost ghostly. She spit, swished, then studied herself again. Nothing a little makeup couldn't hide.

She pieced together an outfit from the mishmash of clothes she'd stuffed in her suitcase and finished getting ready. Concealer proved the hero of the hour, barely beating out Alberto VO5. Damn it all if her hair didn't look fantastic.

Without the checklist of chores taking up the modicum of free space in her mind, she took in the details of the kitchen: a bowl of salad greens on the counter, a loaf of bread sitting on a cooling rack, and a plate of lemon bars with the box of plastic wrap still sitting out. It hit her that Ernestine had been home, going about her morning, only the day before. Maybe it should have been jarring, but she took comfort in it. Like Ernestine might walk in the door any moment with a basket full of eggs.

Although tempted by a lemon bar, she decided her stomach—not to mention the rest of her—would be better served by toast. She cut a couple of slices of bread and popped them in the toaster, then texted Rowan and rooted around in the fridge for the butter before remembering it lived on the counter. She slathered the first piece with way more than was necessary and let out a groan of pleasure at the first bite.

Funny how a nap and some clean clothes could make a girl realize she was starving.

She'd only just started the second piece when a truck rumbled down the driveway. Rowan really was the next-door neighbor. Audrey slung her purse over her shoulder and headed out, toast in one hand and plate of lemon bars in the other.

She walked to the driver's side door, prompting Rowan to put down her window. Rowan accepted the plate but gave her a questioning look. "Did you bake instead of nap?"

"No. I found these in the kitchen and figured they were for you. Ernestine must have finished them before…" She had this image of Ernestine happily puttering around the kitchen, experiencing the first signs of a stroke. The fear that must have gone into the decision to call 911. "You know."

Rowan nodded soberly. "Yeah."

She rounded the hood of the truck and climbed in, realizing it was even more beat up on the inside. Was Rowan a real farmer? That hadn't occurred to her. "Would you rather take my car?"

Rowan, who'd been studying the plate like she couldn't decide if it was rude to dive in, looked at her. "Would you rather take your car?"

It could have been a condescending tone, but it wasn't. Rowan seemed to genuinely defer to her comfort. Which, of course, made her feel like a heel. "I'm okay either way. It's just a bit of a drive, obviously. Mine probably gets better mileage."

"That would be great." Rowan set the plate on the dash and pulled forward, out of the way of Audrey's car. Audrey fished around in her purse and handed over her keys. Before taking them, Rowan freed a corner of the plastic wrap and snuck one of the lemon bars out. She tipped her head at Audrey.

Audrey smiled at the unspoken offer. "No, thank you."

Rowan shrugged and devoured hers in two bites.

"They are delicious. I'm just not sure my stomach can handle them at the moment."

Rowan offered her a reassuring smile. "It's going to be okay."

She wasn't at all sure it was but holding on to hope seemed like her best strategy. "Thanks."

They'd barely settled into the front seat of Audrey's car when Rowan let out a low whistle. She hit the button for the ignition and smiled when the engine purred to life. "Damn."

"It was my gift to myself for making senior associate."

Rowan nodded in general appreciation if not specific. "Nice."

Audrey cleared her throat and resisted the temptation to further explain or justify buying herself a nice car. "She's at Strong. Do you know how to get there?"

"My brother is at the U of R."

She'd gotten the impression Rowan was around her age—early to mid-thirties—but maybe she was wrong. "What's he studying?"

Rowan pulled out of the driveway and headed north. "Molecular biology."

The pride in Rowan's voice made her smile. "Impressive."

"Yeah. I wish I had half his brains." She chuckled. "Or half the looks of my sister who, for the record, is also pretty brainy."

"How many siblings do you have?" The only child side of her had genuine curiosity, but conversation would pass the time, too.

"Four of us altogether. I'm the oldest. My two sisters are only a couple of years younger than me, but then almost a decade between us and my brother."

"Ah." That explained that.

"Yeah. My parents thought they were done and then, surprise."

She knew that sort of thing happened. Her college roommate, for example, had come along when both her parents were forty. It made her wonder how her parents would have handled an unexpected pregnancy. If it was anything like the way they handled other surprises, not well. Like when she brought home the class hamster for Christmas vacation one year. Or when she came out. Or pretty much anytime she did anything not pre-arranged and pre-approved.

"You okay?"

"Oh. Sorry." She scrambled for an explanation that didn't sound like she needed a therapy session. "Just thinking it would be nice to have siblings."

"Only child?"

"Yes. No cousins, either."

"Is that why you and Ernestine are so close?"

Again, simple seemed like the way to go. "One of many reasons."

Rowan offered a reassuring smile. She made conversation as she drove, not filling every second, but asking questions and keeping Audrey's mind from fixating on the worry. The hour and a half passed in no time, leaving her to wonder if Rowan was a natural conversationalist or if she'd been trying to offer distraction.

At the hospital, Audrey took charge, guiding them through the maze of floors and halls and checking in at the nurses' station. Ernestine remained in intensive care. Her vitals were solid, but she'd yet to regain consciousness.

Per standard ICU policy, only one visitor was allowed at a time. Rowan insisted she go in and spend as much time as she wanted. She did, holding Ernestine's hand and telling her all about the morning hijinks at the farm. She included some teasing about the handsome neighbor and jokes about visiting more often for the eye candy.

She emerged just as the doctor arrived on rounds, so she and Rowan stood together in the hallway, getting essentially the same information she'd been given the day before. In addition to searching for answers that didn't exist, her mind did that of out-of-body thing. She imagined herself as the doctor, delivering somber news and vague reassurances to the two of them, just like the family before and the one that would come next. Did she wonder if they were a couple?

When the doctor left, Rowan asked, "Do you mind if I go in for a few minutes?"

She'd half expected Rowan to demur since Ernestine wasn't awake or able to carry on a conversation. The fact that Rowan wanted to see her anyway made Audrey's already wobbly heart melt a little. "Of course. Take your time."

While she waited, she resisted the urge to pace and reminded herself patience was a virtue. She managed about eight seconds before her brain kicked into planning and logistics. Which was fine. She was better at getting things done anyway.

She needed to check in with her boss, let her know where things stood. She had enough vacation and personal time accrued to buy her three weeks before needing to consider big decisions, and she'd already let Vera know she planned to use most if not all of what she had banked. There were plenty of unknowns, but that seemed like a certainty at this point. And somewhere along the way, Ernestine would wake up and they'd have wiggle room to plan for any long-term recovery or rehab she needed.

Until then, she'd take care of the farm so Ernestine wouldn't have to worry. It was a garden and some goats, right? Not rocket science. She didn't know what she was doing, but she'd learn. She'd learned plenty from Rowan already.

The memory of her attempt to feed the chickens played in her mind, making her wonder what Rowan must have thought finding her clinging to the roof of the chicken coop for dear life. She chuckled. She may not save the day, but she'd make do. Especially if Rowan kept showing up, offering her services for nothing more than a plate of cookies.

❖

Rowan pulled out of the garage, waving off the credit card Audrey held out at the payment kiosk. She wanted to offer words of encouragement but didn't know what to say that wouldn't come out as a platitude or something more optimistic than Ernestine's condition warranted. "Do you want to talk about it?"

"I don't know what there is to talk about." Audrey cringed and cleared her throat. "Sorry. I didn't mean to snap. I just, I guess I thought she'd be awake by now."

The doctor hadn't seemed overly worried about Ernestine's unconscious state, but she hadn't been overly encouraging, either. "You don't need to apologize. It's a stressful, sucky situation."

Audrey took a deep breath then let it out in a huff, dropping her shoulders at the same time. "It really is."

Since she couldn't change it, she decided to offer what she could instead. "How can I help?"

Audrey shifted in the passenger seat, tucking one foot under her and smiling for the first time since they got to the hospital. "You mean besides rescuing me from the chickens?"

She took Audrey's ability to joke—especially under these circumstances—as a good sign. "Well, needing to be rescued from the chickens was kind of my clue that you maybe could use a hand."

"Touché." Audrey looked her up and down. "You seem to know your way around the place. Are you and Ernestine close?"

The comment managed to be playful and penetrating at the same time. She weighed how much to disclose. Did Audrey know about her arrangement with Ernestine? Probably not, if Audrey didn't even know her name before today. She wasn't embarrassed or anything, but she didn't need to make the whole conversation about herself. "We've been neighbors for going on five years now. I wasn't kidding when I said I did heavy lifting for baked goods."

That got her a laugh, a real one. "It's kind of you."

"Eh? I'm pretty sure she invents chores for me so I don't feel guilty about how often she feeds me."

"How often does she feed you?"

What was that about being embarrassed? She went out of her way not to add up how many times per week she joined Ernestine for dinner or found a Tupperware of cookies on her porch. "Let's just say more often than a woman of my age and independence should admit to."

Audrey quirked a brow. "Are you helpless or lazy?"

"I prefer to think of it as a mutually beneficial arrangement." One that involved enjoying Ernestine's company as much as her culinary skills.

"Mm-hmm. Mm-hmm. How picky are you?"

"Picky?"

Audrey smirked. "If I'm going to have to cook for you, I need to know what I'm signing up for."

Audrey was obviously teasing her, but it didn't stop the flush from rising in her cheeks. "You don't have to cook for me."

"Fair's fair. I should warn you that my skills in the kitchen don't hold a candle to Ernestine's though."

Rowan tipped her head. "I'm pretty sure most Michelin-starred chefs don't hold a candle to Ernestine's skills in the kitchen."

"Ha. That's the truth." Audrey's expression turned serious. "I mean it, though. If you're going to help out, it's the least I can do."

She got the feeling Audrey needed to offer something in return, a trait she could appreciate. She could also appreciate having a reason to spend time together, not just doing chores around the farm but sharing a meal and some conversation. Despite the circumstances of their meeting, she found herself drawn to Audrey. "Only if you promise not to go to any extra trouble."

"Well, I have to cook for myself so I might as well share."

"Then I definitely won't argue."

Audrey shifted back in her seat and gazed out the window. Rowan longed to ease the worried look from her face but knew it came from things beyond her control. She settled for more distraction, asking about Ernestine and getting Audrey to share good memories. One particular story—about being stuck at Ernestine's in a blizzard and attempting to use a snowblower for the first time in her life—got her eyes sparkling and a genuine laugh out of her. Rowan did her best to ignore the flare of attraction, if for no other reason than it seemed wrong for her attention to be anywhere but on Ernestine.

When Rowan pulled into Ernestine's driveway, Audrey took a deep breath and turned to her with a smile. "Thank you for everything today."

Rowan smiled. "My pleasure."

Audrey shook her head. "You don't have to say that."

"I'm not just saying it." She really wasn't. Despite her initial impression—one that may have involved the word diva—she liked Audrey. And lending a hand while Ernestine remained in the hospital felt like the right thing to do.

Audrey narrowed her eyes. "I'm not sure I believe you. But I won't argue because I don't know how I would have managed the chores on my own."

"How about I'm happy to help?"

Audrey seemed to take that a little more easily. "Having company was nice, too, both for the drive and at the hospital."

She resisted the urge to reach for Audrey's hand—to reassure but also to share a moment of connection. "I probably can't swing that chunk of time every day, but I'd like to go with you when I can."

"Thanks. Hopefully, she'll wake up soon and we'll be able to sort out what comes next."

Audrey got out of the car, so Rowan did, too. She handed Audrey her keys. "In the meantime, don't hesitate to reach out, okay?"

Audrey nodded. "I will. And I'll plan to hit the store when I go up tomorrow so I can hold up my end of the bargain."

"Is that a dinner invitation?" It came out more forward than she intended, but Audrey either didn't notice or didn't mind.

"Seven too late?"

Well, that was easy. "Perfect."

Rowan offered a wave before getting into her truck and driving the short distance to her house. But instead of going inside, or across the street to the cidery, she wandered into the orchard that joined her property to Ernestine's. The apple blossoms had come late but made up for it with a truly spectacular display that lasted into the early part of June. Fruit had begun to form, and with the danger of frost finally past, it promised to be a good season. As long as she could stay on top of pests and blight and windstorms, of course.

She never failed to marvel at the beauty of it, the natural cycles of growth and harvest and rebirth, all dependent on the seasons more than any human strength of will or effort. Some days it felt like folly to hang her hopes and dreams—not to mention her financial security—on such an unstable thing. But growing apples and making cider was in her soul, and she honestly couldn't imagine doing anything else. Even if it left her parents in a state of permanent bewilderment.

She roamed the rows, enjoying the taste of early summer but also checking for signs of strain on the hundred-year-old trees. Had Audrey ever done that? Not the checking, obviously, but the appreciating. Her devotion to Ernestine was unquestionable, but Rowan struggled to get a handle on how much time she'd spent at the farm. Or if, when she did visit, she ventured out of the house much. She seemed eager to take care of things now, but between the chicken coop and Audrey's own admission, her knowledge and experience were essentially nil.

She was glad Audrey accepted her offer because it would be difficult to resist sweeping in to play knight in shining armor. Beautiful women were her kryptonite and Audrey fit the bill in spades. It was also the right thing to do for Ernestine. Even without the generous purchase agreement they'd ironed out, she owed Ernestine plenty. More, Ernestine had become family, offering a friendly ear, a home cooked meal, and a good stern talking-to when the situation warranted it.

She strode back to the little cottage she called home. After snagging a beer from the fridge, she grabbed a notebook and settled into her favorite rocking chair on the front porch. By the time the bottle was drained, she had a list of everything she could think of that needed tending at Ernestine's place, things beyond the daily chores. She couldn't make Ernestine better, but she could ensure things were in good shape for when Ernestine made it home. And if it managed to earn her a few points with the beautiful but unwitting apple of Ernestine's eye, well, that wouldn't be so bad either.

CHAPTER THREE

Audrey set her alarm for six but needn't have bothered. Ferdinand started crowing just after five and didn't let up. A myriad of birds joined in and any hope of more sleep evaporated. People griped about noise in the city, but the traffic outside her apartment had nothing on this.

She hauled herself out of bed, making a beeline for the coffee pot instead of the shower. Matilda sniffed her impatience, so Audrey abandoned that task to let her out. She'd barely managed to grind beans when Matilda returned. Another sniff. "Soon. I promise. Just let me get it started."

She got the old percolator going, got Matilda her breakfast, and considered drinking her coffee on the porch. Then she remembered she'd come downstairs wearing nothing more than a cami and a pair of boyshorts. She grumbled about inefficiency and backtracked to the bedroom to get dressed. After a disappointing survey of the clothes at her disposal, she selected a pair of jeans she could bear to part with and a tank top. If she borrowed one of Ernestine's flannels and work boots, that should do until she could buy some of her own.

Where did one buy farm clothes, anyway?

She made a mental note to ask Rowan and tamed her bedhead into a ponytail. After a quick brush of her teeth, she deemed herself presentable enough for the animals and headed back downstairs. Since the sun was shining already, and she was properly clothed, she decided to have her coffee on the porch after all.

Matilda joined her, settling onto the wide wood planks with a contented sigh. Audrey took a sip of coffee, closed her eyes, and let out a sigh of her own. There, that was better. If she had to be up and running around at this hour, she could at least be civilized about it.

"Good morning."

She sloshed her coffee, swore, then looked up to find Rowan offering her a sheepish smile.

"Sorry. I didn't mean to startle you."

Audrey waved a hand. "I just wasn't expecting anyone at this hour and I'm maybe not fully awake yet."

Rowan grinned and, awake or not, Audrey couldn't ignore how hot she looked in a pair of jeans and a blue Ithaca Beer T-shirt that matched her eyes. "I thought I'd stop by on my way to work. You know, earn my dinner."

She made a mental note to find out what Rowan did for a living. "That's nice of you. I hope you didn't get up extra early."

"No earlier than usual. Figured I'd check in here instead of puttering at my place."

Audrey shook her head. "I so wish I was a morning person."

"Spend a few months here and you might turn into one."

The comment was innocent enough, but it set her thoughts racing. What if Ernestine needed her here for months? She'd do it—no hesitation. What it meant for her life, not to mention Ernestine's, was another matter entirely. "I will in a few days if the rooster has anything to say about it."

"If it's any consolation, Ferdinand wakes me up most mornings, too."

She wouldn't say consolation, but it made her laugh. Like the country version of bonding with your neighbor about the weirdo down the hall. "I'm not sure if I should say thank you or sorry."

Rowan laughed. "Neither. Ferdinand and I made our peace."

With Rowan standing there looking ready to tackle the day, she sort of felt like she should jump off the porch and tromp to the barn, but she couldn't quite muster the momentum. "Would you like a cup of coffee?"

"I don't think I'd ever say no to coffee."

"A woman after my own heart. How do you take it?"

Rowan waved her off. "I can get it."

Right. Because Rowan spent more time here than she did. Rowan disappeared into the house, returning a minute later with a steaming cup. She gave Audrey an expectant look. Audrey closed one eye. "We don't get to sit and enjoy it, do we?"

"We can. I thought you might like to walk through the garden. I know most of what's growing."

And she didn't know peas from parsnips. Well, not the plants that grew them. Or if Ernestine grew either of those. "That would be great."

"And it's more hands-free than the animals. That way you can ease in."

She imagined a leisurely stroll to admire beautiful flowers and perfect vegetables just waiting to be picked but knew enough to know better. "Let me grab my phone so I can take pictures and notes."

Twenty minutes later, her cup was empty and her camera roll had at least a hundred new images. With the exception of early lettuce and spinach, nothing was even close to being ready to pick. More a relief than disappointment, really, since it meant all she needed to do was weed and water. Not her idea of a good time, but decidedly within her skill level.

Rowan walked her through feeding and watering the animals again. With the benefit of both a decent night's sleep and a whole cup of coffee, it felt a lot less daunting. She tweaked the notes in her phone and took more pictures—everything from the correct way to feed the chickens to letting the sheep out to graze. The goats were a new addition from the last time she'd visited, rescued from a bankrupt petting zoo. Ozzie and Harriet had big mouths and even bigger personalities. Audrey found herself equal parts intimidated and smitten. Well, smitten with their personalities. The amount of manure they seemed to produce? Not so much.

"I'll see you for dinner?" she asked when they'd finished.

Rowan smiled. "I'll be here."

Rowan left for work, wishing her luck with her first full day of farming. She smiled with more enthusiasm than she felt, then watered the vegetable patch before tackling the animal stalls. It took a good hour to muck them out and lay fresh bedding—enough time for the pungent aroma to seep into her clothes, her pores, and she'd swear her hair. Oof. People made fun of accountants, but give her a spreadsheet over a poop shovel any day. She told the goats as much before heading in for a shower and breakfast.

Though she usually had yogurt or a smoothie at her desk, she opted for an omelet and more toast. One, because she'd gathered the eggs and picked the spinach herself and it felt ridiculously satisfying. Two, because farming was hard work and she was famished.

On the drive up to Rochester, she imagined telling Ernestine about the things she'd learned and all the ways Rowan was helping out. Of reassuring Ernestine everything was safely in her committed, if not entirely capable, hands. She didn't need Ernestine to be proud of her, but she wanted her to feel like things were taken care of. She wanted Ernestine to be able to rest easy and focus on getting better. Mostly, though, she wanted Ernestine to wake up.

Rowan showered—because she always showered at the end of the workday, not because it was a date. Sure, thinking about whether or not it was a date in the first place might imply otherwise. As did the amount of time it took her to pick a clean shirt and pair of jeans from her closet.

Ridiculous? Yes. Did she still take a few extra minutes to work some product into her hair and style it just so? Also yes.

She stopped at the fridge on her way out for a bottle of cider. They'd released the first batch from last year's press, but it wasn't her absolute favorite. She snagged a bottle of the Russet from the year before—super dry but drinkable with almost anything. It was her favorite of that season, for its versatility as much as its flavor.

Since the evening promised to be cool, clear, and damn near perfect, she walked the quarter or so mile to Ernestine's house. The crickets hadn't started yet, but the frogs were in full force. The peepers had given way to the chirp and thrum of tree frogs, creating a chorus to accompany the red-wing blackbirds sending their final calls for the day.

She studied the spindly rows of her orchard on one side of the road and the stately branches of Ernestine's on the other. Old and new, tradition and innovation. It's what Forbidden Fruit was all about. Really, what she was all about.

She chuckled at the sentimental turn of her thoughts and picked up her pace, preferring to be a minute early over a minute late. Audrey answered the door in a wrap skirt and dark green tee with a deeply scooped neckline. Not dressy, exactly, but it made Rowan glad she'd put some effort into her appearance. Even if Audrey's look had more to do with going to town than having dinner with her. "Hi."

Audrey smiled. "Hi. I hope you didn't get all spiffed up for me."

Oh well. "More cleaned up than spiffed. It was a particularly dirty day at work."

"Was it? I have no idea what you do. You'll have to tell me all about it over dinner." Audrey took a step back. "Come on in."

She held out the bottle of cider and told herself not to be self-conscious. "For the record, I don't show up empty-handed when Ernestine makes dinner, either."

Audrey accepted the bottle and nodded her approval. "Noted."

"It's cold but we don't need to have it with dinner. If it doesn't go with what you made." She cleared her throat, failing epically at the not self-conscious bit. "Or if you don't drink."

"It's lovely. Thank you. And I think it will go better with what we're having than the chardonnay I have chilling."

She had no way of knowing if Audrey meant that or was merely being gracious, but she'd take it. "What are we having?"

"Nothing fancy. I roasted a chicken with some potatoes and the asparagus I picked this morning."

It might not be fancy, but it promised to be better than the rotisserie chicken that made up her dinner at least a couple nights a week. "Sounds delicious."

"You're easy." Audrey's tone was more teasing than critical.

"Yep." She followed Audrey to the kitchen and watched her putter around finishing the meal. She got the update on Ernestine—in a regular room and semi-awake, but not enough to talk or communicate at all really. Not enough to determine how much residual impairment she'd be facing. Audrey seemed more optimistic, though, so that lightened the mood.

"The doctor talked about moving her to a rehab facility in the next week."

"That's a good sign, right?" She tried to focus on that and not how difficult it might be for Ernestine to get back to the life she loved.

"Definitely. Still a lot of unknowns, but progress."

"Are you going to be able to stick around for a while or will you have to get back to your job?"

Audrey tipped her head from side to side. "I've got some time. My company doesn't hesitate to demand sixty hours a week, but the policies around sick time and family leave are generous."

Such a safety net would be nice, even if she wouldn't trade being her own boss to have it. "I think Ernestine mentioned you're an accountant?"

Audrey carved the chicken and arranged it on a platter. "I am. Super glamorous, right?"

"Depends. Do you have a collection of pocket protectors?"

"I do not." Audrey brought the remaining dishes to the table and pointed to the cider. "Would you open that for us?"

"Sure." She focused on the task and hoped the joke hadn't landed the wrong way.

Audrey took her seat. "I do have a designer laptop case, though, that I spent way too much money on. That might be the modern equivalent."

"If it brings you joy in your work, I have no doubt it was worth it." She'd made that exact argument to Dylan about the Japanese grafting knife she'd splurged on over the winter.

Audrey offered a playful bow. "Thank you."

"You do live in Manhattan, though. That seems pretty glamorous."

"I'm not sure about glamorous, but I like it." Audrey gestured to the food. "Help yourself."

She put a piece of chicken on her plate and probably more potatoes than was polite. "I don't think I could handle it. All that concrete, the traffic."

"I work in midtown and it's certainly the case there. But where I live is pretty quiet." She lifted a hand at Rowan's look of disbelief. "In relative terms at least. My whole street is lined with trees."

Yeah, growing from holes cut in the concrete. "Don't get me wrong. I love the restaurants and museums and stuff. But a few days once every year or two is plenty for me."

"I'm always trying to get Ernestine to visit, but she's the same way." Audrey's shrug seemed thoughtful rather than dismissive. She picked up her glass and took a sip. Rowan may have held her breath. "This is fantastic, by the way. Thank you for bringing it."

"I'm glad you like it." Glad, of course, being an understatement.

"So, what about you? What do you do?"

"I'm a cider maker." Five years in and it still gave her a rush to say it.

"Like, hard cider?"

She nodded. "Yep."

"Wait." Audrey gestured to her glass. "Is this yours?"

The surprise in Audrey's voice had Rowan's shoulders straightening with pride. "It is."

"Oh, wow. That's so cool. I know I said it was fantastic, but it really is fantastic."

"Thank you."

"Do you have your own orchard?"

She took a sip, glad she'd gone for the Russet. "Yes and no?"

Audrey set her elbow on the table and rested her chin on her fist. "What does that mean?"

"My partner and I planted five acres when we were starting out, so we have that, but they're just starting to produce, so we also source apples from other orchards in the area. We need the volume, but we also want the variety that comes from older and more diverse trees."

Audrey's eyes got big. "Do you buy Ernestine's apples?"

"I do."

Audrey nodded with enthusiasm. "I knew she had someone taking care of the orchard and managing the harvest. I hadn't put the pieces together."

She wasn't sure why, but Audrey knowing about the arrangement made her feel better. "Our production space is across the street and up a little ways. I bought my house shortly after to be close by and that's how Ernestine and I met."

"I remember how relieved she was to find someone to tend the trees and not just buy the apples once they were harvested."

"She's got some amazing heritage varieties. It's been a boon for us." A godsend, really.

"I love that."

She loved the way Audrey reached across the table and squeezed her hand. The way her eyes sparkled. And maybe more than anything, the way she seemed to appreciate the unlikely bond she and Ernestine had forged from what could have been a basic business arrangement. "I feel really lucky to have Ernestine. For so many reasons."

"You're not the only one." Audrey looked down for a second. When her gaze returned to Rowan, her eyes were glassy with tears. "She's going to be okay, right?"

Rowan wanted nothing more than to offer every reassurance. But the truth of the matter was she didn't know and pretending she did felt too close to lying for her comfort. "I hope so."

"Yes. Hope. Hope is good." Audrey nodded brusquely and picked up her glass. "Until then, I'm glad we're neighbors."

Neighbors. Accurate, even if it fell a little flat. She picked up her glass and lifted it. "To neighbors." Then, taking a chance, added, "And new friends."

Audrey's smile told her it wasn't too much. "New friends."

When they'd finished eating, Audrey let her clear the table but brushed off help with cleanup. She wrapped up the lion's share of the leftovers for Rowan to take home. "Ernestine would insist."

Since she would, Rowan didn't argue. She did, however, join Audrey for evening chores. They got the animals fed and tucked into their stalls for the night, made sure all the chickens were accounted for and safely secured in the coop.

She made the walk home as dusk set in. She let Jack out and gave him his dinner before stripping down to boxers and a T-shirt and putting on the Mets game. She let her body relax from the work of the day, let her mind wander. It didn't take long for her thoughts to turn to Audrey. She was pretty sure the spark of attraction wasn't entirely one-sided, even if the conversation hadn't carried them beyond friends and neighbors territory. No matter what she'd told herself beforehand, for an evening that absolutely wasn't a date, it sure as hell felt like one.

CHAPTER FOUR

Audrey pulled into the garage and tried to be patient as she trolled the levels for an open spot. She'd gotten a call from the hospital that Ernestine was alert but had been stuck in a conference call with her boss and team. Since the meeting was about covering the upcoming clients in her absence, it felt like the least she could do was make sure all that was squared away first. She parked and jogged the now-familiar path to the elevators, tapping her foot the entire ride up to Ernestine's floor.

Monique, one of the regular nurses, caught her eye and she offered a wave of greeting. Rather than return it, Monique flagged her down. "Did you get the call that she's awake?"

Audrey nodded with enthusiasm. "I did. I got here as quickly as I could."

"It's definitely a good sign. I just want you to be prepared."

"Prepared?"

"Her speech is very slow and quite slurred, and she has a lot of paralysis on the left side."

She'd known it could be bad. Honestly, she'd braced herself for worse. "Thank you for the heads up. I want to think I'm ready for anything, but it's one thing to say it and another to see it."

Monique gave her hand a squeeze. "You got this. And Rowan is already in with her, so you'll have company."

"She is?" They'd never gotten around to clarifying their relationship with any of the hospital staff, so Monique's raised brow shouldn't have come as a surprise. "I mean, I texted her when I got the call, but didn't get a reply."

Monique's smile held affection. "She's been here a couple of hours already, so that's probably why."

Audrey nodded again. More surprise than enthusiasm this time, but Monique didn't need to know that.

"I won't say don't stay too long because Ernestine is in and out of consciousness. She'll let you know when she needs rest, one way or another."

Monique went on her way, and she headed down the hall. Outside Ernestine's door, the sound of laughter stopped her in her tracks. Rowan's, if she wasn't mistaken, and a voice that had to be Ernestine's. Only it was softer and raspier than she'd ever heard it.

"Knock knock." She wasn't sure why she felt the need to announce her presence, but it was out of her mouth before she could stop it.

Ernestine's bed had been adjusted to an almost upright position and she had her glasses on. Rowan, who'd been sitting in the chair next to the bed, quickly stood. "Hey."

"Hi." She gave Rowan a quizzical look before turning her attention to Ernestine. "Look who's decided to grace us with her company."

"Audrey."

The slurred greeting had her fighting back tears. Tears of relief that Ernestine recognized her. Tears of worry over the uphill climb Ernestine had in front of her. And probably a few tears she'd been saving up since first getting the call about Ernestine's stroke. Since now was neither the time nor the place to let her emotions run free, she blinked them away and crossed the room to take Ernestine's hand. "How are you? How are you feeling?"

"I've. Been. Better." Ernestine's cadence seemed more about effort than effect.

Audrey fought the urge to ask a million questions. Instead, she focused on Ernestine's hand in hers—frail still but with a gentle grip. Ernestine was back. Everything was going to be okay.

Before she could say anything in return, a nurse came in to check Ernestine's vitals and administer something via her IV. So she turned her attention to Rowan. "How did you know she was awake? Did the hospital call you, too?"

Rowan shook her head. "I had a meeting at a nursery up this way and stopped by after. I'd been here a few minutes when she started mumbling."

Well, that explained that. It also explained why Rowan was looking particularly farm-y. The loose plaid shirt over a snug white tee and gray carpenter pants suited her. Not that she had any business noticing. "Has she said much? How does she seem?"

"She knew me right away, so that's good. She's coherent but kind of fades in and out."

She'd get the official report from the doctors, of course, but glommed onto the good news Rowan seemed to be delivering. The nurse left and she returned her attention to Ernestine. "It's so good to see you awake."

Ernestine nodded and offered something close to a smile. But then her eyes closed, and she seemed to drift off.

"That's really common, apparently," Rowan said.

She didn't like getting news secondhand, but it felt like splitting hairs to worry about that now, so she merely nodded. Because she could use all the reassurances she could get. And because as much as she wished it had been her, she was glad Ernestine got to wake up to a familiar face. It made it feel like she and Rowan were a team.

"Why don't I head out so you two can have some time? She'll probably come around again in a few minutes."

It struck her as odd that Rowan wanted to dart out just as she arrived. But if Rowan had been there a while—longer than she'd intended, perhaps—it wouldn't be all that strange. "You sure?"

"Totally. I'll check in with you later to see what the doctor says?"

"Of course."

Rowan left and Audrey took the vacated spot next to Ernestine's bed. After a few minutes, she started to wonder if she'd missed whatever alertness Ernestine had in her for the day. But just as despondence threatened to creep in, Ernestine's eyes opened as though waking from a nap.

"Hello, dear."

"Hi." She tried not to sound too relieved or too eager and failed on both fronts.

Ernestine looked around "Was Rowan here or did I imagine it?"

"No, no. She just left."

Ernestine seemed to take comfort in remembering correctly. "Oh, good."

"You two were laughing up a storm when I got here."

"That Rowan." Ernestine's features softened into an off-kilter smile.

"Do I want to know?" She absolutely did but didn't want to seem too invested in the answer. Kind of like she didn't want to admit how much Rowan had been on her mind even when they weren't having dinner together or taking care of things around the property.

"She was teasing me about my will."

Ernestine didn't sound upset, but Audrey's brain tripped over the comment. "What?"

Ernestine waved her good hand. "We were joking. She's a good egg. Harmless."

It didn't sound harmless to her. Or even remotely appropriate. She wrinkled her nose in a way she hoped looked playful before pressing for more.

"Oh, you know…" Ernestine seemed to consider that a sufficient answer.

Audrey bit the inside of her cheek and willed herself not to scowl. "No, I don't. Tell me all about it."

The phrase, one Ernestine used on Audrey when she was little, got her a smile. Ernestine began, her cadence slowed by having to concentrate on forming words. "We have a gentlewoman's arrangement."

She liked the sound of that even less than the prospect of Rowan angling to get into Ernestine's will. And it had nothing to do with Ernestine's slurred delivery. "What kind of gentlewoman's arrangement?"

"Well, it all started with a pie."

Ernestine recounted meeting Rowan the first time, Rowan moving in down the road. An apple pie to welcome Rowan to the neighborhood led to Rowan dropping by with a bottle of cider. Rowan dropping by and offering to help with this or that—not unlike Rowan had helped her—in exchange for baked goods and the occasional dinner. Rowan offering to tend the orchard and pay a fair price for the apples she harvested.

All of it was fine. In fact, it matched Rowan's version of the story. Up until the point where Ernestine agreed to sell Rowan the entire orchard for a fraction of its market value.

"She's taking advantage." A more generous statement than what she really wanted to say.

Ernestine shook her head. "She's not. What do I need with the orchard?"

"It's part of the farm and you love the farm more than anything."

"Rowan loves her apples the same way."

Did she? Did it matter? From where Audrey sat, Rowan had ingratiated herself into Ernestine's life for her own gain. And in less than a week, Rowan had done exactly the same to her. "And now she's joking about getting in your will so she won't even have to pay for the land at all?"

Ernestine lifted her good hand and gave Audrey's a pat. "It's not like that. Get to know Rowan. You'll see."

That was the problem. She had gotten to know Rowan. Or, rather, the version Rowan wanted her to see. The charming, funny, version. The version that got Audrey to let her guard down. She never did that with people she just met. Unlike Ernestine. For not taking any shit, Ernestine always saw the best in people. And when it came to people she cared about, she could be generous to a fault.

By the time Ernestine drifted back to sleep, Audrey didn't know what part made her madder—that Rowan had duped Ernestine or that Rowan had duped her. Not that she'd let Ernestine see that. No, Ernestine needed to be calm and happy and resting. But after placing a gentle kiss on Ernestine's forehead and making her way back to the parking garage, she stopped holding her anger in. A growl of frustration, a stream of profanity, and even a few punches of the steering wheel did little to calm her.

Of all the underhanded, low rent, shady things to do in life, taking advantage of an old lady had to be the worst. One of the worst, at least. It was duplicitous. It was unconscionable. It was insulting.

She'd blurred the line between Ernestine and herself with that last one, but it all sort of ran together anyway. She'd fallen for Rowan's chivalry without a second of hesitation. Sure, she'd been exhausted that first day and more than a little desperate, but still. She was a smart, discerning, independent woman. Yet she'd been sucked in by a pair of kind eyes and strong arms. And a way with chickens.

Audrey closed her eyes and took a deep breath. She wasn't one to get angry. Not like this at least. But like a magnet collecting metal filings, everything coalesced and it centered her, centered all the pent-up emotion that had nowhere else to go.

Maybe if she tried really hard she could tease that apart—her worry about Ernestine, her embarrassment over being so easy and flirtations with a practical stranger, her frustration with the whole situation. Only she didn't want to tease it apart. She wanted to give herself to it, to grab on to the ways it made her feel a little less helpless about everything. She let the anger course through her like the first caffeine hit of the day. It felt good. It felt like she was in control.

Okay. First things first. She took another deep breath, not to dispel the anger but to bank it temporarily. She needed to get home and couldn't risk being distracted and having an accident. Because who'd protect Ernestine then? And more pressingly, who would show up on Rowan's doorstep and give Rowan a piece of her mind?

When she got back to Ernestine's, she drove past the house and, sure enough, Rowan's truck sat in the next driveway down. It was a small cottage, really, probably half the size of Ernestine's. It didn't take much to imagine Rowan sizing up the farmhouse every time she came over.

Audrey grumbled a few more swear words as she stormed up to the front door. After a few minutes of banging and yelling that she knew Rowan was in there, she stopped. If Rowan hadn't come to the door yet, she was unlikely to with more threats. She huffed out a sigh and turned around, strategizing her next move. When she did, her eye landed on a squat metal-sided building across the street. It looked new and the words painted on the side said Forbidden Fruit Cider. Bingo.

She left her car and crossed the street on foot, allowing an array of scathing comments to form in her mind. When she was done with Rowan—um, whatever her last name was—there would be no doubt who had whose number. And the gig, as they said, would be up.

At the sound of raised voices, Rowan looked up from the rows of bottles she'd been labeling. One belonged to Dylan and the other sounded vaguely familiar, though she couldn't quite place it.

"You can't be in here. And you definitely can't be in here with open-toed shoes." Dylan's voice had that slightly insulted tone it got anytime someone didn't respect the rules of her domain.

"Don't tell me where I can and can't be. I've got business with your boss whether she likes it or not."

Despite the mystery woman's voice getting both louder and closer, Rowan couldn't suppress a chuckle. Dylan wouldn't take kindly to anyone referring to Rowan as the boss, particularly not some stranger who barged into their production space unannounced and uninvited. She'd no sooner turned to go investigate when Audrey stalked into view.

That explained the vaguely familiar voice.

"Audrey. Hi. Is everything okay?" Since she seemed more angry than sad, Rowan assumed it didn't have to do with Ernestine.

"Don't 'is everything okay' me, you asshole."

Rowan took an instinctive step back. Not in fear of physical harm, but because she was wholly unaccustomed to angry women coming at her. "What's wrong? Is it Ernestine?" Even if she didn't think so, it seemed like the most logical—not to mention safest—place to start.

"Showing up at the farm, being oh so helpful. Playing the part of the friendly and strapping next-door neighbor."

Had Audrey not been shooting eye daggers, she might have taken a second to appreciate the strapping comment. "I am the friendly next-door neighbor."

"You're a two-bit swindler, that's what you are."

Oh. She resented the implication, but at least she understood. "Can we go somewhere and talk? Preferably where we aren't surrounded by my employees and business partner?"

Not that the intern really counted as an employee, but still.

"Does your partner know you're a liar and a cheat? Do your employees?"

"Audrey, please."

"Please what? Please help you steal my aunt's farm out from under her nose? Help you swindle some other helpless old ladies?"

Rowan pinched the bridge of her nose. Audrey implying Ernestine was some helpless old lady told her the ship of reasonable conversation had sailed. Still. She had to try. And hopefully somewhere private. "Come to the office."

She thought Audrey might balk at what was essentially a command, but Audrey glowered and followed her. In the eight-by-eight corner of the building they'd walled up for an office, Audrey's anger concentrated, seeming to take up all the oxygen in the room. Rowan experienced a small bubble of fear for her safety but pushed it aside. That was silly. She hoped.

She took a deep breath and willed the calm to spread. "What happened?"

"Ernestine told me you tried to manipulate your way into her will."

She felt the color drain from her cheeks. "I was joking around, trying to lift her spirits."

Audrey folded her arms and didn't speak. She just stared, incredulous and antipathetic.

For the first time since Audrey arrived, a lick of true worry coursed up her spine. Did Ernestine really feel that way? Even in the moment? Teasing each other was part of their friendship, but maybe that part of Ernestine's mind wasn't working the way it used to. Or maybe her memory was affected.

No. She'd been at the hospital close to two hours. And maybe Ernestine had only been alert for a fraction of that time, but the gleam in her eye had been real. And her smile and the way she squeezed Rowan's hand.

"Is that really all you have to say for yourself?"

Audrey seemed insulted by the idea she wouldn't fight back.

"No. What do you want to know?"

"Everything. I want to know everything."

Audrey might not mean that, but Rowan started at the beginning. "Five years ago, my partner and I started Forbidden Fruit. We bought ten acres of land, the land you're standing on right now. We built this production facility and began planting the rest with heritage apple trees."

She paused, expecting Audrey to tell her to speed it up already. Audrey didn't and her expression turned impassive. An improvement? Hard to tell. But she'd take it.

"We obviously had to source our apples from other orchards when we started. With Ernestine's property right across the street, it seemed like a great place to start. We met, worked out an arrangement to tend the orchard and buy the apple harvest in its entirety." She swallowed and reminded herself she hadn't done anything wrong. "Which you know."

"It's a sound business arrangement benefitting both of you." Audrey sniffed. "Which is probably why you told me that part."

It struck her how that decision, paired with the circumstances, led Audrey to think the worst of her. If she didn't think of Ernestine as family, she'd worry maybe Audrey had a point. But Ernestine was family, as important to her as any of her aunts and uncles, or her grandparents who were no longer alive. "Would you like me to finish?"

"Go on."

"Within a year of starting production, the house across the street—the one technically next door to Ernestine's—went up for sale. It had been a rental and the owners didn't want the hassle anymore and listed it as is and really cheap."

Audrey nodded, seeming bored by the details but not interrupting. "I bought it so I could be closer to our land and Ernestine's. I'm the orchardist, the one in charge of the growing and harvesting and procuring." She'd started to ramble but couldn't seem to stop herself. "Anyway. Ernestine and I became friendly and then we became friends."

"Meaning, you saw an opportunity and you took it."

For some reason, that accusation struck a nerve and her intentions of making nice got swallowed up in defending herself. And Ernestine, for that matter. "Meaning, Ernestine is one of the coolest people I ever met. Meaning, I enjoyed her company and she enjoyed mine. Meaning, I started helping with some of the manual labor at her place and she started making me cookies and inviting me to dinner. Which you know."

Audrey's eyes narrowed slightly, like she was conducting some sort of psychic lie detector test.

"When she offered to sell me the orchard outright, I couldn't pay what it was worth and we both knew it. She offered to sell it to me over time. I could pull together the money more slowly and by the time I was done, Ernestine would be almost ninety. She joked that it would be a good age to downsize."

"But if she dies sooner than that, you want to make sure your bases are covered? Get in her will and save yourself the time and the trouble?"

What remained of her patience snapped. "I get that you've decided to believe the worst of me, but why do you think so little of Ernestine? If you're half as close to her as you say, you should know she's smart and stubborn and has one hell of a bullshit detector. What makes you think I could pull off such a thing even if I wanted to?"

That got Audrey to give, at least a little. The eye daggers faded and she almost—almost—cracked a smile. But she quickly caught herself and glowered all over again. "I don't trust you. And I'm pretty sure I don't like you."

"You don't have to like me." Though, God, Rowan wanted her to. More than she cared to admit or analyze. "And you don't have to trust me because I'm done trying to convince you of anything."

That got her a haughty chin lift that would have been seriously sexy under other circumstances. "Well, then, I think you'd do best to keep the charming neighbor bit to yourself."

Audrey walked out of the office without another word and without a backwards glance. Rowan's shoulders slumped and she pressed a hand to her chest. When had her heart started racing?

Probably when Audrey insulted her integrity. She let out a growl. The whole thing was beyond frustrating. It was infuriating. Because she wasn't a cheat and even if she was, she wouldn't try to cheat a woman like Ernestine. And because, even as Audrey stood there hurling one insult after another, a small part of Rowan's brain reminded her that she'd given more than a passing thought to what it might be like to kiss her. What the hell had she been thinking?

CHAPTER FIVE

Audrey finished filling out the family leave forms shortly before her scheduled call with Vera. She toggled over to her email and clicked the videoconferencing link. She was first to log on, giving her a moment to study her image. Even with makeup and a blazer, she'd swear she looked different. Was it just her? Or would Vera notice?

Vera's face appeared on the screen, relegating hers to a thumbnail in the corner. "Audrey. It's good to see you. How's your aunt?"

Her company's culture wasn't super close-knit, but her boss was an exception. Vera managed to be both friendly and frank without crossing any lines, and she'd served as a mentor as much as a supervisor in the four years they'd worked together. "It's good to see you, too. And thank you for asking. She's being moved to a rehab facility this week. It's going to be a long recovery."

Vera nodded. "My dad was in one for four months after his stroke."

She appreciated the personal detail, even if it made her stomach flip uncomfortably. "I'm prepared for something similar."

"I don't mean to overstep, but have you considered moving her to a place in the city? Since you're not providing in-home care, it would disrupt your life a lot less."

Coming from someone else, she might have taken the question as a veiled insinuation that she shouldn't be considering a leave. Because it was Vera, she knew it had more to do with thoughts of her well-being. Well-being and her timeline to partner, perhaps. But that, in its own way, was looking out for her, too. "The problem is that it isn't her that needs my twenty-four-seven attention. It's her farm."

"Farm?"

"Hobby farm." The clarification didn't lessen the look of surprise—alarm?—on Vera's face. "She has about twenty acres up in the Finger Lakes. Garden, animals, an orchard. The whole deal."

"What kind of animals?" The look on Vera's face was priceless.

"Chickens, sheep, goats. Plus a dog and a couple of barn cats."

Vera shook her head.

"I know. But it's her pride and joy. I have to do this for her. And I think it will help her recovery to know things are being looked after." And protected from the conniving next-door neighbor. She hadn't let go of an ounce of that anger and had no plans to.

"Well, you have the full support of the partners and your team. Your position will be here when you're ready to come back." Vera angled her head and smiled. "And not only because I'm legally obligated to say that."

People talked smack about big corporations, especially in the finance sector. Yes, she worked an obscene number of hours. But she'd always felt like a valuable member of the team. Knowing the company stood by its generous benefit policies and didn't merely pay them lip service only intensified that feeling. "Thank you."

"And thank you for taking the time to meet with me about managing your team in the interim."

It felt like the least she could do. Not to mention in her own best interests to keep things running smoothly. She wasn't guaranteed her exact position, or even to stay in her niche division within the audit branch of the company, but hoped it worked out that way. "Of course."

She spent the next forty-five minutes giving Vera a rundown of the members of her team. Personalities, frictions, ambitions—things not in their annual reviews or official files. She also walked through the clients her team managed. They'd finished a lot of the smaller companies earlier in the year to pair with their tax filings. The larger ones—more cyclical and ongoing than a discreet annual audit—each had a lead besides her, so that helped. By the time they were done, she felt confident things would be okay in her absence. Reassuring if also strange.

"Now that we have that squared away, how are you?"

She smiled. "Can't we talk about something simple like the pending changes to the Professional Practices Framework?"

Vera laughed. "Who said accountants don't have a sense of humor?"

"Right?" Audrey chuckled as well. "Seriously, though. I'm… okay."

"You must feel so out of your element."

Did she? Well, yes. She'd yet to finish a morning of chores without mishap. And she still couldn't don her recent purchases from Tractor Supply—legit work pants and a pair of polka-dot muck boots—without feeling like she was in costume. But she was settling in, holding her own. Sort of a sink or swim situation, really, since she'd sworn off all help from Rowan. Fucking Rowan.

"Audrey?"

She cleared her throat and barely resisted an eye roll. "Sorry. Yes, I do feel out of sorts. It's unsettling to be a novice at something I'm responsible for."

"Spoken like a true raging competent with control freak tendencies."

Her mouth fell open. "I don't have control freak tendencies."

"Honey, it's not an insult. You don't get as far as you've already gotten in this business without some control freak tendencies. Especially if you're a woman."

It was hard to know what struck her more—the pithy assessment or being called honey. Yet again, reassuring but strange. "I'll concede the point. But only because you're both my boss and a woman."

"That's the spirit. Take care of yourself, Audrey. We can't wait to have you back."

Vera ended the call and Audrey stared at her computer screen for a long moment. No files or folders cluttered the desktop; everything was stored in the cloud and backed up in her own highly organized system. She hadn't even bothered to change the factory issued background image to something personal. A few weeks ago, she would have called it efficient. Now, it struck her as a little soulless.

She shook her head. She was being precious. She was not precious.

Vera's words echoed in her mind. Competent. And a little bit of a control freak.

That's why she was so pissed at Rowan. Rowan had taken advantage of her inexperience and eagerness to make sure things were done right. And she'd fallen for it. It still galled her.

But even as she clutched at indignation, Rowan's face lingered in her mind. The look of dismay that turned into defiance as Audrey grilled her up one side and down the other. But also her expression when she talked about her business over dinner. Excitement about the cidery and what had seemed like genuine affection for Ernestine.

No. No going soft.

She had no room in her life for someone like that. Even if that someone didn't seem to mind mucking out the goat pen. And even if—especially if—that someone had a killer smile and made a damn fine bottle of cider.

It was probably foolish to try to make nice with someone who basically believed the absolute worst of her, but Rowan couldn't seem to help herself. It was a matter of principle, sure. She wanted to set the record straight about her relationship with Ernestine and her intentions when it came to the orchard. Her integrity. But there was also the matter of not believing for a second Audrey could handle the farm on her own. As much as she wanted Audrey to like her, her primary loyalty was to Ernestine. And that meant not letting things fall apart in her absence. So, first things first.

She gave Audrey a couple of days to cool off, then scheduled herself for a day of mid-season pruning, a necessary step in the growing season that cleared space for the apples to get enough air flow and light. It gave her the chance to keep an eye on Ernestine's driveway and see when Audrey left for her daily visit to the hospital. That gave her at least three hours, probably four.

If wanting to vindicate herself and win Audrey over made her feel foolish, sneaking over to do chores made her feel—what was the word for extremely foolish? She posited the question to Ozzie and Harriet as she shoveled manure from their pen. "You're no help," she said to their exuberant bleating.

Since Audrey had managed the morning feedings and collected eggs, she headed to the flower garden. She started with the beds, pruning the lilac bushes and deadheading some of the early bloomers that were now on their way out. After weeding and spreading some fresh mulch, she turned her attention to the vegetable patch. The first peas were almost ready to pick, and both the beans and tomatoes needed staking.

She made a mental list and headed to the barn. Sure, it would be nicer to do this with Audrey the way she often did with Ernestine, but that was okay. Things would work out in the end. And be taken care of in the meantime.

She popped in her earbuds and pulled up her power ballad playlist since Dylan refused to let her play it on the production floor. She gathered a bunch of bamboo canes and a roll of twine, stepping back into the sunshine just in time for the final chorus. She belted out the deep truths with abandon—roses and thorns, nights and dawns, and of course cowboys with their sad, sad songs.

She looked over to see if the goats were heckling her or singing along. But instead of their cheerful mugs, she found herself face-to-face with Audrey. "Gah."

With the music blaring in her ears, she couldn't hear whether Audrey made a similar sound. But if the look on her face was anything to go on, she did. Or maybe she swore. She didn't hear the stakes clatter to a jumbled pile at her feet either, but they definitely did. Along with the twine. Ugh.

Audrey started to speak, but the song changed and the words in Rowan's ears had to do with midnight trains going anywhere. She yanked out the earbuds and fumbled for the pause button. "What?"

Audrey's surprise had dissipated, leaving pure irritation in its place. Irritation laced with suspicion. "What are you doing here?"

She wanted to ask Audrey the same question but resisted. "Helping."

"I thought I made it clear I don't want your help."

The dismissive tone got her hackles up, despite her desire to channel calm. "I'm not here to help you. I'm here to help Ernestine."

That got her a derisive snort.

"I thought you'd left to visit her and would be gone for hours." It sounded rational in her head, but out loud, it made her seem creepy.

"I'm going up later. I went to the post office." Audrey's eyes closed like she was kicking herself for deigning to explain her activities.

"The tomatoes need staking. I thought I'd be done before you got back."

Audrey sneered. "And you figured I wouldn't notice?"

"I was going to leave a note." Why did this plan suddenly seem so dumb?

"Was it going to say, 'Hi, I trespassed and by the way, you suck at gardening?'"

She shouldn't take the bait. "No. It was going to say something nice. Because I'm a nice person."

Audrey rolled her eyes.

"Oh, my God. Why are you being so stubborn about this?"

Audrey folded her arms. "Why are you?"

"You might have decided I'm the devil incarnate, but I'm not. I care about Ernestine. The arrangement we have for the land was her idea, not mine."

Audrey unfolded her arms and planted her hands on her hips—the universal sign of a woman upping the ante of her ire. "You're planning to buy it from her for a fraction of what it's worth."

"Because I dumped all my savings into the business and don't have the capital. I'm still going to pay her a reasonable price. A price she suggested, I might add." When Audrey shook her head, she plowed on. "And because I love the land and Ernestine knows that. Because Ernestine would rather her pride and joy go to someone who will appreciate it and take care of it and not some rich chump from the city who decides having a place in the Finger Lakes would be charming but only comes up a couple of times every summer."

Audrey's expression turned stony. "You need to leave now."

It occurred to Rowan about two seconds too late that the end of her tirade was a step too far. She'd inadvertently implied Audrey was one of those rich people from the city. "I wasn't talking about you, you know. Ernestine always talks about how often you visit and how proud she is of everything you've accomplished."

Audrey blew out a breath and resisted the urge to pinch the bridge of her nose. Between the shock of running face-first into a singing Rowan, immediately falling into an argument with her, and the feelings stirred up by her meeting with Vera, the low-grade headache she'd been nursing swelled to a pulsing throb. "I don't need you to make me feel better about my relationship with Ernestine."

"I wasn't trying to do that, either."

"She's my family. She's been the most important person in my life for as long as I can remember. I was here the day she bought this place. I've seen what she's put into it." Even as she defended herself, she loathed Rowan for making her feel compelled to.

"I haven't been around as long, but I'm around a lot. I see it, too."

"No. You don't get to waltz in and insert yourself into that and become her best friend because you live next door."

Rowan's features softened. Audrey hoped it was the first sign of her backing down and maybe even backing off. "Are you upset about the land or about the fact that I know how things work around here? That I'm more a part of Ernestine's day-to-day life than you are?"

She felt the blood drain from her face. As tightly as she'd been clinging to rage, it abandoned her all at once. Like a balloon that's been filled too far and pops without warning. She opened her mouth, but no words formed.

"I didn't mean—"

She shook her head. "Please go. Please."

Rowan looked down. Whether cowed by her own intrusiveness or realizing she was about to have a crying woman on her hands, Audrey couldn't be sure. But she picked up the scattered poles and set them in a neat pile next to the barn door. "I'm still here if you need anything. Whether you want to believe it or not, we're on the same side."

Without another word, Rowan walked down the driveway and turned right, in the direction of her house. Audrey watched her disappear. It was what she asked for, begged for practically. But for the life of her, she couldn't remember a time she felt more alone.

On a different day—or a different planet—she might have been able to take Rowan's question as a gentle inquiry into her insecurities or her messed up childhood or how Ernestine was more of a mother to her than her own had ever been. But this was not that day. Today it was a poke to her most tender and vulnerable parts and no way in hell had Rowan earned that privilege.

Still. What did it say about her that she was jealous of the relationship Ernestine had formed with her neighbor? That regardless of Rowan's intentions, she was more involved in Ernestine's life than Audrey. Rowan might be angling to protect her interests, but Audrey was the one who'd lulled herself into weekly phone calls and visiting only every few months. Telling herself she was busy; telling herself there'd be more time after she became partner.

What if there wasn't more time?

She stood in the driveway for a long while, debating whether to scream or cry. In the end, she did neither. She went into the house and googled how to stake tomatoes. Then she went outside, gathered the supplies Rowan had abandoned, and got to work.

CHAPTER SIX

Rowan resisted the urge to sneak over to Ernestine's and do more chores. She even resisted checking on things when she knew Audrey was out. At least for the time being.

She obviously struck a nerve about being more involved in Ernestine's life than Audrey was. She hadn't meant it as a jab. She just wanted Audrey to see she was overreacting. Admit that her emotions had gotten the better of her and that those emotions had to do with more than being protective of her aunt. She should have known better. Those kinds of conversations never went well if the person in question was angry. Even less so if there wasn't a foundation of trust to begin with.

Rowan chuckled at her slip into counselor speak. Her social worker sister was rubbing off on her. She didn't need to figure Audrey out; she needed to give her space. Hopefully, Audrey would come around.

Which was why she put off her chores in the orchard in favor of helping Dylan in the bottling room. It would save her from wandering in the direction of Ernestine's or constantly looking that way to see if Audrey was puttering about. It would also give her something to focus on, since tending the trees gave her mind ample room to get itself into trouble.

"To what do I owe this pleasure?" Dylan asked when she strode in.

"You're bottling. You always want help with bottling."

"And you always avoid it."

She didn't always. She simply preferred being outside with the trees. "But bottling is important and if I help you, Jamal can cap."

"He does love the capper."

Their intern, courtesy of the county's vocational exploration program for high school seniors, was enamored with the capping machine. Rowan couldn't blame him. It was almost hypnotically satisfying to use. "What time is he in?"

"Just about—"

"Morning, bosses." Jamal bounded in with far more energy than the average teenager at nine in the morning. "What magic are we working today?"

Dylan relayed the plan, and he whooped his approval. The whole thing made Rowan smile, especially Jamal's eagerness to be relieved of the sticky job of filling bottles. She was pretty sure he was going to find a niche in hospitality management, or maybe marketing, more than food and beverage production, but she remained glad he'd been paired with them.

They got to work on the Rustica, a dry pét-nat style that included apples from both Ernestine's land and their own fledgling orchard. It was one of the first ciders made with apples that were one hundred percent theirs. Watching the golden liquid flow into bottles—bottles that would be bought and enjoyed by hundreds of people around the state and maybe even beyond—always made her heart feel a little too big for her chest. Knowing it contained apples from trees she planted with her own hands? Next level.

When Jamal pulled the lever to cap the last bottle, they exchanged fist bumps. Jamal even played along with the cheesy dance she and Dylan had been doing since college to celebrate victories large and small. "Now what?" he asked.

"Now I wheel these over to the rinsing station and we leave them to dry overnight."

Jamal made a face. "Does that mean I have to stick labels tomorrow?"

"Nah," Dylan said.

Rowan raised a brow, pretty sure labeling needed to happen if they were going to get everything boxed in time for cider subscription deliveries and the scheduled pickup from their distributor. Dylan offered her a wink before turning back to Jamal. "It means you get to stick labels tomorrow."

Jamal shook his head. "Not cool, bro. Not cool."

Rowan swallowed a laugh and Dylan seemed at least slightly remorseful. "How about I buy you lunch on Friday after we do subscription shipping?"

Jamal, with far more savvy that she could even pretend to possess at that age, lifted his chin. "Bake My Day?"

The bakery—now café—was far enough away to prevent it from becoming a daily habit. But close enough, and addictive enough, for Jamal to know it wasn't a big ask. Dylan didn't even pretend to consider. "Deal."

They let Jamal head home early and took a late lunch outside at the beat-up picnic table she'd snagged at a yard sale for fifty bucks. She tried not to be sad about her tuna sandwich and lack of dessert. Thoughts of Bake My Day, home of the world's best eclairs, didn't help.

"So, is the hottie with the short temper still mad at you?"

Since she wasn't in the business of having women angry with her, it didn't take much deduction to know who Dylan was talking about. Still. She didn't appreciate Dylan referring to Audrey as the hottie. Even if Audrey objectively fit the description. "Her name is Audrey and she's Ernestine's niece." She paused. "And yes."

"Dude, you need to get back on her good side. Who knows how long she'll be running things over there while Ernestine recovers."

"I know."

"What if she tries to keep us from harvesting?"

The thought had occurred to her. She and Ernestine had put their agreement in writing, but it wasn't vetted by a lawyer or anything. She had no idea if it would hold up if Audrey tried to revoke her access. "She won't. Besides, it's a long way off. Hopefully, Ernestine will be home and she'll be long gone before we need to worry about it."

Even as she said it, a knot remained in the pit of her stomach. Partly because Audrey could make things difficult if not impossible for them, and they didn't have the time or resources to spare to deal with difficult. But equally unnerving was having Audrey think the worst of her. It shouldn't be weighing on her, but it did.

"I hope you're right."

"I am."

"Do you think you should try to make nice just in case? You said Ernestine was going to need extensive rehab."

She hadn't mentioned to Dylan that she'd tried to make nice, or that she'd snuck over to do some chores and been caught. And she most definitely didn't mention inadvertently denigrating Audrey's relationship with Ernestine. "I'm going to give her some time to cool off. Then we'll see."

Dylan grinned. "If anyone can win her over, it's you."

"Ha ha." Dylan was teasing, but the fact of the matter was that she did win people over, almost invariably. She had a genuine curiosity about people and what made them tick, paired with empathy and a preference for listening over talking. She'd never been what she'd call popular, but people tended to like her.

That was the problem, really. Audrey had liked her at first. They'd done the friendly—bordering on flirty—thing for days. Only when Audrey jumped to conclusions about her intentions did things go sideways. She didn't know how to counter that, especially since Audrey shut down her attempts at helping.

"Has she told you to stay off the land?"

"Actually, no." Just to stay away from her.

"That's good. You can keep the crop from going to hell in the meantime."

"Yeah." She knew better than to tell Dylan that was the least of her worries, even if it was.

What time Audrey didn't spend working on the garden and doing chores in the barn, she spent reading and researching. She watered and weeded. She mucked and scrubbed. She pruned, potted, and polished. She even taught herself to make jam with the raspberries that were ripening faster than she could eat them. And she did it all without a single second of help or advice from Rowan.

She was pretty sure every pore had absorbed the stench of manure. It followed her everywhere. And every muscle she had—including a few she didn't know she had—ached. It was all she could do to stay awake long enough to shower and eat dinner. The upside was that her body overruled her brain and she slept. Hard.

The days dragged but that was okay. She was biding her time and taking care of everything that mattered to Ernestine until Ernestine could take care of it herself again. And she'd find a way to get help for the things Ernestine wouldn't be able to do herself anymore. Help that didn't come with an ulterior motive.

More than once, her mind wandered down the path of reconsideration, of believing Rowan's intentions were noble and her relationship with Ernestine sound. Each time, she stopped herself. She hadn't made peace with falling for Rowan's charms in the first place. She wasn't about to entertain being wrong. It was a matter of principle, not pride. Well, except for the pride and the satisfaction of holding her own at the farm. A rather grim satisfaction but satisfaction nonetheless.

It was that satisfaction she held on to as she drove to Rochester for Ernestine's move to the rehab facility. Well, satisfaction and optimism. Ernestine transitioning to rehab would bring her one step closer to coming home. It was a good day, even if she had to keep reminding herself of the optimism part.

"You look tired, dear."

Audrey paused her unpacking and arranging. "I just want everything to be nice for you."

Ernestine, settled in her new recliner and wearing her own clothes, smiled. "It's not a hospital room. It's plenty nice."

"It's not home, either, but that doesn't mean we can't make it homey." She set a framed photo of herself and Ernestine in Province-town next to a black-and-white one of Ernestine and her brother.

Ernestine frowned. "You're doing too much."

Audrey squeezed her hand. "I'm doing exactly what I want to be doing."

Ernestine might have limited used of her facial muscles, but her incredulous look came through loud and clear. "Rowan says you yelled at her and won't let her help out."

Really, Rowan? Air the dirty laundry to the old lady who should be focusing on her recovery? "I didn't yell." She kind of had.

"She didn't say yell, but I surmised."

"I feel like she's taking advantage of you. And she was dishonest with me."

Whatever Ernestine may have lost in mobility or speech did not affect her ability to express disapprobation without uttering a word.

"I'm not saying you're naive. I'm saying she manipulated the situation. She's trying to steal your land out from under you."

Again, no words. Just the stare. But damn, it was effective. Honed by thirty years of teaching.

"Okay, maybe I jumped to conclusions. You're perfectly capable of making decisions and doing what you want." Even if that wasn't entirely true in the moment, the general sentiment was. And she'd been sufficiently cowed that she wasn't going to split hairs, at least not out loud.

"Thank you."

She wanted to say more, to understand more of the why and the how, but Ernestine was worn out from the move. She wasn't at her best either. "It's been a big day. You get some rest and I'll see you tomorrow."

Ernestine offered a semblance of a smile and closed her eyes. Audrey waited a beat, but Ernestine's breathing evened out and she was clearly down for the count. Audrey bit the inside of her cheek to keep the tears at bay. It had only been a couple of months since her last visit, when Ernestine was up at the crack of dawn and working circles around her right through dinner. Even with the progress she'd made, it was getting harder to believe Ernestine would be getting back to that anytime soon.

She finished unpacking the suitcase of Ernestine's clothes into the small dresser and closet, tidied the framed photos and tchotchkes that didn't need tidying. Not home but a big upgrade from a hospital room, right? Right.

She waited another minute, until the hovering made her feel silly, then headed to the nurses' station to check in one last time. They already had her info, but she was able to glean when shifts typically changed, when meals were served to residents who needed assistance feeding themselves.

It was all so…what? Normal. Routine. It gave her confidence. Maybe it should have given her comfort, too. It didn't.

Audrey offered the nurses and CNAs a good night and made her way to the front door. She got into her car but didn't start the engine. She took a deep breath, told herself it was going to be okay, and then proceeded to break down. Not a few elegant tears, but a long, hard cry. The kind that left her eyes red and her nose running. The kind she hadn't had in years.

She'd been excited for Ernestine's move, what it symbolized. But seeing her loaded into an ambulance for the transport only intensified how fragile her condition remained. And the facility—a lovely, modern sort of place with state-of-the-art technology and a caring staff—felt so much like a nursing home, it was all Audrey could do to hold it together while Ernestine got settled into her room.

It was part of the recovery process. She knew this. She'd researched for days and assured herself it was Ernestine's best shot at regaining her strength and her independence. She'd assured Ernestine, too. She also knew that some people never left. Their need for higher-level care meant they were safer and healthier in a facility and not at home. That could wind up being Ernestine. And that didn't even take into account Ernestine's elevated risk of another stroke.

She'd known all of that and had kept her chin up. She'd smiled and managed to remain upbeat and optimistic. And yet, somehow, seeing Ernestine in a sun-drenched room with art on the walls and one of her own quilts on the bed did her in.

Was it because it was supposed to feel like home and so very much wasn't? Or that it made her come to terms with the possible permanence of Ernestine's situation? Probably both. The whole Rowan mess didn't help, either. She didn't want Rowan's company, but she couldn't shake the sense of being profoundly alone.

Whatever the trigger, once the floodgates were open, the torrent of tears and feelings and fear came pouring out with the speed and strength of a tidal wave and she was powerless to stop it. She cried and lost track of time and cried some more. When the tears finally let up, it was like being deposited on the shore after a storm—battered, drenched, and weak. She fished a tissue out of the center console and wiped her eyes. She blew her nose and looked around, almost surprised that she still sat in the parking lot.

A woman in scrubs walked by and they shared a second of eye contact. The woman offered her a look of sympathy but didn't come over. Probably because people crying in their cars happened often around here.

Oof. Okay. Enough. Pity party over. Ernestine was in excellent hands and, since the move had taken most of the day, she had a mess of chores waiting for her at home.

She started the drive and debated what, if anything, to tell Rowan. She was slightly tempted to say nothing, let Rowan show up at the hospital and find out the hard way. But that was petty. Even if she wanted to drive home the point that she was Ernestine's family—not Rowan—it made her feel small.

Since she was the kind of person who couldn't sit with a decision and not act on it, she pulled over and dashed off a text to Rowan. Okay, dashed might be an exaggeration. Agonized might be more accurate, but whatever. She included the name of the facility and Ernestine's room number, along with the visiting hours and times she was scheduled for PT and OT.

Satisfied she'd made a decision, if not entirely satisfied with the decision she'd made, she drove the rest of the way home with the music turned way louder than she usually allowed herself. And if she tuned in to a vintage rock station because she hadn't been able to get Journey out of her head since her collision with Rowan outside the barn, well, no one but her needed to know.

CHAPTER SEVEN

Audrey stuffed the armful of hay into the hopper. "No offense, but you guys aren't the best conversationalists."

Ozzie and Harriet, who'd bounded over at the promise of breakfast, bleated not quite in unison.

"I mean, don't get me wrong. You're enthusiastic and pretty decent listeners, but I can't help but feel like things are one-sided."

Ozzie munched and Harriet gave her a "Maaah."

"I know. It's me, me, me. I don't know about you, but I'm getting a little sick of me."

"Meeaaah."

"Are you saying I need to make friends?" Perhaps the fact that she posed the question to a pair of goats was its own answer.

Ozzie threw his head back and screamed.

"Yeah." If it wasn't his usual way of communicating, she might have taken offense.

"Beah." Harriet's gentler reply seemed like her attempt to agree.

"Thank you. You're at least trying to be helpful."

Ozzie screamed again. This one was more of a moan.

"You, sir, are not helpful."

She made her way to the sheep pen and the chicken coop. No one else seemed to have opinions on the matter. Perhaps they were relieved that, after two days of swearing and grumbling about Rowan, she'd moved on to something else. Not that she wasn't still mad because she absolutely was. She'd started to get on her own nerves, though, so she did her stewing in silence.

After watering and weeding the garden, peeking at the progress of the cherry and peach trees, and tidying the barn, she headed inside to shower and dress for the day. Since she hadn't bothered with breakfast, she made an early lunch. Then cleaned the kitchen. And the refrigerator. And the stove.

Since it was barely noon, she pulled out her computer and checked her email. With her work account disabled—because they were sticklers about that—she didn't have much more than the daily offerings from Zappo's, Ann Taylor, and her other online retailers of choice. Sigh.

She cleared out her inbox then toggled over to social media, where she was promptly reminded of why she avoided social media. She hadn't been serious when kvetching with the goats, but maybe there was something to it. Maybe she did need friends.

Like Rowan.

But not Rowan.

Ugh.

Rowan had been perfect because of proximity and because she was friends with Ernestine and because she knew how to do stuff. Their meeting had been organic. Not the result of her trying too hard. Which was how she often felt in social situations.

But unlike when she arrived—thinking her stay might not be more than a week or two—she'd signed herself up for at least the next couple of months. Maybe as many as six. Even her socially awkward, introverted self would start to get twitchy if her only source of conversation was Ernestine. And, of course, the goats.

Maybe she should break her promise to Ernestine and go back to visiting every day. No. She'd promised, at Ernestine's insistence. And she could appreciate Ernestine's discomfort with being fussed over so much, on top of her ongoing difficulties with speech. She just hadn't counted on being bored. And, if she was being honest, lonely.

She spent a minute feeling pathetic and gross and sorry for herself. It only took that long for her to feel better. Because she might not like her situation, but now she had a plan. And she could implement the fuck out of a plan.

Half an hour later, she cruised along Route 96 with the top down and the radio up. Rather than heading north like she did to visit Ernestine, she drove south, her sights on Ithaca. Smaller and quirkier than Rochester, it had a world-renowned farmer's market, funky shops, and an impressive slew of restaurants. She might not make friends, but she had no doubt she'd have a good day.

She was still a good half hour shy of her destination when she slowed for yet another small town with a thirty mile per hour speed limit. But unlike the towns she'd passed through so far, this one seemed to boast more than a traffic light and a post office. Oh, it had those things, but it also had a pizzeria, what appeared to be a furniture and gift shop, and a bakery. When she passed the sign for the bakery—Bake My Day—a giggle escaped her. And even though she wasn't prone to spontaneity or changing her plans or anything of that nature, she pulled over, turned the car around, and did just that.

The inside of the bakery looked new or at least recently redone. Two beautiful glass cases displayed cookies, cupcakes, and a plethora of pastries. Definitely the right call.

She joined the line and used the wait to survey her options. Was it wrong to have a cupcake and a cookie? She chewed her lip, enjoying the delicious indecision. When it was her turn, she settled on the cupcake to have now but got a few cookies to go. A reasonable compromise in her book, especially since she hadn't been baking. Because she had no one to bake for.

Fucking Rowan.

She settled at a small table by the window, near a group of women knitting. Or crocheting. She didn't know which was which.

She sipped her latte, ate the best red velvet of her life, and tried not to eavesdrop. But her gaze kept wandering back to the group. The needles clicked in time with the rhythmic movements of the women's fingers. Most of them didn't even look at their work, save the occasional inspection or adjustment of the piece they were working on. It was surprisingly graceful and more than a little hypnotic.

"Do you knit?"

She started. She wasn't sure who'd asked the question, but it had obviously been directed at her. She shook her head. "No. I'm sorry. I didn't mean to stare. I just don't think I've ever watched people doing it before. I got a little entranced."

"Do you want to knit?" The voice came from the older woman of the group, her voice a little softer than the initial asker.

"I couldn't..." Couldn't learn? Couldn't try? She wasn't sure.

"Pretty sure you could." The woman who spoke—who'd asked her if she knit—looked to be around her age.

"I mean, maybe. I've never tried. And I'm not crafty or artistic or anything."

"Doing it, trying it—that's what makes you crafty." The assertion came from the third woman at the table, the one whose fingers she'd been most entranced by. "I've only been doing it a couple of years."

"Um." She was quickly running out of excuses. And while she could simply excuse herself and leave, she didn't want to.

"There's a group of us that get together every Saturday. Seven or eight total, whoever can make it any given week. You could join us." The older woman offered an encouraging smile. "Do you live around here?"

Did she? Loaded question. "Sort of. For now at least."

Rather than press, the women offered her nods and smiles. The woman who looked to be her age started rooting around in her bag. "I've got some extra needles. I can cast on for you and show you the basic stitch and you can give it a try."

She lifted both hands. "I wouldn't want to use your yarn. I might ruin it."

"Oh, honey. You won't ruin anything. And I've got enough to spare."

The older woman laughed. "Enough to fill a spare room, you mean."

"That's true. I'm Gretchen, by the way." She extended her hand.

Audrey took it. "Audrey."

"Lydia and Natasha." Gretchen indicated the older woman and then the younger.

"It's nice to meet all of you."

Natasha smiled. "It's nice to have you."

Lydia scooted over to make room for Audrey to pull up her chair. "Welcome to the Stitch 'n' Bitch."

A flutter of panic danced in her chest. What was she doing? She didn't chum up to strangers and she sure as hell didn't knit.

And then she remembered the reason she left the house in the first place. She had no idea if these women would become her friends, but they seemed happy enough to welcome her into their circle. And having an activity—literally something to do with her hands—might make getting to know them feel a little less awkward.

Even if she had no idea what she was doing. Even if she might turn out to be terrible and the thought of trying filled her with nerves. Because nervous or not, she'd managed to find exactly what she was looking for.

❖

Rowan put down the windows of her truck and blasted the one FM station the old dial managed to pick up. Randy Travis crooned and she smiled. Driving was literally the only time she listened to vintage country, but it suited the backroads and the '87 Chevy just fine.

She didn't need eclairs. Then again, who did? That was the beauty. They were an unnecessary treat. An indulgence. And given her complete lack of indulgences over the last week, she was as close to needing as a person could get. Plus, she needed tomato food and getting a couple of capfuls from her usual supplier wasn't happening. Which made it a legitimate errand and not just a sugar run. And it was a nice day for a drive.

Not that she needed to justify any of it. She was a grown woman with a sweet tooth and there was nothing wrong with that. Especially in moderation. And she'd cleared all the pruning detritus for shredding and composting with no help from Dylan or Jamal so she'd kind of earned it. She turned into the small lot of Bake My Day, chuckling at her unnecessary mental gymnastics.

She no sooner pulled into a parking spot than her eye caught a familiar car two spaces down. What was Audrey doing here? It was Audrey, right? How many BMW convertibles could there be in this little corner of upstate New York? Probably more than she cared to admit, given the influx of rich folks buying up lake property in the last ten years. Maybe it wasn't Audrey after all.

She had half a thought of leaving, not chancing a run-in. But eclairs. She'd come all this way and had her heart set on them.

Rowan shook her head. She was being ridiculous. She didn't have a problem with Audrey, save perhaps Audrey's unyielding stubbornness. And Audrey's beef with her was rooted in that stubbornness and not any real contention. If anything, bumping into each other casually might be her best shot at smoothing the waters.

Rowan chuckled again. Why was she overthinking everything today? It so wasn't her style. Because Audrey. Because Audrey had gotten in her head and was making her question things, big and small. It was asinine. And it needed to stop already.

She strode into the bakery with purpose, practically tasting the decadent custard filling on her tongue. Inside, the aromas—butter, chocolate, coffee, and who knew what else—enveloped her in a sugary hug. Oh, yes. There was no coming to Bake My Day and leaving empty-handed.

There was no line, so she walked right up to the counter. Amanda, the owner, offered her a warm smile. "Long time no see."

Rowan smiled in return. "For the record, I've been here like a dozen times and you've been baking or delivering or honeymooning."

Amanda beamed. "Fair enough. How have you been?"

"Really good. Keeping busy. You?"

"Same, same. How's the tasting room coming along?"

She blew out a breath. "Stalled for the moment. We spent a big chunk of our building budget on new fermentation tanks."

Amanda chuckled. "Been there. Well, with an oven, but still."

The bakery had undergone a major renovation and expansion the year before and she remained in awe of the transformation, not just aesthetically but in terms of how much it seemed to boost clientele. "If I can pull off something half as good as what you've done here, I'll be thrilled."

"You'll get there."

She appreciated the vote of confidence, especially from another small business owner. Even if that business owner had a decade more experience. "Thanks."

"So, what'll it be?"

"Eclairs for sure. Four, maybe?" And since she rarely got the pleasure of being served by the owner, she added, "And baker's choice. Surprise me."

"Coming right up."

Amanda boxed up her order and rang her out. She took a surreptitious glance around to see if Audrey was in fact the owner of the convertible outside. What she found was Audrey sitting with a group of women, hunched over a pair of knitting needles. The look of concentration on her face was so intense, it was almost as though her life depended on doing it right.

Not that she wanted to get into the habit of staring, but it was difficult not to. It reminded her of Audrey's expression when Rowan walked her through the process of feeding the animals or weeding the vegetable beds. When Audrey was eager to learn and maybe a little flirty. Before she decided Rowan was a con artist.

Would they ever get back to that? Get to know each other more? She hoped so.

Because things always seemed to pan out that way, Audrey looked up a fraction of a second before Rowan could tear her gaze away. Surprise, suspicion, and irritation played across her face in rapid succession. Well, hell.

Audrey got up from the table and came over. Rowan stood there, holding her box of goodies and probably looking awkward as hell. "Hi."

"What are you doing here?" Audrey whispered. Not technically a hiss but pretty damn close.

Audrey looked slightly perturbed and utterly gorgeous, and Rowan smiled before she could stop herself. "Eclairs."

Audrey's eyes narrowed. "You're not following me?"

Seriously? Why did she like this woman again? "I'm not following you."

Audrey frowned, like maybe she realized how ridiculous she sounded. "Sorry. I just…Never mind."

Unsure what to make of the shift, Rowan tipped her head in the direction of the table. "Avid knitter?"

"Huh?" Audrey looked at her with surprise. "Oh. No. Learning. Or trying to."

Knitting was pretty much the last hobby she expected someone like Audrey to pick up, but who was she to judge? She clearly didn't know Audrey at all. "Nice."

"Yeah. I'm going to get back to it."

"Don't let me keep you." It sounded snarkier than she'd meant, but since Audrey already seemed perturbed, it probably didn't make much difference.

Audrey lifted her chin and smirked slightly. "Enjoy your eclairs."

The comment could have been snarky back but it almost— almost—felt like Audrey was flirting with her. Which was confusing. And enough to make her second-guess herself. Which was annoying. She needed to cut her losses and let it go. "Have fun knitting."

Audrey walked away and Rowan stood there for another moment, feeling foolish but unsure why. Then she headed to the door, shaking her head and wondering how the interaction had gone sideways. Not entirely bad, just sideways. Though, sideways seemed to be par for the course with Audrey. Maybe she needed to stop trying to figure her out and accept that they were never going to see eye to eye on anything.

The idea dampened her mood. She wanted Audrey to like her. She'd maybe, eventually, make peace with Audrey not liking her. This weird, almost hot and cold vibe from Audrey simply baffled her.

Despite every intention of devouring the first eclair in the parking lot, she didn't linger. Fortunately, the Tractor Supply wasn't far and had a nice big parking lot where she could get up close and personal with one of her pastries without worrying about an audience. Because she wasn't known for patience when it came to sweets. And after that bizarre conversation with Audrey, she could use a sugary distraction more than ever.

CHAPTER EIGHT

Audrey pulled the camisole-style nightgown over her head and smiled. There was something extra delicious about clean pajamas after a hot shower. And, as she was learning, something extra delicious about a hot shower after the sweat and dirt of an afternoon of farming. Well, gardening. Mostly weeding. Essential part of the gardening process, if not the most exciting. Though, there was something profoundly satisfying in yanking unwelcome things out, root and all.

She padded downstairs and into the kitchen. She needed dinner but mostly wanted a glass of wine. She tipped her head this way and that, having the sort of argument with herself she imagined many people had with their kids. She settled on some hunks of baguette with cheese and a handful of grapes, because it counted as dinner and went well with wine.

She slipped on a pair of flip-flops and took her plate—and her well-earned glass of sauvignon blanc—out to the front porch. Having inhaled her dinner in about twenty seconds, Matilda joined her, happy to be outside together and ever hopeful of crumbs. She pulled the door closed behind her and let out a contented sigh. The sun had set and the first fireflies of dusk dotted the yard.

She'd no sooner settled into her favorite rocking chair when the most awful noise pierced the quiet evening. She set her glass down and leaned forward, as though that might help her sort out what it was or where it had come from. It came again, a sort of plaintive wail that had to belong to an animal in distress. Her insides twisted. It seemed to be coming from the barn.

After a moment of hesitation—because that sounded better than paralyzed indecision—she put Matilda in the house and grabbed her phone. Halfway down the porch steps, she realized what she was wearing and turned around. The sound came a third time and she turned around again, heading to the barn with only a detour to pull on her muck boots. A compromise of sorts.

Once inside the barn, she hesitated again. If a wild animal had somehow gotten in and gotten stuck, she had no idea what to do about it. Then again, if it was one of Ernestine's animals sick or hurt, she wouldn't know what to do with that either.

When the sound came again, it seemed to envelop her. It was definitely a bleat. And it was coming from the goat pen. Shit.

Audrey hurried over, stomach in her throat. "It's okay, guys. I'm here."

Ozzie was nowhere to be seen but Harriet lay on her side, looking both lethargic and miserable. Was she hurt? Sick?

Her heart raced, helplessness and fear pulsing through her veins as much as blood. Who was Ernestine's vet? And did they answer the phone after hours?

She darted back to the house, imagining a list of emergency numbers stuck to the fridge with a magnet. Unfortunately, Ernestine had joined the digital age and the only thing on the refrigerator were postcards from Prague—her last vacation—and Antigua—her parents'. She headed back to the barn, afraid of what she'd find but even more afraid of what might have happened in her absence.

Harriet was unchanged, though Ozzie had come in from their fenced area to investigate the situation. Audrey groaned with frustration. She needed a vet. Any vet. Well, any vet who'd answer the phone. Preferably one who made after-hours house calls.

House calls.

For some reason, the phrase made Rowan's face appear in her mind. She groaned again, though it came out as more of a growl. Was there a person on the planet she wanted to ask for help less than Rowan?

Harriet bleated again and Audrey would swear on a bible it sounded like a please. She pulled up her last text exchange with Rowan—the one before she'd learned Rowan was a conniving jerk—and tapped the phone icon to initiate a call. She'd ask if Rowan could recommend a vet and be done with it. It would be ten seconds. She could suck it up for ten seconds.

"Hello?"

Based on the surprise in Rowan's voice, she should probably be grateful Rowan picked up. "Hi."

"Is everything okay? Is it Ernestine?"

Fear must have lowered her defenses because the concern in Rowan's voice softened her. "It's Harriet. She's sick or injured or something and I don't know what to do."

"I'll be right there."

"I was looking for the name of a vet. You don't have to—"

"I'll be right there."

The call ended before she could argue. And she would have argued, on principle at least. In reality, she was relieved. And glad Rowan was coming.

The crunch of tires on gravel announced Rowan's arrival only a minute or two later. "In here," she called, even though it wasn't necessary.

"Okay, what seems to be the problem?" Rowan—solid, steady, and calm—appeared at her side.

"I don't know. She's clearly in pain but I didn't want to poke at her and make it worse."

Without comment or hesitation, Rowan unlatched the gate and stepped into the stall. She knelt next to Harriet and brought the back of her hand to Harriet's nose before giving her a gentle pet. She moved her hand to Harriet's middle and Harriet's whole belly rippled. Audrey's did a lot more than ripple.

Rowan turned to her with a smile. "She's not sick. She's in labor."

"What?" Audrey's voice pitched louder and higher than she would have liked.

Rowan stood. "I completely forgot until just now, but Ernestine mentioned something about her being pregnant. It was a surprise to her, too, because the place she adopted her from said both Ozzie and Harriet were, you know, past their prime."

A laugh bubbled up and escaped before she could stop it. Not that it was funny. No, it was anything but, given that she had no idea how to deliver a baby goat. But the almost manic sound perfectly reflected her barely lessened panic. As if to drive home the point, Harriet let out her saddest bleat yet. "We have to call a vet."

"I don't mean to burst your bubble, but I don't think most vets will come out for a standard birthing, especially at this time of evening."

"Do you mean we have to take her to the hospital? Is it okay to move her?" Her disquietude intensified. "Are there goat hospitals?"

Rowan put a hand on her arm and though Audrey would be dead before she'd admit it, the warmth of her touch proved more reassuring than her words. "No. I mean we keep an eye on her and let her do her thing. Animals are pretty good at this."

Even if a tiny part of her logical brain accepted that, believed it, the panicky part didn't let it get a word in edgewise. "But how do we know if everything is going how it's supposed to go?"

Rowan lifted a shoulder, almost sheepish. "I mean, I've done it a few times."

"You have?"

"With sheep mostly, and cows. But it's pretty similar I think."

Similar or not, it was about a billion times more experience than she had. She swallowed—both her pride and the lump that had worked its way into her throat. "Would you stay?"

She didn't think Rowan would abandon her entirely, but maybe a "call me if there are these signs of trouble." At the very least, she expected a sort of smug satisfaction at having the upper hand. But Rowan's smile was gentle. "Of course."

The squeeze she gave Rowan's arm had a trace of desperate mixed in with the grateful, but she didn't care. No point pretending she was anything else. "Thank you."

"I'm guessing it's going to be a few hours. Why don't I do some quick internet research and you can look around for supplies. I'm guessing Ernestine was prepared before..."

When Rowan didn't finish the thought, Audrey nodded vigorously, both in agreement and to make it clear she didn't need to say more. "On it."

Rowan smiled again. This one seemed to hold mischief, though Audrey couldn't imagine why. "And you might want to change your clothes."

Only then, when she looked down, did she realize she was standing in the middle of the goat pen in muck boots and a gauzy summer nightgown that just barely squeaked out of the negligée category. "Shit."

To her credit, Rowan didn't laugh. She did raise a brow, though, and her eyes danced with humor. "Not that it isn't a really nice look on you."

She deserved that. So whatever issues she had with Rowan, this wasn't the time or the place to be prissy about it. "I appreciate you pointing that out. Are you okay for a few minutes?"

Rowan nodded. "It really is going to be a while."

As self-conscious as she now was about her attire, she went poking around the barn. It didn't take long to find a plastic storage tote labeled "kidding kit." She brought it to Rowan and they shared a moment chuckling over the name and Ernestine's penchant for being prepared. And for her label maker. She turned to go but remembered her abandoned dinner and paused. "Have you eaten?"

Rowan shrugged. "Not yet. Big lunch, though."

Something told her Rowan was just being gracious now. "I can bring you something."

"Don't go to any trouble." This affable, easy Rowan reminded her of the Rowan she met, not the one she swore to loath for all eternity. In fact, the Rowan she swore to loath was getting harder and harder to pin down.

"I'm not offering anything fancy. Just bread and cheese." She tipped her head. "And wine."

"That sounds fantastic."

She hurried back to the house, taking a second to check out her reflection in the back door glass. Not that she needed to. She closed her eyes for a second. Yep. Ridiculous.

She toed off her boots and went inside, replacing the nightie with jeans and a T-shirt. She retrieved her makeshift dinner from the front porch and made a second plate, poured a second glass of wine. Balancing it all on Ernestine's breakfast tray made her feel silly, but the ship of self-dignity had sailed so why worry now?

By the time she'd tugged her boots back on and made her way to the barn, Rowan had pulled two of the Adirondack chairs over from the fire pit, creating a makeshift seating area just outside the barn. With the dusky sky and view of the garden, it looked downright charming. If poor Harriet wasn't bleating away, it could easily hop right over charming and land squarely in romantic. Well, Harriet's bleating and the fact that it was Rowan, of course. "Is it weird to have a picnic while an animal is in labor?"

"I don't think Harriet cares one way or the other. Besides, we're going to need our strength."

She regarded the tray. "Does that mean you don't want wine?"

"Oh, I want wine."

She appreciated Rowan's humor almost as much as her calm. She handed Rowan a glass and picked up hers. "Cheers."

Rowan tapped her glass to Audrey's and they both drank. They settled into the chairs and ate mostly in silence. It should have felt awkward and tense, but it didn't.

Rowan asked a few innocuous questions about her work. She did the same. The unresolved accusations she'd hurled at Rowan felt a bit like the elephant in the room, but Rowan didn't seem interested in bringing them up. A myriad of overtures and apologies flitted through her mind, but none of them felt right, so she kept them to herself.

They took turns checking on Harriet and commenting on the beauty of the night sky in early summer. She asked at least a half dozen times if Rowan was sure she was okay staying. When it got to the point where Rowan's only reply was a smirk and a slightly exasperated look, she stopped.

❖

"My turn." Rowan hefted herself from her chair and turned. Audrey smiled and made a sweeping gesture with her hand that said by all means. Not an apology, exactly, but she'd take the mix of humble and grateful. It was nice, for whatever it was worth, to feel like they were back on the same team. They'd sort out the rest later.

She headed into the barn, checking her watch. It was going on two. How had that happened?

Rather than pondering how easy it was to spend time with Audrey—even while technically still feuding—she focused her attention on Harriet. The white mucus had given way to blood, and she could make out the amniotic sac beginning to emerge. Despite the confidence she'd tried to channel for Audrey, her heart leapt into her throat.

Confident or not, they were doing this.

"I think we're getting close." Rowan had no sooner finished the sentence than Audrey appeared at her side.

"How do you—oh." Audrey's mouth fell open.

"Often, kids are born with the amniotic sac intact."

Audrey's head swiveled back and forth slowly. "Wow."

Rowan nudged Audrey to the barn sink so they could wash up and be ready. Harriet pushed and Rowan prepared herself to jump in at any sign of distress. She let herself take occasional glances at Audrey, who had so many emotions playing across her features Rowan couldn't even begin to name them.

The sac emerged intact, bursting only when it hit the bedding on the ground. Rowan knelt next to the kid, a buck, rubbing it all over and offering words of encouragement and praise to mama and baby alike. She shifted the kid closer to Harriet and she immediately went to work licking and cleaning him.

"Oh, my God." Audrey knelt on the ground next to her. "That really just happened."

Harriet's body contracted. Rowan smiled. "It looks like it's about to happen again."

Harriet struggled more with the second kid. His front legs emerged, but his head got stuck. Rowan said a prayer of thanks—for the gloves and lubricant in Ernestine's kidding box and for the summers she spent pulling calves at her aunt and uncle's dairy farm.

She worried Audrey might balk, if not pass out. She never wavered, though. For not having a clue what she was doing, she pitched in like a champ, even cutting the umbilical cords and dabbing them with iodine.

When there was nothing left for them to do, they sat back in the straw and simply watched. It didn't take long for both kids to fumble to their feet. Harriet nosed, nudged, and continued to lick them both and then it wasn't long before they started to nurse.

"How do they know what to do?" Audrey asked.

"I think it's instinct."

"Is it wrong that I find animals way more impressive than humans in this moment?"

Rowan laughed. "No. That seems about right. At least in the moment."

Rowan stood and extended her hands. Audrey took them and let Rowan haul her to her feet. Audrey had a smile for her, but her attention immediately went back to the kids. "Now what?"

"We let mama do her thing and keep an eye on everyone. And call Ernestine's vet. The after birth care I read about seemed a little more complicated, so I defer to the experts."

Audrey seemed reluctant to leave but followed Rowan outside. The sun hadn't officially risen, but the eastern sky was a riot of pink, orange, and purple. Rowan took a minute to soak it in. She wasn't always up at dawn this time of year, but often enough. Even by farmer standards, this one put on quite a show.

"What time is it?" Audrey asked.

She'd tucked her watch away so she pulled it out now. "Not quite five."

Audrey turned to face her, expression serious. "I've kept you here all night."

She smiled. "It's okay. I knew what I was signing up for."

Audrey clearly hadn't. She shook her head once again. "I don't know how to thank you."

"You already have." At least twenty times over the course of the night.

"You know what I mean. I want to do something to thank you." Audrey looked at the ground before making eye contact. "And to apologize."

"How about dinner?" She'd meant to imply a return to the way things had been, but the phrasing made it sound like she was asking Audrey on a date. Based on Audrey's incredulous look, it sounded like that to her, too. "Friendly dinner, I mean."

"Dinner would be a small price to pay for your services last night." Despite the reference to the night before, Audrey seemed to be talking about a lot more.

"Yeah, but I'll gladly take it." The payment, the implied apology, the promise of a détente—she'd take it all.

"I'm sorry if I've ruined you for whatever you needed to get done today."

Rowan waved off the apology. "Perk of owning my own business. I can knock off early for a nap."

"Still. I literally don't know what I would have done without you here."

"I was happy to help. I promise."

"Well, I'm grateful. Like, don't even have words to say how grateful."

She was filthy and exhausted but suddenly didn't want to leave. "You sure you're okay on your own?"

"I am. I'll call the vet as soon as they open." Audrey's smile reached her gorgeous brown eyes. "And I have you on speed dial."

"Indeed you do. Don't hesitate, okay?"

Audrey seemed to consider before saying, "I won't."

"Get some sleep, too. It was a long night but an intense one, too."

Audrey laughed. "Massive understatement."

"Is it okay if I check in later?" She figured it would be welcome but wanted Audrey to confirm it, to say it out loud.

"That would be great."

Since she'd officially crossed the line into stalling, she lifted a hand. "All right, then. Take care."

Audrey nodded with more feeling than the situation warranted, leaving Rowan to wonder if it was fatigue or her own version of an awkward good-bye. "You, too."

She headed to her truck and climbed in, resisting the urge to let her head fall back and her eyes close. She drove the thirty or so seconds to her house and pulled into the drive. Fully out of Audrey's line of sight, she indulged. Just for a second.

She might have dozed off. And she might have jerked awake and banged her knee on the steering wheel when Ferdinand crowed. She laughed and slid out of the truck. What a night.

Inside, Jack lifted his head from the sofa, looking equal parts bored and judgmental.

"Don't give me that look. I wasn't on some hot date."

One eyebrow lifted, then the other.

"I mean, she was hot, but it wasn't like that. We were bringing life into the world, man."

Jack got up from his spot and came over, tail wagging. It probably had more to do with being happy to see her—and wanting to be fed—than her explanation, but she didn't mind.

She let him out and started coffee, let him in and gave him breakfast. The aroma of the coffee made its usual promises, but she headed for the shower first. She could sit and enjoy the first cup before heading to work.

She was scheduled to help with disgorging and corking today, which was too bad. Maybe she could convince Dylan to flip-flop the schedule. Partly because she wanted to spend the day outside, partly because she didn't trust herself to do finicky tasks on no sleep.

Whatever the day held, she'd try to make it over to Ernestine's at least once. To check on Harriet and the kids, of course. She rinsed shampoo from her head and lathered soap over her body. It was a thin excuse. She wanted to see Audrey, plain and simple. Wanted to make sure she was okay. Wanted to reinforce whatever peace they'd made.

And, okay, she wanted to see the baby goats.

CHAPTER NINE

When Rowan left, Audrey headed inside, bypassing the kitchen and heading right for the bathroom. She would have expected getting that up close and personal with animal body fluids would gross her out, but it hadn't. Not in the moment, at least. She'd been so caught up in the wonder of it, she'd barely noticed.

Now was a different matter. She was crusty, grimy, and didn't even want to think about what she must smell like. She cranked the shower and climbed in, letting out an audible moan of pleasure. The hot water pelted her, managing to feel like heaven and draw her attention to sore and stiff muscles at the same time.

After, she padded to her room and crawled into bed. Stretching out in the clean sheets felt glorious and she spent a few minutes rolling around and reveling in it. But when she settled onto her side and tried to fall asleep in earnest, nothing happened.

Well, not nothing. Her mind flitted about, barely landing on one thing before moving on to the next. Ernestine would be sad to have missed the birth, but it would be fun to tell her all about it. Had Ernestine picked out names? Had she known there would be two? What had Rowan thought when her phone rang with Audrey's number? She still couldn't believe Rowan showed up—and stayed all night—without a second of hesitation. What was Rowan doing now?

After several minutes of this, she tossed the covers aside and got up. Maybe she could take a nap later. Maybe.

She pulled on clean clothes and headed downstairs to get the coffee started, then realized she was starving and made herself a real breakfast. With bacon. She even squeezed a glass of orange juice. Ernestine would be so proud.

When eight o'clock rolled around, she started calling every vet in a twenty-mile radius. Fortunately, there were only three and it didn't take long to track down which one was Ernestine's. And, best news of the day, they made house calls. She got a list of instructions and things to watch out for, along with an appointment the following day.

Despite wanting to spend the whole day in the barn watching the kids nurse or sort out the tricky business of walking on four legs, she allowed herself only a peek and a hello before morning chores. Since she'd finally managed a peace treaty with the chickens, she didn't want to do anything that might jeopardize it. She fed and watered—animals and plants—then picked lettuce, cucumbers, and cherry tomatoes so she could have a salad for lunch.

Satisfied with her accomplishments, she returned to the goat pen, prepared to while away most of the day watching them. Harriet seemed to be doing great. Her bleating had returned to its usual conversational cadence and she seemed to be a proud and happy mama. Ozzie was no help, but she sort of expected that.

No surprise, the real stars were the babies. They bumbled about, making the cutest little noises and running into each other, Harriet, and occasionally the wall. They also seemed to be nursing well. A huge relief given the dozens of websites she'd read in the wee hours of the morning, trying to wrap her head around signs of trouble while she and Rowan waited.

"It was quite a night, you guys."

Harriet continued to chew her hay, but her expression changed. Like Audrey had a lot of nerve to be the one saying that.

"For all of us but mostly for you."

That seemed to satisfy Harriet and she pulled another wad of hay from the hopper.

"Aren't you glad you weren't stuck with only me?"

Harriet bobbed her head up and down. To be fair, she did that a lot. Still.

"Rowan really saved the day, didn't she?" She'd convinced herself Rowan's goodwill gestures—from the chicken coop rescue on—were no more than ploys to get in her good graces. Mostly convinced herself, at least. All to bolster her determination to think the worst of Rowan. Now, the whole thing made her feel foolish.

In the span of one very long, eventful night, Rowan had laid all that to rest and proven herself to be a decent, caring human being. Admitting it meant swallowing her pride and owning she'd been both judgmental and downright mean. A humbling thought, but better than thinking she'd been hoodwinked by little more than some broad shoulders and a flirty smile.

Audrey sighed. It was the fear of being duped that had done her in. She'd made it all about Ernestine, but really it had as much to do with herself. She wasn't suspicious by nature, exactly, but guarded. And Rowan had slipped in and made her comfortable in ways that still baffled her. She hadn't wanted to reconcile that, so she let herself assume the worst and went off the deep end instead.

And now, the memory of Rowan in action—her strong, competent hands and the look of fierce concentration—sent ripples of, well, something through her. She could pretend it was gratitude, or an emotional manifestation in response to her own crippling helplessness. But pretending would be a lie and she wasn't in the habit of lying to herself, at least not knowingly. She was attracted to Rowan. Since that was something she wanted to deal with even less than admitting she'd been wrong, she decided to start with the latter.

She took a deep breath and squared her shoulders. Okay. First things first. Apology baking.

She pulled her hair back, cranked some tunes on the portable speaker she'd given Ernestine for Christmas, and got to work. An hour later, the kitchen smelled like butter and sugar and chocolate. She'd just finished cleaning up when the timer beeped. After opening the oven and indulging in a long inhale, she slid the pan out and set it on a rack to cool.

Should she bring dinner, too, or was that overkill? Probably overkill. She'd already offered a dinner of gratitude. The brownies were pure apology. Best not to muddle the two.

She checked on Harriet and the kids, took another shower, and did a little bit of pacing and thumb twiddling to pass the time. She was pretty sure Rowan didn't keep precise regular business hours, but waiting until five seemed likely to increase her chances of finding Rowan at home. She stepped outside to a breezy, sunny afternoon—the kind with giant puffy clouds that slowly changed shape.

She'd always enjoyed watching them, even if her ability to see people and animals and scenes fell a bit flat. Maybe she'd try again, with a blanket and a picnic and nowhere to be for an afternoon. Where had that come from? Lack of sleep, probably. She'd never been one to rock an all-nighter. Even when studying for the CPA exam, she was meticulously structured with her time management. And during the busy seasons at work, it was her social life that suffered more than her sleep schedule.

Anyway. Rowan. Brownies. Making nice. That was the task at hand.

Despite the nervous butterflies that had taken up residence in her stomach, she enjoyed the short walk. The pit bull mix she'd seen ambling through the orchard lounged on the porch, which she took as a good sign. Since he offered her a goofy smile and his tail wagged with enthusiasm, she gave his head a scratch on her way to the door. But she'd no sooner knocked when it occurred to her maybe Rowan had gone to work and come home and was now trying to get some sleep.

Before she could stress about it or think of a plan B, Rowan's face appeared in the glass and the door swung open. "Hi."

"Hi." Why was she so nervous?

Rowan smiled but looked mildly concerned. "Is everything okay?"

"Oh. Yes. Great."

"Good."

Pull it together. "Sorry. I didn't mean to disturb you, but I wanted to say thank you again for last night."

Rowan's smile took on a playful edge. "Baked goods thank you? I thought you were going to make me dinner."

"Yes. I will. I want to, I mean." Heat rose in her cheeks, making her feel silly. "I wanted to do something else, though."

"I feel like I should say you shouldn't have, but if there are baked goods involved, it would be disingenuous."

She continued to blush but for a completely different reason. "I'm pretty sure I should have."

"Well, thank you." Rowan accepted the plastic-wrapped plate of brownies and searched Audrey's face for meaning. Was this her way of apologizing? Or just laying it on thick with the thank you? It killed her not to know but she couldn't bring herself to ask.

"I'm sorry." Audrey looked up and her eyes held even more remorse than her words.

"Okay." Was it rude to ask what exactly she was apologizing for?

"I was wrong."

Something gave her the feeling that wasn't a phrase Audrey uttered very often.

"I don't like the fact that you seemed to be withholding the specifics from me, but I don't think you're trying to swindle Ernestine out of her land. I think you're a good friend to her and you were trying to be a friend to me."

It was a hell of a lot more than she expected to get from Audrey, even after the last twenty-four hours. "Thank you."

"I'm also sorry for hurling those accusations as belligerently as I did and that I did it at your place of business."

For some reason, the overly formal language made it seem authentic rather than forced. "Thank you for that, too."

"I hope I didn't make things difficult for you."

She laughed. "You did, but not in the way you're thinking. My partner's been teasing me about having a talent for getting myself into trouble."

"Ah." If the look on Audrey's face was anything to go on, it was the absolute wrong thing to say. But since Audrey stood on her doorstep with a peace offering, she didn't worry about it overmuch.

"Anyway, thank you, both for the brownies and the apology."

"You're welcome." Audrey shifted her weight from foot to foot, looking both uncomfortable and unsure of how to make a graceful exit.

"I'd love to chat, and hear how the babies and mama are faring, but I'm afraid you're catching me on my way out."

Audrey managed to look startled and relieved at the same time. "Oh. Of course. I'm sorry. Don't let me keep you."

"I wouldn't normally be such a stickler about it, but my mother does not look kindly on anyone who holds up dinner. Even her favorite child."

"Yes. Yes, you wouldn't want to keep her waiting." The comment seemed to put Audrey at ease. Whether it was the mildly funny mom joke or the roundabout reassurance she wasn't rushing off on some hot date, Rowan couldn't be sure. It shouldn't really matter, but she wondered nonetheless.

"Would it be all right if I stopped by tomorrow?"

Audrey's gaze, that had drifted down to her feet, shot up. "You should come for dinner."

"Really?" She didn't think Audrey would back out of her offer, exactly, but well, maybe.

"If you don't have other plans, of course."

She visualized the day of bottling, capping, and labeling that waited for her tomorrow. And how nice a decent meal and some charming company would be at the end of it. "That would be great."

"Good. Okay. Yes. I won't keep you then."

She turned to go but Rowan couldn't help herself. "Audrey."

"Yes?"

It was wrong to think about how beautiful Audrey looked in that moment, right? Hair loose and eyes sparkling with what felt like eagerness. "I'm looking forward to it."

"Me, too."

Audrey offered a shy smile and a parting wave, leaving Rowan standing on the porch with a plate of brownies so decadent the aroma of chocolate wafted up at her through the plastic. The nap she'd fantasized about but didn't get, the delicious dinner waiting for her at her parents' house—all of it took a back seat to wanting to spend the evening with Audrey. Alas. She didn't bail on family dinners. And Audrey had invited her over tomorrow, not tonight. She could be patient. If being an orchardist had taught her anything, it was that.

She went inside to set the brownies on the counter and grab her keys. She hesitated only a second before snagging one. One wouldn't spoil her appetite, right?

She polished it off in the ten or so steps it took her to get to her truck. As she backed onto the road, possibilities danced through her mind. Would she and Audrey become friends? Would that flirty energy return? Would that flirty energy turn into something more?

Not for the first time since she'd found Audrey perched on the top of the chicken coop, she wondered how Audrey's mouth would feel under hers, how Audrey's body would fit against hers. On the drive, her thoughts continued to wander, though they all seemed to be moving in a singular direction. A few degrees south of strictly platonic.

Audrey had barely decided not to hate her. Indulging fantasies of kissing—and a whole lot more than kissing—was the last thing she should be doing. She let out a chuckle and turned up the radio. So much for being patient.

CHAPTER TEN

Just like that first night Audrey invited her for dinner, Rowan spent a little too long deciding what to wear. And just like that night, she snagged a bottle of cider from the fridge on her way out. She went with a wild crab this time, thinking the subtle effervescence and balance of sharp and sweet matched the delicacy of their relationship.

There was a slight possibility she was overthinking it.

She knocked on Ernestine's side door, hoping the move was casual in a good way and not familiar in ways that had gotten her into trouble with Audrey in the first place. When Audrey opened the door with a tentative smile, she let out a sigh of relief that bordered on overkill. "Hi."

"Hi." Audrey's look turned questioning. "Is everything okay?"

Should she admit having a tiny fear that Audrey would change her mind and slam the door in her face? "Yeah. For sure. I was thinking about the goats."

A ridiculous answer but one that could cover any number of sins.

"Do you want to go see them first? You won't hurt my feelings."

The playfulness in Audrey's voice took the edge off her uncertainly. And since declining would essentially blow her cover, she nodded. "I do."

Audrey reached for the bottle in her hand. "Here, I'll take that and put it in the fridge. You go on and I'll be right out."

She headed over to the goat pen. The kids hadn't mastered jumping yet, but they were already trying, and their awkward attempts made her smile. As did the fact that they were already exploring the yard, running back to Harriet every few seconds, but not hiding behind her.

When Audrey joined her, they stood at the fence side-by-side and she could almost forget they'd been feuding. Did Audrey feel that way, too? "Have you named them yet?"

Audrey shook her head. "I feel like Ernestine should get to."

"Yeah."

"But I confess I've been thinking of them as Bert and Ernie." Audrey turned to her with a shrug. "I can't decide if Ernestine will appreciate having a namesake."

"She'd never do it herself, but she'll probably get a laugh out of you doing it."

"We'll see." A sadness passed through Audrey's eyes, but it disappeared as quickly as it came. "Dinner's ready if I can tear you away."

"You can tear me away from pretty much anything for a good meal."

"I'll remember that."

Audrey insisted the roasted pork loin was nothing special, but it knocked her socks off. As did the sweet potato wedges and apple and celery slaw she served with it. In between stuffing her face, she asked about the visit from the vet and how Harriet was doing. Conversation remained light, keeping mostly to a rehash of their unexpected night of midwifing and being too old to stay up all hours.

Dessert was an elaborate affair of meringue, berries, and cream that Audrey called a pavlova. It managed to be light and rich at the same time and Rowan didn't hesitate to note that she could probably finish the whole thing if left to her own devices. After a full second helping, she attempted restraint. Conversation lulled. Perhaps it—along with the apology and the brownies and dinner—meant all was well, but she wanted to hear Audrey say it. "So, we're friends again?"

"I'd like that." Audrey looked at her tea for a moment. "If you would."

Rowan sighed. "I never didn't want to be friends."

"Right." There was sadness in Audrey's eyes, paired with something resembling regret.

"I mean that in a good way."

Audrey nodded. "I appreciate that. And how much you help Ernestine. Trying to do everything myself has been brutal."

"It's a lot." She honestly wasn't sure how Ernestine kept up.

"Ernestine is lucky to have such a good neighbor. And I know she'd be loathe to take your help if she wasn't giving you something in return." Audrey looked into her eyes. "Something more than dinner and sweets."

That's what made the arrangement so perfect. It meant a lot to have Audrey finally see that, appreciate it. "It helps both of us."

"I get that now."

"Does this mean you'll let me help without yelling or chasing me off?"

"I didn't chase you off."

"No?"

"Okay, I kind of chased you off." Audrey cracked a smile. "But not with a pitchfork or anything."

The image of Audrey wielding a pitchfork angry villager style should have made her laugh, but it sent a ripple of discomfort through her. "I want to help. Ernestine as much as you. And not just because of the orchard."

Despite the friendliness of the conversation, Audrey scowled. "The only way I'm accepting your help is if you accept something of value in return."

"You mean besides baked goods and the occasional dinner? I consider that pretty damn valuable."

"It's not the same. You're doing things I'd pay someone to do."

Rowan's lip curled before she could stop it. "You want to pay me?"

Audrey blew out a breath and considered. "I'd rather not. Can we work out a trade of some kind? Tit for tat?"

Audrey didn't seem to be joking so she resisted the urge to laugh at the phrase. She cleared her throat and tried to keep her expression serious. "What are you offering?"

"I don't know. Do you need an accountant?"

That might have been a joke. Or not. Either way, her mind started turning. "Kind of."

Audrey's eyes narrowed. "Are you making fun of me?"

"No. We can't afford a finance person, so Dylan and I tag team the books. And not to insult my own intelligence or hers, but we're pretty terrible at it."

"Cash basis or accrual?"

Thanks to the class she and Dylan took at the cooperative extension, she at least knew what those two things were. "Cash because it's easier, but I think accrual would be better for us financially."

That got her a slow nod. "Probably. But if you switch you have to commit to it. You can't go back and forth without raising red flags."

One of several reasons they hadn't taken the leap. "I think we could maintain it if we had a good system in place. We just haven't been able to afford a professional to get us there."

Audrey seemed to appreciate the mention of a professional, or perhaps the acknowledgment that it was the sort of job that warranted a professional. "If it was done well, you could maintain it."

A backhanded compliment at best, but she wasn't about to split hairs. Especially if it got her some accounting services for free. Or rather, in exchange for things she was already planning to do. "Is that your way of offering?"

Audrey scratched her temple. "Maybe."

She let the idea sink in—having her books whipped into shape by someone who did that sort of thing for a living and got paid God knows how much to do it. With or without being friends with Audrey again, it was enough to make her giddy. Not that she wasn't eager to be friends again. Maybe they'd never get back to the easy, flirty vibe of their first few interactions, but she'd take what she could get. "I'm willing to sweeten the deal with more farm chores." When Audrey narrowed her eyes once again, she added, "If that would seem fairer or whatever."

"We'll see."

"I'm sure your time and skills are very valuable. That's all I meant." Wanting to see more of Audrey, wanting to spend time with her, didn't have anything to do with it.

"All right." Audrey nodded slowly and a smirk seemed to play at the corners of her mouth.

Rowan swallowed the hum of attraction that buzzed in her ears and, well, elsewhere. She needed to run this by Dylan, but she had a hard time imagining Dylan would turn her nose up at free bookkeeping help. She also wanted to lock Audrey in before she thought better of it—offering her help, accepting help in return, as well as what it implied about their relationship going forward.

Relationship.

The word pinged around her mind like a pinball and had her imagining all sorts of things beyond a professional arrangement. She shook her head. They'd barely managed a truce. She was getting ahead of herself. If by "ahead" she meant another galaxy.

"What? Changing your mind?"

"Huh? Oh, sorry. Not at all. My mind, you know, wandered?"

She expected an eye roll—or a comparable expression—but Audrey's smirk bloomed into a full smile. "I'm familiar with the condition."

Was Audrey flirting with her? No. Friendly. She was being friendly. And friendliness was such a stark contrast to how testy she'd been. That had to be it. "So, what next? Do you require a formal contract?"

Audrey folded her arms. "I can tell you're teasing me, but it would be a good idea. At least on your part. You've got a lot at stake."

Her delivery was matter-of-fact, but Rowan appreciated the underlying consideration it implied. Maybe it fell under basic CPA code of ethics or something, but she let herself think it was more. Again, friendly. She wasn't looking for anything more than friendly. "I'm going to defer to your expertise."

Audrey nodded, all business now. "I'll write something up. Keep it simple, but in case you ever get audited or start working with an accountant more formally, there will be a paper trail."

"Audited?" The word caught in her throat like stale bread.

"I'm not saying you will, but it's a crap shoot with the IRS. Especially if you aren't turning much of a profit for several years running."

That was Forbidden Fruit, to be sure. "Okay."

Audrey reached over and put a hand on her arm. "Relax. Everyone freaks out about audits. They happen. It doesn't mean you did anything wrong. And unless you have done something egregiously wrong, the worst that can happen is you'll owe money."

Owing more than they already paid was pretty awful in her book, but she knew what Audrey meant. "Sorry. I promise that was layperson panic and not cooking the books panic."

Audrey sat back in her chair and laughed, surprising herself. The way Rowan made an accounting joke surprised her. Hell, this whole evening was surprising her. "I assumed that to be the case, but it's nice to hear you say it out loud."

"Oh, good. I'm not saying we haven't screwed up the books in some way, but I swear it wasn't intentional."

Now that she'd gone back to giving Rowan the benefit of the doubt, it wasn't a stretch to add, "My guess is you're not taking all the deductions and credits you're allowed. It's a common small business mistake."

"Really?"

One of the reasons she'd considered opening a practice for small businesses back in her grad school days. But the stability and security of a big firm had won out, not to mention the salary and promotions that came with it. "This is where I give you the lecture that a good accountant will likely save you more than they cost you."

Rowan shook her head. "That's what Dylan says about marketing. With revenue not savings, but you know what I mean."

"I do." She angled her head and tried to read Rowan's expression. "Do you disagree?"

"No, no. I just grew up in a family that was all about self-sufficiency, so it feels like cheating to pay people to do things I can do myself."

"But if it takes you twice as long, aren't there more valuable things to do with your time?"

Rowan pouted and it shouldn't have been cute but it was. "Are you in cahoots with Dylan? Did she set you up to say that?"

"Cahoots?" That was even better than the pout. "No. But speaking of your partner, you should probably run this plan by her."

"I'm sure she'll say yes, but you're right."

"Well, given her first impression of me." She cringed at the memory.

"How about you come over? We can give you a tour and pretend that first time never happened, especially since you technically didn't even meet."

The idea of a do-over appealed. "It would be good to talk through what you're looking for, the scope of work."

Rowan nodded with enthusiasm. "Exactly. We can do a proper tasting, too. You can see what Forbidden Fruit is all about."

It almost felt like Rowan wanted to impress her. Or maybe, show Audrey that she ran a legitimate business. Which gave her a pang of guilt. "I'd love that, but I don't want you to feel obligated."

Rowan smiled. "I don't. We don't get the chance to show off much. It'll be good practice for when we start tours and open up the tasting room."

That made it better. "Well, if you need the practice."

"We do. So, it's settled."

It was. Or, at least, that was. She still had a few things needling her, though. And now was as good a time as any to deal with them. "I feel like I need to acknowledge what you said to me the other morning. About me being jealous of your relationship with Ernestine."

Rowan shook her head. "I shouldn't have said that. It was crossing a line."

"Maybe. But it was—is—accurate. I didn't want to admit that anyone could be closer to Ernestine than me, but in a lot of ways you are." It hurt her heart to say it, but that was her issue, not Rowan's.

"Closer because of proximity and how often we see each other. Ernestine loves you."

She didn't doubt that. And for so much of her life, Ernestine's love and acceptance and pride filled the gap left by her well-meaning but emotionally absent parents. But for some reason, it felt shallow now. At the very least, one-sided. She wasn't that lost little girl anymore. She was a grown woman, full of gratitude but capable of so much more.

"Was that the wrong thing to say, too? I'm sorry if it was. It's not my place to say that."

It might not be, but the truths stirred up by the initial question wouldn't change or go away. Again, her problem, not Rowan's. "No. It's fine. I overreacted and I wanted to apologize for that, too."

Rowan didn't say anything. Her expression held understanding and not pity exactly, but maybe patience. Like she'd happily play therapist if Audrey wanted to bare her soul.

Ugh. No, thank you. "Anyway, since we're clearing the air, I wanted to clear all of it."

"Okay." Rowan smiled but Audrey would swear disappointment flashed in her eyes.

"Okay, good. So, you let me know when I can come by to meet your partner. Other than the days I visit Ernestine and my Saturday knitting group, I'm pretty much free."

Rowan's head angled slightly. "You joined the knitting group at the bakery?"

"I did." She enjoyed Rowan's surprise as much as the change of subject. "I'm pretty terrible so far, but it's fun."

"It's good to do things you're terrible at sometimes."

It could have been a dig, but it didn't feel like one. It felt like casual observation. Encouraging even?

"It exercises parts of your brain you're not used to using." Rowan winked. "And it keeps you humble."

She grinned. She'd take mild teasing over a heart-to-heart any day. "Like farming."

Rowan tipped her head. "Like farming. Speaking of, are there particular things you want me to do?"

If a small part of her wanted to hand off mucking duty, the rest of her fair and logical brain knew that wasn't the point. "There's a section of fence that looks like it's going to go. I'd hate to hunt down a contractor for such a small job."

"I'm sure we can handle it."

"And I need some real lessons in the vegetable garden and the kitchen orchard. I'm not sure what each thing needs beyond knowing they're all different, and I don't want to mess anything up beyond repair."

"You won't mess anything up. But tending things the right way should yield you a nice crop, so why don't we set the bar a little higher?"

It sounded like a challenge. That, she could get behind. And a much better mindset than wondering if she'd be here long enough to have a crop to harvest. "Deal."

CHAPTER ELEVEN

W ait, wait, wait." Dylan lifted a hand. "Let me make sure I'm getting this right."

"All right." Rowan folded her arms. She'd been perfectly clear. Dylan was merely ribbing her.

"So, she calls you in a panic. You go over. You stay all night while Ernestine's goat has babies. And now she's not mad at you anymore."

"Basically."

Dylan lifted the beaker of cider she was checking and gave it a swirl in the light. "That's the most absurd thing I've ever heard."

Well, phrasing it like that sure did. But she didn't want to give Dylan the satisfaction. And she'd already told Dylan that part when she walked into work yesterday looking like a zombie. "It's not absurd. Stressful situations often bring people together. This was stressful and included the miracle of life."

"The miracle of life." Dylan used a pipette to collect a few drops of the cider and did whatever she did to test for sugar and alcohol levels, scribbling the results in the leather-bound journal she used in lieu of a computer. She didn't bother to make eye contact or hide the sarcasm in her voice.

"Have you ever seen anything born?"

Dylan shuddered. "No."

"You're such a city kid."

"I grew up in the suburbs of Buffalo."

Rowan shrugged. "Same difference."

"Whatever." Dylan set the sample aside. "Back to the subject at hand. So, you have a moment. She bakes you brownies. You go over for dinner. You make up. And now she's going to be our accountant?"

"You're trying to make it sound ridiculous." Which totally wasn't cool since the end result would benefit them both.

Dylan tipped her head to the side. "Or maybe it is ridiculous."

"No. We made up and I asked if that meant she'd let me help out again. You know, around the farm like I do for Ernestine. And I think she's the kind of person who has a hard time with people doing nice things for her, so she insisted on trading something for it." Since she'd done her best to set aside her attraction to Audrey at the time, she didn't bother mentioning it now.

"Uh huh."

"And she made a joke about asking if we needed an accountant and I said we did."

"Only you, Rowan. Only you."

She did have a way of connecting with people—in ways that turned out to be mutually beneficial—maybe more often than most, but it didn't strike her as all that strange. "Are you saying you don't want her help?"

"Oh, no." Dylan shook her head with vigor. "I'm not saying that at all. I absolutely want her help."

"So, maybe don't give me such a hard time, then."

Dylan pressed a hand to her chest. "But if I don't, who will?"

"I'm pretty sure my siblings would be only too happy to step in." They'd been harassing her long before she and Dylan ever met.

"Right, right." Dylan, one of three, nodded sagely. "I'll stand down. If for no other reason than I'm legit ecstatic you got us an accountant."

Regardless of her arguments to Dylan, even she could admit it had come about rather strangely. Still, she wasn't going to look a gift of financial expertise in the mouth. She'd just have to resist the urge to look too much at Audrey's mouth. And think about what it would be like—taste like—to kiss her. "She's going to come over tomorrow to talk with both of us."

Dylan grinned. "Don't worry, I'll be charming."

"That's not what I'm worried about." If anything, she worried Dylan might be a little too charming.

"Are you scared I'm going to ask her out?"

Teasing or not, the question cut a hair too close to the direction of her thoughts. "You can't ask her out."

"I know, I know. If anyone is going to ask her out, it's going to be you."

"No one is asking her out." Not that she hadn't thought about it. And a hell of a lot more.

"Blah, blah. Professional. Blah, blah."

Because Dylan was egging her on, she shrugged. "One of us has to be."

That did the trick. Dylan's features sobered and her shoulders straightened. "I'm professional."

Dylan had a maverick approach to cider making. It helped her make a name for herself but also raised the ire of some of the more traditional, established members of the cider community. It was a small enough world that it had gotten them snubbed a few times and Dylan took that to heart, even if she had no intentions of changing. "You are."

Dylan frowned. "I trust you on this. You take the lead and I'll follow."

Trust was as implicit in their business model as it was in their friendship. Even when they goaded each other, she never lost sight of that—of how important it was and how much she valued it. "I think we're both going to be following hers."

"Doing what a smart, beautiful woman says? I can think of worse things."

"Easy for you to say. She didn't yell at you." Apologies or no, she wouldn't be forgetting the fire and brimstone anytime soon. She planned to stay clearly on Audrey's good side.

"Be honest. You like 'em fiery."

It was her turn to frown. "I don't."

"Kidding. I know you go for the soft and sweet any day of the week. It's a good fit for your knight in shining armor routine."

She'd dished it out plenty through the years, especially when it came to dating and relationships, so she accepted it was her turn to take it. Especially since Dylan wasn't wrong. "I resemble that remark."

"Seriously, though. You're better with the books than I am, and you have the connection. It's going to be your call."

"That's a low bar but thank you. We'll see what she has to say."

"Indeed we will." Dylan lifted her chin. "You going out to baby the trees?"

She'd planned to do a visual inspection before the next round of microbe spray went on. Mostly an excuse to walk the orchard, but Dylan let her get away with it in exchange for not having to help with her proprietary brew that was organic and effective but smelly as all get-out. "I am."

"Have fun, farmer. Give my best to the apples."

"I will." She headed for the side exit, grabbing her favorite ball cap from the hook by the door. And with a smile on her face—for her arrangement with Audrey as much as the task at hand—she walked out into the sunshine.

Audrey loaded an armful of hay into the hopper in the sheep pen. She gave Scooby and Shaggy each a pat on the head and a good morning before doing the same for the goats. Ozzie and Harriet trotted over, kids in tow. The kids had learned that feeding time for Mama meant a perfect opportunity to nurse. She shoved the hay in, then leaned her elbow on the fence. "Another day, you guys. Another day."

Ozzie and Harriet bleated their agreement.

"No real news about Mama E, but your friend Rowan will start coming by again."

"Maah."

"I know. We made up. And I'm going to help her with something she isn't good at, so it'll be more even."

This time the babies joined in.

"I know you don't appreciate math or money, but they're important. No money means no hay. No grain, either."

She'd swear the bleats took on a level of urgency.

"Exactly. But you don't have to worry. Your humans take care of all that and you'll never want for anything. Except maybe an extra apple or two."

"If I'm interrupting, I can come back later."

The sound of a human voice made her jump. She turned to find Gretchen standing several feet away, a thoroughly bemused look on her face. "Hi."

Gretchen grinned. "Hi."

"I, um. I talk to the goats. To keep them company."

"Sure." Gretchen continued to smile.

"I started doing it to help clear my head. Now, I think it's mostly habit. And to be fair, they're pretty good at talking back." Unlike the sheep. They seemed happy to listen, but their tendency to stare at her with big brown eyes and remain quiet left her too much to her own devices.

"See, that's nice. I talk to my dog all the time and mostly she raises her eyebrows at me. I think she's judging my life choices."

Audrey laughed. "I'm sure she's offering moral support."

Gretchen pointed at her. "You haven't met her. The rescue said she was a cocker spaniel mix, but I think she's at least a quarter cat."

"Oh, well, in that case. She's definitely judging you."

"Thanks." Gretchen rolled her eyes and let out a chuckle. "Anyway. Am I interrupting?"

She thought of the chores waiting. Some were starting to grow on her, but even they remained chores. "Let's call it a welcome interruption."

"I'll take that."

"Can I offer you some coffee? Tea?"

"Yes, but not before you introduce me to the babies."

Audrey folded her arms. "Is that really why you came over?"

Gretchen angled her head. "Maybe. But I come bearing gifts for you, so it's not rude."

Delight warred with the discomfort of receiving a gift for no reason. "What kind of gift?"

"I'll show you after you introduce me."

And with that single, borderline silly comment, Gretchen wiped away her unease. "Right this way."

At the sight of a new human, the kids bounded over. Gretchen gasped. "Oh, my God, they're literally the cutest things I've ever seen. And I've seen a lot of cute things."

Since she agreed, she didn't argue. "They're as entertaining as they are cute."

"Can I pet them? Can I go in with them?"

"I can't promise you won't end up covered in dirt, but absolutely." She'd gotten used to the dirt that came from sitting on the ground, letting them climb all over her and nibble her hair. She'd started to enjoy how earthy it made her feel. But she didn't presume that about anyone else.

Gretchen waved off the warning. "Here, hold your present."

Audrey unlatched the gate and took the tote bag from Gretchen's outstretched hand. "Do I get to peek?"

"Go ahead. It's not a real present. I just didn't want to show up empty-handed."

Gretchen's attention turned fully to the goats and Audrey peered into the bag. It held at least a dozen skeins of yarn in varying shades and textures. Instinctively, she reached in to touch them and let out a sigh. She was still learning, but she knew enough to recognize it as wool and not the cheap stuff she'd picked up at the craft store in Rochester. "I can't take all this from you."

"Of course you can." Gretchen was already cross-legged on the ground, with Bert climbing across her lap. "Besides, I need to get rid of it."

"Get rid of it?" She couldn't fathom why.

"I got my hands on some cashmere that was on sale and if I don't clear out some space, Jenny is going to have my head. She's made me promise that more yarn leaves the house than comes in."

If she hadn't spent the last several Saturdays learning the ins and outs of Gretchen's yarn addiction, she'd question whether that was a sign of a healthy marriage. Since she had, she merely laughed. "Does that make me your knitting beard?"

Gretchen snorted. "I prefer to think of it as yarn rescue. I'm rehoming some of mine so it can be appreciated and cared for by a new owner."

"You should at least let me pay you."

Gretchen spread her arms. "Payment enough, friend."

Even with all the work that went into tending the animals, she'd fallen hard for the whole pack. The kids simply took things to the next level. "I won't argue but only because I don't want to interrupt your fun."

Ernie balanced his front hooves on Gretchen's forearm and licked her face. "Yeah. Don't interrupt my fun."

After getting her baby goat fill, Gretchen extricated herself from the pile. Audrey smiled at the wistful glance Gretchen gave them as she let herself out of the pen. "I'd love you to stay for coffee, but I also understand if that was your real reason for coming by."

Gretchen's huff of exasperation was almost comically dramatic. "I came to see you, too."

She wouldn't have thought she needed that reassurance, but it was nice all the same. "I made blueberry muffins this morning. You can help me eat them."

"Yes, please. You bake on random Tuesday mornings?"

She shrugged. "Well, since I'm not working right now, it's not like I have anywhere to be, really."

Gretchen followed her into the house. "Still. I think I'd put my feet up and read a book."

"I do that, too."

"Woman of leisure, eh?"

Audrey frowned.

Gretchen lifted a hand. "Kidding. I know you have a real job, and taking care of this in the meantime is plenty of work, too."

She shook her head. "No, you don't need to take it back. I was actually thinking about needing to find some things to occupy my brain as much as my hands."

"I feel you. I milk every minute of summer vacation but if I didn't go back every fall, I'd be bored out of my mind."

"Yeah." She'd sort of expected that to kick in by now. But as much as she wanted something besides manual labor to keep her busy, she hadn't started to miss the office.

"Maybe you could help me. I'm setting up an online shop to sell some of my wares and the money part of it freaks me out."

"I'd love that."

"Okay. I'm not there yet, but soon."

The idea, along with the work she'd be doing at the cidery, made her smile. "I'm ready when you are."

"Awesome. Jenny will be thrilled, too."

"Is she hoping it covers the cost of your yarn habit?"

Gretchen tipped her head. "Every little bit helps is what she says. Though I think it's about yarn taking over the house more than money."

"For the record, I'm starting to empathize with how that could happen."

"Ha. I'm so telling her you said that. Speaking of domestic disputes, how goes the feud with the sexy neighbor? Still maintaining the cease-fire?"

Audrey sighed. She was glad to be back on good terms and was looking forward to her meeting at the cidery that afternoon, but she was a long way from sorting out her tangle of feelings when it came to Rowan. "Yes."

Gretchen's eyes narrowed. "You don't sound sure. I'm really striking out on the conversation topics today."

She laughed. "No, no. It's not that."

Just as quickly as her expression had turned serious, Gretchen's brows lifted and her eyes danced with mischief. "Did you hook up with her?"

"No." Her answer came a little too loud and a little too quick. She cleared her throat. "Why would you think that?"

"You seemed a little zingy at the bakery. I thought maybe you found some creative ways to make up."

Relieved to be spared a line about protesting too much, she rolled her eyes. "It is not that kind of arrangement."

Gretchen sighed. "That's too bad. I'd hit that. Or maybe I should say, I wouldn't mind getting hit by that."

"Gretchen."

"Relax with the stern mom voice. I'm happily married. And I was kidding. Mostly."

She didn't even know she had a stern mom voice. "Sorry."

Gretchen merely laughed. "I'm just saying. It might, you know, smooth things over."

"How can you make the most mundane phrase sound sexual?"

Gretchen shrugged. "It's a gift. Largely wasted as a third grade teacher, I might add."

She'd never call herself uptight—okay, maybe a little uptight—and she had friends. Mostly work friends, but friends. Even off the clock, when they were having drinks and talking about life and dating and whatever, it was never like this. Easy, but also like nothing was off limits. Strange, but nice. Liberating. "I'm really glad we met."

Gretchen gave her a quizzical look, the kind the abrupt change of subject warranted, but then smiled. "Me, too."

"Tell me about your latest yarn haul."

Gretchen's eyes lit up. "Oh, my God. It's gorgeous."

She hadn't been desperate to talk about something else, but Gretchen launched into descriptions of the different colors and textures and Audrey was perfectly content to listen. She asked questions about choosing the right fiber for a project versus deciding what to make with an exquisite skein. She filed away the details, knowing she'd be able to pull them from memory on command. Like learning a new language, but one that clicked for her. Mentally at least. The actual knitting remained a work in progress. Her brain knew what to do, but her fingers were a bit slower to catch on. She lamented this fact to Gretchen as their conversation meandered.

"You're probably thinking too hard."

Well, at least she was consistent. "It wouldn't be the first time."

Gretchen nodded. "Like with your sexy neighbor."

"What makes you think I'm overthinking that?"

"Are you going to hook up with her?"

"No."

Gretchen lifted a shoulder and angled her head to meet it. "Remind me why not, again?"

The thought had crossed her mind. Rowan was gorgeous. And kind. And right next door. Between being friends again and having more free time than she knew what to do with, it had taken considerable effort to keep her imagination out of NSFW territory. "Because."

"Because you get laid so often you've got your bases covered." Oh, and that. There was definitely that. "I wish."

"Maybe you should consider it."

She absolutely should not. "I don't think that's a good idea."

Gretchen smirked. "There you go with your thinking again."

"I'm pretty sure thinking has kept me out of trouble more than it hasn't."

"Yeah, but sometimes a little trouble is what you need."

Was it? No. Her life might not be the most exciting, but it was free from drama. Relatively speaking. That's what mattered. Even if it left her feeling like a stick in the mud.

"Seriously, you're both good-looking, consenting, single adults. Have some fun and let your married friends live vicariously through you."

"She might not be single. I don't really know." Why did it sound like she was making excuses?

"You could ask. I'm guessing, if there was someone, you'd know it by now."

Not that she was keeping tabs, but Rowan's truck rarely left her driveway and never at night. And she'd never noticed another car. Hmm.

"See? You're agreeing with me even though you won't say so."

Audrey shook her head. "Has anyone ever told you you're relentless?"

"Mmm. Most people. You complaining?"

Whether or not she wanted to be nudged in Rowan's direction, she couldn't deny how lovely it was to find herself with the kind of friend who would do that sort of needling and nudging. She took a deep breath, bracing herself for the doors her answer might open—now or in the future. "No. No, I'm not complaining at all."

CHAPTER TWELVE

Dylan angled her head. "Why do you look first date nervous to meet with our new accountant?"

Rowan mirrored the movement to drive home how obnoxious Dylan was being. "Because someone who knows what they're doing is about to look at our books. What if they're worse than we think they are? What if we're doing something illegal?"

"Dude, chill. I was yanking your chain."

"Well, don't, maybe. This is a big deal."

"I don't see why. We're not professionals, but we aren't stupid. She's a math nerd accountant and she knows we aren't. Are you afraid she's going to think less of you?"

That was part of it, but a less problematic part than how much Audrey had been occupying her thoughts. And her dreams. "She only just decided I'm not a two-bit swindler. I want her to take me—us—this—seriously."

Dylan watched her indicate their surroundings and didn't say anything. Funny how silence could imply all sorts of things.

"I want her to like us." A cheesy thing to admit, but not unreasonable, right?

Dylan's eyes got big. "You want her to like *you*."

The almost comical emphasis Dylan put on the *you* conveyed all the things she was doing her best to ignore. "Of course I do. I'm pretty sure her opinion carries a lot of weight with Ernestine and I don't want to be on either of their bad sides."

"Yeah, but you already sorted that out. This isn't about good sides or bad sides. It's about wanting to get underneath, or maybe on top of, our new accountant."

She wasn't drinking but managed to choke anyway. "Christ, Dylan. You're so crass. Also, I'm not an idiot."

Dylan grinned. "We're all idiots in love."

"Love?" She wanted to sound dismissive, but the word came out as a squeak. "Don't be a jerk."

"I'm not being a jerk. And I don't mean love." This time, the emphasis was on love and she threw in air quotes for good measure.

Ribbing each other had been part of their friendship since college, so she didn't really have grounds to be irritated. Or at least not more irritated than usual. She tried to play it cool instead. "Then what do you mean?"

"I mean, being attracted to someone can mess with your head even if there's nothing to it. Basic physiological response. Nothing to get your boxers in a bunch over."

She could feel the scowl form on her face. "I'm not some horny teenage boy who only thinks with his dick."

"I never said you were. And to be fair, most grown men only think with their dicks, too."

She didn't want to crack a smile but did. "I'm still offended."

"Fine, fine. I'll lay off. I don't want you all worked up before she even gets here."

She didn't deny being worked up, but only because it would make her sound petulant. And worked up. "So, you're going to give her a tour of the operations, then I'm going to show her the space for the tasting room."

"And then we'll do a tasting." Dylan didn't hide her amusement over Rowan's reviewing the plan again. "And then she'll be tipsy and less likely to judge our bookkeeping practices."

"Stop. We're not getting her tipsy." Even if a tiny part of her wanted to see Audrey softened by a couple of drinks.

"Dude."

Dylan didn't need to finish. "I know. I'll fucking relax."

Whether she managed to or not became irrelevant. Audrey walked in, dressed in a skirt and blouse that reminded Rowan of the day they met. Her hair was done up in a twist and she had on these heels that made the whole package somehow prim and sexy as hell at the same time.

While she collected her tongue from where it had landed on the floor, Dylan stepped forward and extended a hand. "Audrey. Dylan. Thank you so much for coming today."

Audrey shook Dylan's hand. All business, but Rowan couldn't help the twinge of envy over the moment of physical contact. "It's my pleasure. I'm looking forward to working with you both."

If she hadn't been so busy drooling over Audrey, she might have laughed at how they were both pretending Audrey hadn't stormed in, yelling and swearing, little more than a week ago.

"I hope you didn't dress for us. I confess we're a bit rough and tumble even on our good days around here." Dylan's smile was easy. Borderline flirtatious.

Audrey waved a hand. "This is business light for me."

Dylan bowed slightly. "I did iron my shirt this morning. I guess that means we're meeting in the middle."

She'd been so preoccupied fending off Dylan's teasing, she hadn't even noticed. The twinge of envy took on an edge of something closer to jealousy. Completely unwarranted and completely ludicrous, but there all the same. She cleared her throat. "We were hoping you'd indulge us in a brief tour and tasting before talking business."

"Yes, we never get the chance to show off," Dylan said.

"And we figured seeing the operations firsthand would help the vocabulary in the books make a little more sense." Why did she suddenly feel like an eager suitor, competing for the attention of the girl everyone wanted?

Audrey smiled, either not noticing or used to such shenanigans and therefore unfazed. "I'd love a tour and I'll never say no to a tasting."

Dylan made a sweeping gesture with her hand. "Excellent. Right this way."

Audrey followed Dylan, taking the opportunity to study the differences and similarities between her and Rowan. Dylan was a bit lankier, and her brown hair had the unruliness of natural curl compared to Rowan's sleeker, albeit still casual, style. And huge relief, Dylan seemed to be ignoring their initial pseudo-meeting when she'd stormed in and given Rowan a piece of her mind. She hadn't really noticed her surroundings then, so she paid extra attention now. And did her best not to glance back at Rowan, who brought up the rear of their little group.

"It's smaller than I imagined," she said, more out of wonder than anything negative. "I mean, it's impressive what you do with the space you have."

Dylan turned and flashed her a thousand-watt smile. "Nice recovery."

"I really did mean it as a compliment."

"I believe you." Dylan stopped and indicated a very scary looking machine. "This is the grinder. It turns the apples to pulp so we can press the juice from them."

"Remind me to stay on your good side."

Dylan chuckled and Rowan looked uncomfortable. Was Rowan not glad she was there?

"I promise we only use it for apples," Dylan said.

"And the occasional pear." Rowan smiled and seemed almost relieved to have contributed to the conversation.

Dylan tipped her head. "Or quince." Dylan moved them toward a row of large metal tanks, flanked by what appeared to be wine barrels. "The cider is allowed to settle and is fermented with various yeast strains before being aged."

Next came the bottling area. Dylan showed off the way champagne-style ciders were stored upside-down so the sediment could be removed—disgorged—and the bottles could be topped off before their final corking. It reminded her a lot of the winery tours she and Ernestine had done on some of her visits. This seemed scrappier, though. A smaller operation, but also more playful. It made her wonder if that had to do with size, with cider making in general, or with the proprietors of Forbidden Fruit.

After looping the production area, Rowan led them into what they hoped would be the retail space and tasting room within the next few years. Rowan took over the talking, making her think maybe they'd sorted—if not rehearsed—it ahead of time. Their pride was evident, along with what felt like a trace of nerves.

Like they were trying to impress her.

Something about it made her warm to both of them. Not that Rowan didn't already leave her a little hot and bothered when she let her guard down. This was different, though. They were clearly passionate about what they did. And she might be getting swept up in the moment, but they seemed to be doing it with integrity and care.

"It's really quite impressive."

Dylan beamed. "High praise before the tasting. I like it."

She returned the smile. "To be fair, I've tried a few of your ciders already. And loved them."

"Have you now? Rowan, you didn't tell me our guest was a fan."

"I shared a couple of last year's favorites when we first met."

Given the ups and downs of the few weeks they'd known each other, she appreciated the generosity of the broad strokes Rowan used to describe things. It made her wonder how much Dylan knew. Or perhaps more accurately, how Rowan would frame it. "I'm looking forward to tasting more."

Just like in the production area, Dylan took the lead. It made sense, really. Rowan had mentioned being more focused on the growing and the sourcing. An orchardist, she'd said. That would logically make Dylan the expert at making and explaining the cider. Dylan poured three samples, a still and two sparkling, and talked her through the apples that went into making them and the process used.

She'd always enjoyed wine tastings. And though she was far from an expert, she enjoyed learning some of the science behind it. Dylan's explanations managed to straddle the line perfectly—teaching her something without venturing too far over her head. It helped that everything she tried was delicious.

"This has been lovely. If I was an investor and you were looking for one, I'd be all in."

Dylan elbowed Rowan in the ribs. "We need to get us one of them."

Rowan lifted her chin at Audrey. "If you know anyone, send them our way."

She sort of wished she did. One, because then they could buy Ernestine's land for what it was worth and she wouldn't have to deal with any residual ickiness over that. Two, because businesses like theirs deserved to thrive. "Alas, you've found yourself an accountant not a venture capitalist."

Rowan smiled. "It's okay. We're pretty thrilled at the prospect of having an accountant. Even for a few hours."

"Speaking of, why don't we get to it?"

Both Dylan and Rowan sat up a bit straighter. Rowan cleared her throat. "We have an office, but it's basically a closet with a computer and a file cabinet. Do you want me to grab you the computer?"

She wondered if Rowan forgot that's where she'd done some of her yelling or was generously pretending it didn't happen. "Actually, I thought we could agree to parameters. What you're willing to give me access to, the scope of advice you're looking for. That sort of thing."

Rowan glanced at Dylan before continuing. "We admit we're a little clumsy but have nothing to hide. You can have access to whatever you'd find useful, and we're open to any help or suggestions you have."

Dylan lifted a finger. "Ideally something we can maintain when left to our own devices. Hiring a professional is still a few years out, probably."

She nodded. "I get it. I will say, though, you don't need a fancy accountant. A lot of good bookkeepers take small jobs on the side. And because they haven't jumped through the educational and licensure hoops of a CPA, they can be quite affordable."

Both Rowan and Dylan gave her a curious look.

"I'm not going to say I'm overpaid for what I do, but if you were paying me, you'd be paying for a skill set you don't entirely need. Especially after I overhaul your system."

"I promise we'll take that under advisement." Rowan nodded. "We want to get it right."

"So, let's talk about what you want."

"Um." Rowan looked startled by the question.

Dylan cleared her throat. "Seriously. We want whatever you're willing to give us."

Since Rowan appeared at a loss for words still, she focused her attention on Dylan. "I understand you're still using cash basis."

Dylan cringed. "Yeah."

"It's okay. A lot of startups do. But I get the feeling you're more than ready to convert."

"We are," Rowan said.

"Excellent. We'll start with that. I'll want to look at your current year balance sheet and your taxes from the last two years, if you're okay with that."

"Of course." Rowan and Dylan answering in unison was kind of adorable.

"Do you have preferences for whether I work in the morning or afternoon? I'd like at least one of you around to answer questions."

"I'm here pretty much all day, every day," Dylan said.

"And I'm rarely far away at this time of year," Rowan added.

It would be unlike any work she'd done before, not to mention unlike any work environment. But she was looking forward to putting that part of her brain back to work. "Then I'll plan to see you tomorrow morning."

Both Rowan and Dylan nodded with enthusiasm.

"I'd say eight but I'm kind of running a farm right now, so how's nine?"

"Whenever," Rowan said. "Nine, ten, eleven."

"Nine should work. It's not like Ferdinand lets me sleep past five these days."

Rowan laughed. "Tell me about it."

"I feel like I should apologize for that." They'd joked about it before, but still.

Rowan waved her off. "He did it long before you showed up."

Right. Because Rowan's life was here and she was merely a guest. An extended guest, perhaps, but a guest nonetheless. She would have expected that little reminder to bring relief, and maybe a moment of longing for her quiet apartment and courteous neighbors. But for some reason, she couldn't shake the thought of being in bed—stretching and rolling over as Ferdinand did his thing and the sun crept above the line of trees in the orchard—knowing Rowan was doing the same.

CHAPTER THIRTEEN

Audrey marched her way through morning chores with purpose. She showered and dressed, spent a little too long standing in front of the tiny closet where she'd hung the clothes she'd brought with her. Okay, the clothes she'd brought with her and the clothes she'd ordered online because she hadn't packed nearly enough.

She settled on a flowing skirt with a vibrant floral print—nothing she could ever wear to the office but that made her feel prettier than the super casual things she'd taken to wearing around the farm. And slightly less starchy than what she'd worn to her meeting the day before. She paired it with a sleeveless top and a pair of slingback sandals and told herself she didn't care if Rowan and Dylan teased her. Or noticed her.

She tucked her own laptop into her bag in case she needed backup and, since the sun was shining, opted to walk down to the cidery. The side door was propped open, so she walked right in. Rowan's and Dylan's voices wafted through space, seeming to come from behind the row of fermentation tanks.

She followed the sound and found them with their heads pressed together, staring into glasses holding liquids of different shades of gold. It made her wonder if Ernestine ever visited the cidery. "The two of you look like mad scientists right now."

Rowan looked up and smiled. "It's all her. I watch. And taste."

Dylan lifted her chin in Rowan's direction. "I'm glad we finally agree on who's the brains of this operation."

"I didn't say that. My brains just don't happen to be in the chemistry department."

Audrey chuckled. She'd always considered her office culture friendly, but it had nothing on this. "Do you antagonize one another all the time or only when you have an audience?"

Dylan gave one of those bobbing head nods. "Oh, no. We do it all the time."

Rowan tipped her head back and forth. "Pretty much."

"I want to know what you're doing, but I should probably get to work."

"Nonsense," Rowan said, just as Dylan let out a pfft. "We're checking some of our early season varieties to see if they're ready for bottling."

Even though she was itching to get her hands on the books, curiosity won out. "How do you do that?"

"Gizmos that test for alcohol levels, acidity, that sort of thing," Rowan said.

Dylan brought her fingers and thumb together and waved them like an old Italian guy, or maybe more accurately, someone pretending to be an old Italian guy. "But we also get a feel for it. Her color and the way she feels on the tongue."

Something resembling a giggle escaped Audrey's lips and Rowan rolled her eyes. "Okay, Romeo."

Dylan let out a tsk of dismissal. "Body, aroma—these things are science. But they're art, too." She made a sweeping gesture at Rowan. "Not unlike how you predict a frost by the smell of the air."

Rowan bowed slightly. "Touché."

For all that they harassed one another, it was easy to see why they were partners. And friends. It made her a little sad that her job didn't work that way. Or maybe it was that she didn't work that way. "Something tells me the two of you manage to blend the art and science of it perfectly."

Dylan bowed this time, and with much greater flair. "My dear, flattery will get you everywhere."

Rowan coughed. "But I'm sure you'd rather get to work than stand around watching us argue about flavor profiles."

She angled her head. "Do you argue about flavor profiles?"

"Not really." Rowan hooked a thumb at Dylan. "She doesn't tell me how to grow the apples and I don't tell her what to do with them after the fact."

"Mm-hmm." She didn't want to admit it, but it would be easy to fritter away the morning with them.

"It's why we're such a good team." Dylan's chest puffed out slightly like a proud little kid.

"I'm enjoying the show, but I probably shouldn't encourage you, so lead me to the books."

"Happy to." Rowan made a comment about leaving Dylan to her various tests and assessments and led Audrey to the office. "I'm sorry it's so small."

"I spent the first five years of my career in a cubicle. I'm good." Rowan visibly winced. "Right."

"But now my office overlooks Times Square."

"Really?"

She wasn't sure why she shared that fact. The whole point was to assure Rowan she was okay with the small space, not brag about her climb up the corporate ladder. "Yes, but what I mean is it doesn't matter. I can work anywhere."

Rowan nodded, looking even less convinced than before. "Okay. Well, all the passwords are on a sticky note next to the computer."

"You know that's not remotely secure."

"I do. I'm also banking on you being the kind of woman who picks her battles."

The joke, along with Rowan's sly grin, broke any tension that may have been there. "Indeed I am."

"Holler if you have questions or can't access something you need. I'm going to get back to work and leave you to it."

She preferred that to hovering but got the sense Rowan's discomfort exceeded her own. "Does this freak you out?"

Rowan hesitated. "It's like getting blood drawn. I don't mind it happening, but I can't watch."

She laughed. "Excellent analogy."

"Yeah. So." Rowan shrugged. "Good luck?"

She knew better than to offer reassurances before getting a handle on how bad things were, so she went for a decisive nod. "Thanks."

Rowan disappeared, leaving her in the tiny space alone. She could just make out music coming from somewhere else in the building. Not loud enough to place the song even, but between that and the occasional muffled voices of Rowan and Dylan going about their work, it made for the perfect white noise. She spent an hour simply reviewing the data and running reports, drafting a running list of questions she wanted answered before making any changes. She got up to find Rowan but practically ran into her in the doorway. "Do you have a minute?"

"All the minutes you need." Rowan made a face. "Unless something's wrong and you're going to yell at me. If that's the case, three minutes, tops."

She laughed in spite of herself. "No yelling."

Rowan followed her back into the office. "I'm trusting you."

"No promise you're going to like all the questions, though."

Rowan let out a dramatic sigh. "Okay. Lay it on me."

Audrey scanned the balance sheet she'd gotten the software to generate, then pointed at the screen. "You've got all this equipment, but you're not depreciating any of it. It's skewing your expenses."

"I know."

She shook her head. "You're starting to bring in income. If you don't offset it better, you're going to have a huge tax bill."

"I know."

"It looks like you haven't started paying estimated quarterly taxes, either. You're almost to the point where they're going to come after you for that."

Rowan closed her eyes. "I. Know."

"Sorry." She pulled her hands away from the keyboard and laced them together.

"I warned you it was a mess."

She sighed. "It's not a mess. I've seen worse."

"Is that supposed to make me feel better?"

She lifted a shoulder and smirked. "No, because a lot of those companies were in hot water for unethical practices and, on at least a couple of occasions, fraud."

Rowan's shoulders slumped. "You think less of me, don't you?"

"I don't. I swear."

"We were planning to hire a professional this year, but we were able to get the new fermentation tanks at auction for half what we'd pay retail. So, we put it off."

It was a decision so many people—as individuals or businesses—made. Kind of like car maintenance. It didn't seem urgent, got put off, and cost way more in the long run. "I get it. But I'm telling you right now and I'm going to keep telling you, hiring someone who knows what they're doing is going to save you money. It's an indisputable fact."

"Yes, ma'am."

She tried for a withering look. "And don't call me ma'am."

"Yes, Ms. Adams."

"You're being cheeky now. I'm serious."

Rowan had the decency to look cowed. "Sorry. I deal with uncomfortable situations with bad humor."

The honesty, paired with the deadpan delivery, had her cracking a smile. "Apology accepted."

"Really, thank you for doing this. Despite how Dylan and I have handled things, we know it's important."

The shift to sincerity caught her by surprise. She thought she'd softened all the way when it came to Rowan, but apparently not. Or maybe she was slipping deeper into liking her territory. Not the worst thing, though she didn't need to be broadcasting it. "You're welcome."

"Anything else?"

"Not at the moment." At least nothing she was prepared to discuss with Rowan.

Rowan tipped her head. "I'm going to let you work then. I'll be in the bottling area with Dylan if you need me."

Having set her thoughts about Rowan aside, her mind returned to the books, wanting to tease things apart and put them back together in ways that made sense. "Will do."

"Don't work too hard, okay? We don't want you burning out."

She laughed, thinking about the multi-million-dollar corporations that comprised her portfolio. "Do you not understand what I do for a living?"

Rowan frowned. "I do, but—"

"I'm good at what I do and—"

"I never said—"

She raised a hand. "I'm good at it and I like it. I'm going to need you to trust me."

For the second time that morning, Rowan looked cowed. "Sorry."

Given the majority of their interactions so far—ones in which Rowan knew what she was doing and Audrey didn't—there was something fun about flipping the dynamic. "You don't need to apologize, but you do need to go away so I can get to work."

Rowan pressed her lips together, clearly suppressing a smile. "Yes, ma'am."

Rowan pulled the door and disappeared before Audrey could complain again about being called ma'am. She rolled her eyes but chuckled. And then she rolled her shoulders a few times, flexed her fingers, and dove in.

Rowan helped Dylan clean up from the tasting and testing. Jamal arrived and she corralled him into helping her wash and prep bottles for the Dabinett-Golden Russet blend Dylan deemed ready for its secondary fermentation. She never quite forgot that Audrey was nearby but didn't obsess about it. She even managed to lose track of time until Jamal started asserting that he was starving and someone better feed him already.

After a bit of internal struggle, she concluded it was only right to include Audrey in their communal lunch. Or at least offer. She stood outside the office door for a full minute at least, debating whether to knock. It was her space, technically, but also now Audrey's. She didn't want to startle Audrey. Or make her feel like she was being checked up on. But after this morning, she didn't want to come across as any more timid and unsure than she already had. Of course, if Audrey could see her standing there hemming and hawing, timid wouldn't be the half of it.

She gave the door a few taps with her knuckle but didn't wait for an answer to open it. There. Was that so hard?

Audrey looked up, eyes wide. So much for not startling her. She blinked a few times, like she needed to coax her vision to refocus, then pulled off her glasses and smiled. "Hi."

"Hi. Everything okay?"

Audrey nodded. "It's great. Things aren't as bad as you made them seem."

"I have a feeling you're being generous, but I'm not going to argue."

"Your system isn't serving you as well as it could, but you're getting all the data in. That's more than I can say for some people."

She chuckled at the various games and bets they used to determine who'd be stuck entering receipts and paying invoices. "We do try."

"I'm starting with some new categories and codes that should make data entry faster right off the bat. It'll help me organize, but should make your lives easier, too."

"Music to my ears."

"Are you always this easy to impress?"

God, it would be so easy to imagine them back in flirting territory. She knew better, but damn. "I'm going to go with no."

Audrey's smirk was playful at the very least. "Good answer. You never want to be too easy."

Okay, seriously, how was that not flirting? "Speaking of easy, I'm popping home to make sandwiches for lunch. Nothing fancy, but I thought I'd see if you wanted to come up for air long enough to join us."

Sure, she'd have preferred "me" to "us" but whatever. "What time is it?"

"A little after one."

"Really?"

Why did it not surprise her that Audrey lost track of time with work? "Really."

"Lunch would be great, though I feel bad to have you make it for me."

"Like I said, just sandwiches. But if it would make you feel better, you can join the little rotation Dylan and I have going and take a turn." There. That was better. Nothing flirtatious about rotating who brings lunch to work.

"I could get on board with a lunch club."

The conversation might be entirely banal, but Audrey's smile continued to send Rowan's thoughts in directions that were anything but. "Great. Turkey and Swiss okay?"

"My favorite."

"I'll be back in about fifteen minutes."

Audrey nodded. "I was going to leave around three to go visit Ernestine if that's okay, since I missed her yesterday."

"Um, every minute you give us is a gift. You get to set your own hours."

The exasperated look, complete with huffy breath, shouldn't have been attractive. But it was. "I know. But we're colleagues now, in a way. There's some basic professional courtesy there."

It was her turn to huff out a breath, though it had nothing to do with exasperation. No, it was the metaphorical bucket of cold water reminding her of one more reason being attracted to Audrey was a bad idea. "Well, then, thanks for letting me know."

Audrey's eyes narrowed. "What's wrong?"

Besides being an idiot? "Nothing."

"Okay. I've got some questions for you and Dylan if you don't mind a working lunch."

"Sure."

"Perfect."

Audrey returned her attention to the computer, clearly unfazed by the whole interaction. Rowan closed the door, shaking her head as she headed for the exit. Idiot.

CHAPTER FOURTEEN

It didn't take long to settle into her new routine. Most mornings, Audrey woke before her alarm, courtesy of Ferdinand. She worked her way through the morning farm chores, then drank her coffee on the porch or while chatting with the goats. She went to the cidery on Mondays, Wednesdays, and Fridays, leaving Tuesdays and Thursdays open for visits with Ernestine and weekends for knitting group and an all-day trip to Rochester where she could visit Ernestine but also spend an hour or two getting groceries and running errands. If part of her worried that Ernestine didn't seem to be improving, she shoved those worries aside, reminding herself that these things took time.

She fell into an easy rapport with Rowan and Dylan, even if her interactions with Rowan still seemed to have a trace of something she couldn't put her finger on. It wasn't residual tension, at least as far as she could tell. Well, not bad tension. Maybe tension of a whole different sort. The kind of tension that had her staring at Rowan's hands for longer than she cared to admit. The kind that had her wondering what Rowan's mouth would feel like on hers. Or the rest of Rowan's body, for that matter. Unfortunately, Rowan didn't appear to share in her train of very distracting thoughts.

It was probably for the best, really. She had her hands full. And if she was cognizant of how long it had been since she'd had sex with anyone, well, she was no stranger to dry spells.

So, she did what she did best. She channeled her energy into depreciation schedules and streamlined accounts payable structures, finding places of efficiency and, more often than not, savings. It flexed her brain in all the ways she'd been missing, yet managed to be novel at the same time. More satisfying, if only because it felt more personal.

On this particular Wednesday, she emerged from the office around three, having eaten her salad without leaving her desk, and went in search of either Rowan or Dylan. She found Dylan and the intern, Jamal, loading bottles into cardboard boxes. "Ooh, finished product."

Jamal raised a bottle for display. "What do you think of the label? I designed it myself."

The pen and ink drawing had been printed on what looked like parchment. With the Forbidden Fruit logo across the bottom, it looked both artistic and professional. "Did you do the drawing, too?"

His chest puffed up. "I did."

"It's really nice."

Dylan bumped Jamal's shoulder with hers. "I keep telling him he can come back after college and run our marketing department if he decides not to become a cider maker."

Jamal rolled his eyes. "Dude, you don't have a marketing department."

Dylan shrugged. "Exactly. You could be the marketing department."

Audrey laughed at the exchange. "If you want to talk with someone who does marketing or graphic design, I have a couple of people I could connect you with. They're in the city, but I'm sure they'd be happy to talk to you."

Jamal beamed. "Yeah? That would be sick."

Did sick mean cool again? She hoped so. "Let me send a couple of emails."

"Thanks."

"So, how's the accounting department today?" Dylan shot her a wink, though she couldn't tell if it was gratitude for offering to hook Jamal up or the reference to her as the accounting department.

"Good, good. I need to do some research, but you might be able to consolidate some of your purchasing and get better volume discounts."

"Really?"

Dylan's unabashed delight at the prospect made her smile. "Really."

"For that, you should take the afternoon off."

She tried to roll the computer hunch tension from her shoulders. "You know that's no way to run a business, right?"

"Ha ha. Seriously, though. Work hard, relax hard. It's a beautiful afternoon. You should spend it outside."

Audrey shrugged. "I did chores outside this morning and I'll have more when I get home."

Jamal shook his head. Dylan did, too. "I mean play outside."

"Play." She understood the word, obviously, but it didn't compute with anything she'd do. "Does sitting on the porch count?"

"Eh? Borderline. Lie in a hammock. Stare at the clouds."

She had a flash of herself staring at the sky, willing creative frivolity that simply wouldn't come.

"Okay, you don't need to make that face. If it's not your thing, it's not your thing."

She let out a sigh. "Sorry. It's not you. It's me."

"If I had a nickel for every time a woman said that to me." Dylan tutted and gave a slow shake of her head.

Something told her Dylan didn't find herself on the receiving end of that talk very often. "I have a hard time with idleness."

"Seriously? You're one of those workaholic women who can't relax?" Dylan's question seemed genuine, which was cute.

"Does this really surprise you?"

Dylan offered a casual shrug. "I forget you're a city girl at heart."

She wouldn't disagree, though it felt jarring to hear it. The city felt so far away, and not just in terms of physical miles. "Well, creature of habit at least."

Dylan pointed a finger at her. "You should spend the afternoon with Rowan."

Ignoring her attraction to Rowan was becoming second nature, but it still took effort. The idea of spending the afternoon together might appeal, but it wouldn't be relaxing. "Why?"

"She's walking the orchard and could keep you company. It would be like pseudo idleness. Ease you into it."

"Pseudo idleness." It sounded both ridiculous and brilliant.

The door to the production room opened and Rowan strode in. Dylan winked again. "Speak of the devil."

Dylan called out a greeting and Rowan headed their way. Rowan offered hellos but launched into a series of questions for Dylan about a new foraging spot she had a lead on. Audrey took the chance to study them. Dylan flirted with her freely, but it was playful. Innocent. Like they both knew neither of them meant anything by it. Unlike Rowan. With Rowan, things were friendly but then sometimes stilted. Like they couldn't decide whether or not to flirt. Okay, not entirely accurate. Rowan definitely flirted. And she flirted back, but then caught herself and backed off. And then acted weird. Which made Rowan act weird. She sighed. The whole thing was…awkward.

"What do you say, Audrey? You game?"

"Huh?" Speaking of awkward.

Rowan gave her a curious look. "I said I'd love you to walk the orchard with me. But no pressure. Obviously."

"Oh. Yes. That would be fantastic."

Rowan looked from Audrey to Dylan, searching for a clue about why Audrey was saying yes but looking completely disinterested. Or at least distracted. She could think of little she'd enjoy more, but only if Audrey actually wanted to. "Are you sure?"

"Yes. Absolutely. I've been meaning to ask for more of a guided tour anyway."

She was pretty sure Audrey hadn't, but it seemed silly to argue. "Great."

Dylan told them to take their time and enjoy the sunshine. Rowan grabbed her hat and led the way outside. She started toward the orchard, then stopped. "Do you want to go home and change?"

Audrey looked down, then at Rowan. "Depends. Are you going to put me to work?"

"I wasn't planning on it." But damn if the idea of Audrey on a ladder, reaching to grab a perfectly ripe apple, didn't get her juices flowing.

"I'm good then. This is pretty casual for me."

She had a hard time filing anything involving a skirt in the casual category. "If you say so."

"It's like the warm weather equivalent of jeans."

"Pretty sure those are called shorts."

Audrey folded her arms and her left hip jutted slightly. Rowan reminded herself to find it charming, not sexy. "I don't wear jeans to work. I'm sure as hell not going to wear shorts."

"Totally your prerogative. I'm merely arguing the equivalency." It was one of those arguments that wasn't really an argument. The kind friends would have. Or people who were flirting.

Audrey let out a dismissive sniff. "Fine. This is the girly warm weather equivalent of jeans."

Why was she having so much fun with this? Because it felt like flirting more than friendly banter, that's why. "So, what's the girly, cool weather equivalent?"

"There isn't really. You can push jeans a little with tall boots. Or thick tights under a skirt."

"And that's still casual?"

"Well, it's not pantyhose, I can tell you that."

For some reason, the mention of pantyhose had her imagining Audrey in thigh-high stockings, complete with a garter belt. She cleared her throat. "I'm going to take your word for it."

Audrey narrowed her eyes but didn't argue.

Rowan tried for a smile but coughed. And because her thoughts also included what it might be like to slide those stockings down Audrey's legs, she couldn't bring herself to make eye contact. She angled her head. "Let's start here, then we can go across to Ernestine's land."

Audrey smiled a smile that made it clear she had no idea where Rowan's mind had gone. "Works for me."

Rowan opened the gate and waved Audrey through. "There are seven acres currently fenced and about five of them are planted. I have enough grafted scions to plant one more acre next spring and we should be able to do the last acre the year after that."

"What's a grafted scion?"

"Sorry. It's an apple tree, or any fruit tree really. In horticulture, you graft the apple variety you want to grow onto a rootstock that is adapted to your climate and will give you the size of tree you want."

"So, a Franken-tree?"

"Yes, but it's not mad science or anything. Fruit trees aren't true to seed, so that's how they're grown."

"But I thought you were organic."

"We are. I'll be happy to wax poetic about the trials and tribulations of that if you're interested. Grafting is organic, non-GMO, all that. It's literally sandwiching two trees into one. Quite an ancient practice, really."

Audrey looked incredulous. "Do you do the sandwiching?"

"Not always, but I enjoy it. I'd be happy to show you sometime." Though saying it made her realize Audrey wouldn't likely be around in the early spring when grafting happened.

"I'd like that."

She couldn't tell if Audrey's mind simply hadn't gone down that path or, perhaps more likely, didn't have a sense of the growing calendar. Not that it mattered.

"So, tell me about the trees."

Rowan let her gaze return to Audrey. "Do you really want to know or are you being polite?"

"I want to know. Like, what kinds they are. What makes them different."

"All right. I'll warn you I can get carried away, so stop me if it's too much."

"You've listened to me talk about accounting, so you've earned some leeway."

Rowan grinned. "You might regret that, but okay."

"Try me."

There were so many things she wanted to try with Audrey. "We have a mix of species native to New York and traditional European varieties, mostly French and English."

"Because that's where cider started?"

"Cider is much older than that, but those climates are similar to ours, even if our winters are harsher."

Audrey snorted. "I'll say."

"It's nice because we get to select apples for the exact flavor profiles we want—acids, tannins, sugar." It had been one of the most exciting and most daunting parts of the whole process so far, at least for her.

"I like cider but confess I've never given it much thought."

"It's okay. Most people don't." She didn't need them to. "I'm hoping more start to think about what kinds they like so they can find and enjoy more of it."

"Like wine." Audrey cringed. "Sorry. Is it bad form to compare cider to wine?"

"Not at all. There are a lot of similarities. Way more than between cider and beer. And it's a nice entry point for a lot of people."

Audrey nodded. "That makes sense. Common language and all. Will you take me through Ernestine's orchard, too? I hate that I know so little about it."

Rowan smiled. See? They could do this. No weirdness, no irrepressible urges to kiss Audrey and ruin everything. "Of course."

They crossed the street and walked directly into one of the rows. Audrey stopped. She looked back at Rowan's orchard, then Ernestine's. "Wait a second."

"What?"

Audrey pivoted her head back and forth before returning her gaze to Rowan. How had she never noticed that? "Ernestine's orchard isn't fenced in."

"Her trees are tall enough and established enough that the deer can't do more than steal what's on the lower branches."

"Oh." That made sense. Honestly, it never would have occurred to her to fence in an orchard until she'd seen Rowan's.

"Don't get me wrong. I'd love to fence in her orchard. But it's not worth the cost and Ernestine's convinced sharing apples makes the deer less inclined to obliterate her veggies."

She got this flash of Ernestine griping about bunnies and groundhogs stealing her squashes and tomatoes. It had seemed so foreign at the time. Now she knew. "I suppose there's a certain logic in that?"

Rowan gave her a not you too look, followed by a shake of her head. "I leave it in the category of Ernestine's prerogative."

"I'm not going to lie, I love that 'Ernestine's prerogative' makes up an entire category of things in your mind."

Rowan shrugged. "I'm not stupid."

She thought about her own spirited debates with Ernestine through the years. Rarely did feelings get hurt, but damn, the woman was stubborn. Especially when it came to something she wanted. Like jumping into hobby farming at nearly sixty, which to Audrey's mind, had bordered on preposterous. "I learned long ago to pick my battles."

That got a chuckle out of Rowan.

"So, are the trees in Ernestine's orchard the same varieties, just older?"

"There's some overlap. Russets and Pippins, mostly. Ernestine has some that weren't meant to be cider apples but they're old enough that the fruit has the complexity to stand up to the process."

"Does that mean they aren't good for eating?"

"You could eat a few of them, but they're quite sharp. Or bitter. Or both. Ernestine sticks with the kitchen orchard for her eating and cooking apples."

She was familiar with those trees, planted in an octagon around the small yard that held the chicken coop. In addition to apple trees, Ernestine had peach, cherry, quince, and pear. The harvest from those yielded more pies and preserves than Audrey could wrap her head around. "You've got me craving pie now."

"Does that mean you're baking?"

Things were starting to ripen, and she'd need to do something with all the fruit. "I think it does."

They walked the rows and Rowan talked about the differences between the trees and the apples they produced. Not just flavor and texture—her two primary considerations—but subtle distinctions in size and ripening time and something called Brix. How all those things affected the cider.

Listening to Rowan talk about the trees drove home how much she loved them. Like, genuinely loved each tree, along with the orchard as a whole. Beyond the monetary value of the apples and the cider those apples would become. She loved them the way Ernestine loved her garden and her animals, the way Ernestine loved the land. Seeing this side of Rowan made her realize how truly wrong she'd been. How similar Rowan and Ernestine were in so many ways. How lucky Ernestine was to have Rowan in her life.

"You okay?"

She looked from the trees to Rowan, who eyed her with concern.

"Of course."

"You looked about a million miles away. I've crossed the line into too much information."

"You haven't, I promise."

"No?" Rowan smiled, like she'd be okay even if the answer was yes.

"No." It only seemed fair to share the trajectory of her thoughts. "I was imagining you doing this with Ernestine, nerding out together about land and agriculture and the weather. I'm sure you two are quite the pair."

"We've definitely lost hours doing that."

"Not lost." Though that's exactly the word she'd have used to describe it only a few weeks ago. "I love that she has you. Not just the business arrangement or even the friendship. You're kindred spirits."

Rowan chuckled. "I think we are."

As close as she and Ernestine might be, she'd never been that. "I'm sorry I misjudged you."

Rowan would have been completely within her rights to get in a dig, or at least a gentle poke. But she didn't. "You're protective of her. I get it. I'm kind of protective of her myself."

Audrey laughed. "She'd kill us both if she heard us talking like that."

"I won't tell if you won't."

"Deal."

Rowan offered a decisive nod. "Deal."

She waited for Rowan to resume the walk, but she remained still. Her gaze went to the trees and her features relaxed into a smile, leaving Audrey with a jumble of feelings. "Would you like to come to dinner tonight?"

Rowan's focus returned to her. "Really?"

They hadn't gotten together outside of the cidery since the apology dinner. She missed it, but now that they had their arrangement worked out, dinner seemed to imply something more. She'd held off inviting Rowan for just that reason. Well, that and about a dozen others that all felt insignificant now. "Or tomorrow. Whenever."

"Tonight is good."

She couldn't quite read Rowan's expression but got the feeling Rowan had been waiting on her to bridge that gap. It made her wonder why she'd waited so long. "Perfect."

CHAPTER FIFTEEN

Rowan knocked on Ernestine's back door and waited. She assumed she and Audrey were back on friendly enough terms that she could walk right in but decided not to chance it. Standing there, freshly showered and clutching a bottle of cider, made it feel once again like she was waiting for a date. Only this time she secretly wanted it to be a date. Hoped it was.

Before she could convince herself how laughable that was, the door opened. Audrey stood on the other side in a striped sun dress and flip-flops and offered her an easy smile. "Hi."

Any chance she had of not hoping it was a date went flying out the window. "Hi."

"Come on in." Audrey returned to the stove instead of hovering at the door.

Steam wafted from one pot and another sizzled. "I probably shouldn't ask first thing, but it smells amazing in here and I'm dying to know. What are we having?"

Audrey grinned. "It's perfectly acceptable to ask, especially if the question includes a compliment."

"I see."

"Risotto. There were some gorgeous mushrooms at the market and the thyme is coming in so beautifully."

"Mmm." She opted not to admit she didn't think anyone made risotto at home.

"Though, to be fair, you're mostly smelling onions and garlic in butter and olive oil."

Yep. "Why does that always smell so good?"

Audrey didn't hesitate with her answer. "Magic."

"Right, right."

"The only downside is that I need to tend it, so you're going to have to help yourself to wine."

"I think I can manage." Especially if it came with getting to hang out in the kitchen and watch Audrey cook.

"There's an open bottle of chardonnay from what I put in the risotto, but there's cider, too."

"Wine sounds great." Though she appreciated Audrey keeping cider on hand, whether for her or as a general rule. "Can I pour you a glass, too?"

"I confess I was pre-gaming, but you can top me off." Audrey winked before returning her attention to the stove, where she added a ladle of broth to the pot and stirred.

She tried to ignore how adorable she found strait-laced Audrey using the term pre-gaming and opened the fridge. She poured a glass for herself and refilled the half-empty one on the counter next to the stove. "Is there anything I can do to help?"

Audrey picked up her wine and took a sip. "You could toss the salad. Or stir so I can."

"I'm pretty sure I can't mess up salad." She wasn't sure she could say that about risotto.

"The fennel is already marinating in the dressing. You just need to add arugula and shave in some parm."

Not a salad she'd made or had, but the tasks landed safely in her wheelhouse. "On it."

"Perfect." Audrey added another ladle to her pot and continued to stir.

It wasn't long before they sat at the table together. Since they'd seen each other a mere couple of hours ago, there was little to cover on the how was your day front. Rowan decided to take a chance on a slightly more personal topic. "Is it weird to do accounting on such a small scale? I mean, I assume most of your clients are big corporations."

Audrey considered. "It is. But nice. I'm usually doing audits to make sure the numbers add up and the appropriate procedures are happening. I like being able to see the whole picture, understand the people and products behind the line items."

"I wouldn't have thought about it that way." Though it was exactly why she did what she did instead of working for some large-scale producer.

"You know, I wouldn't have, either. I mostly think of accounting as auditing or tax. I forget there's the whole internal side of things."

She only had a vague notion of the difference between the two, but the appeal of novelty? That she understood. "Would you ever do something different than what you're doing now? Full time, I mean."

Audrey sighed. "I've thought about it. One of the perks of starting at the Big Four is that if you can make it through the first five years, you can go almost anywhere."

"Okay, help a layperson out. That sounds like a good thing but you seem wistful."

That got her a laugh. "It is a good thing. And I still can. I'm just doing well enough where I am that I haven't been inspired to look elsewhere."

Aha. "Well, as long as you're content and not merely complacent."

"Yeah." Audrey's tone seemed to imply the two may have blurred.

Rowan coughed. "I don't mean to poke. I was just curious."

Audrey's smile was definitely wistful now. "Don't apologize. You got me thinking is all."

Hard to say if that was a good thing or bad, but Audrey didn't seem upset. Thoughtful, maybe. Still, she didn't need to stir things up. "Well, you probably would just as soon not talk about work either way. How are the kids?"

Audrey shot her a look of amused exasperation. "Really? Change the conversation to goats and you're off the hook?"

"Depends. Did it work?"

Audrey smirked. "Maybe."

"Don't get me wrong. I love talking about big thoughts and big feelings, but only if it's a welcome conversation." Audrey seemed to really consider that, and Rowan couldn't help but wonder if she might be overdue for some processing. But she'd gotten herself into trouble before, so she left it at that.

In the end, Audrey merely nodded. "Thanks."

They talked about the garden and the animals. Audrey joked about becoming the woman who carried on conversations with goats. Rowan shrugged. "If it makes you feel better, I'd be concerned if you didn't have conversations."

Audrey laughed. "I think it does."

She asked about Audrey's knitting. Audrey asked about the family dinner she'd been running off to the other night. Rowan congratulated herself on only thinking about kissing Audrey every so often and not the entire time. Though, to be fair, the wanting to kiss Audrey never wavered.

After the main course, Audrey whipped out a plate of lemon shortbread. "I confess they were an afterthought. I'm dying for peaches, but I've accepted they need another week or two."

"You can serve me afterthoughts anytime."

"I'm hoping I can count on you to help me demolish a pan of peach cobbler. I could do it myself, but I'd probably regret it."

Rowan smiled at the idea of Audrey abandoning her self-restraint. "Maybe if you did it in one sitting at least. Count me in."

"I like that you're such a team player."

"Always." She snagged one more cookie from the plate. "And as always, dinner was amazing. You have to let me do the dishes."

"Other than the pot, it's just loading the dishwasher."

"Still. It's the least I can do." She headed to the sink before Audrey had the chance to argue. And thanks to her many dinners with Ernestine, she knew her way around and didn't even need to ask questions about what went where. They washed and dried, put things away. "I'm glad we're friends again."

"Me, too." A simple statement, but the feeling behind Audrey's words was palpable.

Rowan walked to the back door with more than a trace of reluctance. She stepped over the threshold but turned. She told herself it was to say thank you one more time, to tell Audrey she hoped they could do it again soon. Maybe, even, that she'd take a turn making dinner. But the truth of the matter was that it was more instinct than choice. She found Audrey beautiful all the time, but tonight Audrey's mouth had her fixated. Wondering how Audrey would taste. How Audrey's lips would feel under hers. "So, thank you."

Those perfect lips turned up at the edges. "You already said that."

"It bears repeating."

"Ah. Well, you're welcome. It's nice to have company." Audrey looked down, then back into Rowan's eyes. "It's nice to have your company."

Rowan leaned in. No more than an inch, but she caught the slightest hint of Audrey's perfume. Something light, both citrusy and floral. A tease and an assault on her senses at the same time. In the span of a second, her mind went from the possibility of a kiss to imagining Audrey naked and under her. Or maybe on top. Either way, it was all bare skin and roaming hands and seeking mouths.

She pulled back, startled by how quickly her thoughts got away from her.

Audrey's gaze remain fixed on hers. Was she anticipating a kiss? Were her lips parted in invitation or to protest? Not knowing was almost as bad as not kissing her. And not kissing her was, at least in this moment, pretty damn awful.

"I'll see you tomorrow?" She at once admired her restraint and loathed herself for it.

Audrey nodded slowly. She smiled but her eyes seemed full of questions. "You will."

"Okay. Well, then, um, good night."

"Good night."

She nodded without having a reason to and went down the porch steps, probably looking more purposeful than made sense. When she turned to offer a parting wave, Audrey remained in the doorway, a playful smile on her face. She nodded again. Then, thoroughly unsure she'd made the right decision, she turned back toward the orchard and started the walk home.

❖

Audrey closed the door behind Rowan, flipping the lock more out of habit than anything else. She allowed herself one peek out the window and watched Rowan's moonlit form disappear into the trees. Then she turned and slumped against the frame, complete with wistful sigh.

Was it possible to be utterly content and thrumming with pent up sexual energy at the same time? Obviously it was. She was living proof.

In truth, that wasn't really the question of the moment. No, the matter at hand had a lot more to do with whether Rowan felt it as much as she did. And whether that almost kiss was a shared experience or a figment of her imagination.

With neither answers nor any immediate way to get answers, she hefted herself upright and went to the kitchen to finish cleaning up. Since there was nothing left to do, she wiped the counters and flipped off the light, figuring she could read for a while if the work and excitement of the day didn't have her eyes heavy in a matter of minutes.

She'd showered before dinner but indulged in another. Just a quick one, to replace the cooking smells on her skin with the rosemary and grapefruit of her new favorite soap. Because it relaxed her. Because clean skin on clean sheets was one of life's most basic pleasures. Not because she was hunting for Rowan's woodsy cologne, wondering and wishing a little of it had rubbed off on her.

Cool, mostly dry, and completely naked, she padded to the bedroom. Matilda, who'd come in for the night, gave her the once-over before shuffling downstairs to claim her rightful place on the sofa. Audrey wished her a good night, no longer pretending she didn't talk to all of the animals like they were people at this point.

Of course, doing it made her think of Rowan. Rowan's playful assurances and kind eyes. Her easy smile and the way she could ask hard questions and make them seem not all that hard. Her ridiculously sexy hands and the way her mouth parted slightly when she hesitated at the door.

Sigh.

Audrey climbed into bed, feeling like a teenager with a crush. She laughed. When was the last time she'd felt that way?

She brought a hand to her throat, let it trail down between her breasts. Over her rib cage. Across her stomach. Around the curve of her hip.

At the apex of her thighs, she hesitated. Forget the crush, when was the last time she'd been turned on? Felt sensual?

Apparently, if she was a teenager with a crush, she was the horny kind.

It wasn't like she never masturbated. If anything, it was her preferred method of getting off. Reliable. Efficient.

God, where had her passion gone?

She pushed the question out of her mind and invited Rowan back in. Her laugh. The calloused skin of her thumb when their hands brushed over the bottle of wine. That look of longing in her eyes so intense Audrey still couldn't believe Rowan hadn't kissed her.

With those images flitting around, she moved her hand lower. She gasped, at the sensation of her index finger sliding over her clit and realizing how wet she was. How hard.

Little circles, then big. Long, lazy strokes that didn't stay lazy for long. She brought her left hand to join the party, pressing two fingers inside. She clenched them, pulled them deeper. Imagined they were Rowan's.

The promise of release built quickly. But instead of chasing it—the way she usually did—she changed angles, slowed down. Let herself build again. Would Rowan touch her like this?

Despite her intentions to draw it out, the question made the idea of Rowan fucking her so vivid, so visceral, the orgasm crashed through her. The moan that accompanied it was both uninhibited and unplanned. Her body arched, tensed, then collapsed into a pile of sated release.

She had about four seconds of that blissfully sated feeling before Rowan's comment about Ferdinand careened into her like Ozzie at dinnertime. Had she been louder than a rooster crow? Was there a chance Rowan heard her?

Oh, God. Oh, God. Oh, God.

She yanked the pillow from under her head and covered her face. Confident she'd managed to muffle herself, she let out a groan of mortification. She set the pillow aside and allowed her head to list side to side. Maybe Rowan had her television on. Or her windows closed. The latter was unlikely. It was a gorgeous night and her own were thrown wide.

Sigh.

If she had, she had. It wasn't like Audrey could ask her one way or the other. No, she'd just show up at the cidery tomorrow, blushing and wondering and unable to make eye contact. Not like it was the first time she'd thoroughly embarrassed herself. Rowan was probably used to it. It would be fine.

She shook her head. In her normal life, she was so put together she had a reputation for being downright prim. Here, all traces of that seemed to go right out the window. Good thing all this was temporary. Right? Otherwise she might very well forget who she was.

Chapter Sixteen

Ferdinand's morning pontifications pulled Audrey from a sound sleep. Well, a sound sleep and a particularly explicit sex dream about Rowan. She burrowed deeper under the blankets and groaned.

Usually, the burrowing had to do with wanting another minute or two of sleep. Not today. Not only had the sex dreams—and her own efforts—done little to satisfy her ever-expanding attraction to Rowan, they left her fully alert and as revved up as a cup of coffee.

Too bad she wasn't ready to face the day. Or, perhaps more accurately, ready to face Rowan. Because even if Rowan hadn't heard her last night, she knew what she'd been up to. With Rowan front and center in her mind. Not to mention the almost kiss and whether she'd imagined the whole thing or if the palpable sexual tension would remain.

She groaned again, but this time threw back the covers and climbed out of bed. After using the bathroom and pulling her hair into a messy ponytail, she tugged on her work clothes and headed downstairs. Matilda out, coffee on. Matilda in for breakfast, first cup of coffee at the kitchen sink. Just like the last fifty or so mornings. But also, inexplicably, different.

Okay, not inexplicably. Last night changed things. Just like Harriet's giving birth to Bert and Ernie made her see that Rowan was a good person, dinner last night made it so she could no longer pretend her attraction to Rowan was some casual, passing thing. She had the hots for her next-door neighbor, plain and simple.

Audrey went about her morning chores, mulling over that realization. Or acknowledgment. Whatever. Did it change things? Did it have to? Did she want it to?

With more questions than answers, she showered and got ready to head to the cidery. She hemmed and hawed over her outfit, took extra care to put on makeup but have it look subtle. The idea was to feel put together and confident, but all she managed to accomplish was a case of nerves that felt like a first date.

Oh, well.

Since the weather was damn near perfect, she grabbed her things and walked the quarter mile down to Forbidden Fruit. Inside, she found Rowan, Dylan, and Jamal prepping bottles for disgorging and corking.

"Good morning." Was she blushing? Was it obvious?

Dylan offered a wave, but Rowan turned with her full attention. "Good morning."

Despite her predictions of being unable to make eye contact, she couldn't seem to tear her gaze away from Rowan. Though, if she was being honest with herself, it had little to do with embarrassment and a whole lot to do with wanting. "How's it going?"

Rowan smiled. "Good, good. Did you sleep well?"

It could have been a perfectly innocuous question. Or a thinly veiled way of saying I know what you were up to after I went home last night. Since there was no way to know—short of asking and she sure as hell wasn't going to do that—she'd have to play it cool. "I did."

"Gorgeous night, wasn't it? Good sleeping weather. I love how even in the middle of August, the nights start to flirt with fall."

Neither Rowan's tone nor her expression held innuendo. Was she playing it cool because Dylan was there? Trying to make her squirm without making it obvious? Rowan didn't seem like the type to do that, but then again, how well did Audrey really know her?

Perhaps more likely, she was obsessing about absolutely nothing. And, as always, overthinking everything.

"You okay?" Rowan asked.

"Yes, of course. I was thinking about…um, a random dream I had." Only when the lie was out of her mouth did she remember the very real, very erotic dream she did have.

Rowan's smile was kind. "Those will get you."

If she only knew. "Yeah. Sorry. Don't mean to be spacey."

"There's coffee in the kitchen if you need an extra boost."

"Thanks. I think I'll take you up on that." More to have something to do with herself than any notion caffeine would solve her current situation. "Can I get anyone anything?"

Dylan shook her head, Jamal lifted his bottle of Mountain Dew, and Rowan indicated she'd just topped off her mug. Audrey fled to the nook that housed the coffee pot, microwave, and mini fridge. She grabbed what she'd started to think of as her mug from the row of hooks over the sink and poured herself a nice steaming cup of joe.

"You sure you're okay?"

Rowan's voice—quiet but close—startled her so badly she sloshed in way too much cream and sent the contents of her mug spilling over the top. "Gah."

"Sorry. I can't seem to get out of your way today."

She chuckled at her own ridiculousness. "Pretty sure I'm managing that all on my own."

"I wanted to make sure we were okay after last night."

Panic swelled in her chest and she grasped, without success, for something to say. "Last night?"

"I had a really great time and, I don't know, it felt like we had a moment there at the end. But then I worried maybe I overstepped or maybe I didn't step far enough. And now you seem uncomfortable and if that's my fault, I wanted to apologize and clear the air."

She barely managed to cover up the snort of laughter with a cough. "I'm good. We're good. I promise."

Rowan narrowed her eyes, but more out of suspicion than concern it seemed.

"I woke up in a weird mood, but I'm already feeling better." Not a lie.

"All right. You'd tell me if something was wrong?"

Rowan's genuine concern—not to mention her willingness to listen, to talk about whatever it might be—sent a ripple of warmth through her that had nothing to do with a sex dream. It might complicate things in the long run, but for now, she'd take it. "I'm really good. Thank you for asking. It's sweet."

"That's me." Rowan smiled, but a crease formed between her eyes. Like she was on the fence about whether to take it as a compliment.

"Okay, well, I guess I'll get to work."

Rowan's nod seemed curious, but again, probably more about her behavior in the moment than anything she may have overheard the night before. It was fine. It would be fine. Besides, she had plenty of work to do.

First up, finishing her research on a small business grant she was pretty sure would be a perfect fit for Forbidden Fruit. If she could focus on that, she could pitch it to Dylan and Rowan that afternoon and chase away any residual awkwardness. Even if that awkwardness seemed to be hers alone.

Dylan lifted her chin. "I'm not going to go check on her. You go check on her."

Rowan sighed. Audrey had been radio silent since heading to the office, not even emerging for lunch. On top of that, Audrey's energy had been weird enough for even Dylan to notice, causing Dylan to prod at her until she spilled the beans about almost kissing Audrey the night before. And now Dylan had taken to egging her on, telling her she needed to finish what she started. "You're so not helpful."

"Well, if you aren't going to kiss her, at least make nice. Offer to get her coffee or something. I don't want to lose her brains any sooner than we need to."

"Again, not helpful." Especially since she couldn't tell if Dylan meant Audrey might be mad about the almost kissing her in the first place or the almost kissing her and not. "But since I seem to be the grownup of this operation, I'll see how her day is going and make sure she doesn't need anything."

"Like a kiss."

She glowered in lieu of a comeback and headed to the office. After a light knock to announce her presence, she opened the door to find Audrey smiling at her with a gleam of excitement in her eyes.

Rowan couldn't decide whether to be relieved or suspicious. "How's it going?"

"Good." Audrey tapped her pen on the desk, clearly thinking about something other than pleasantries. Or kisses. "Have you heard of the Upstate Agricultural Development Program?"

Rowan closed one eye and tried to summon specifics from the recesses of her mind. Nothing. "I don't think so."

"It's a state program that gives funding to small farms that are developing retail experiences."

"Retail experiences?" She resisted a lip curl.

"Yes, like markets. Cafés." Audrey looked at the ceiling and tipped her head back and forth like she was pulling examples from thin air. "Tasting rooms."

The sneer dissolved. "Tasting rooms?"

"Yeah. You know. Like the one you're trying to build."

From where she sat, or stood, it sounded too good to be true. "Does it say that or are you extrapolating?"

Audrey shot her a look of exasperation. "Do you think I'd mention it if I hadn't done my homework?"

The question hadn't factored in Audrey's obsessive attention to detail. "Well, when you put it that way."

"Thank you." Audrey made a playful bowing gesture. "I actually emailed the contact on the website, and she confirmed it's absolutely the kind of project they support."

Getting the tasting room open for business didn't seem like an agricultural endeavor to her, but who was she to argue? "Okay."

"The idea is marrying agricultural and other economic development. Things that will create jobs but also boost tourism and help generate revenue across industries and sectors."

That actually made sense. "Rising tide."

Audrey made a lifting gesture. "Lifts all boats."

"How complicated is the application and what are the odds of getting it?"

Audrey returned her attention to the computer. "Not too complicated, especially for an existing business that is looking to expand."

Like they were. "And what's the catch?"

"If you're doing construction, you have to go through a bidding process that ensures access to women and minority owned contractors."

"Which I'd do anyway."

"And you have to have a plan to expand payroll by twenty percent over three years. I worried that might be the sticking point."

She did some quick calculations in her head. Based on what she and Dylan took in terms of salary and the meager size of their staff—an intern and some seasonal help—it wouldn't be a reach. Especially over three years. "That's doable."

"Excellent. I took the liberty of starting an application with the financials I have access to and what I know about the cidery otherwise. I just need you and Dylan to fill in the blanks and sign it."

"Seriously?"

"Yep. I'll print a copy for you two to review and I can finish entering the data once you give it to me."

"Where did you even learn about this?"

Audrey's face scrunched up. "I did this webinar sponsored by the cooperative extension and someone mentioned it."

Rowan shook her head. When Audrey negotiated helping with the financials, she expected a few hours of whipping their bookkeeping software into shape. Somewhere along the way, Audrey had taken on a hell of a lot more. It gave her a strange and not entirely unpleasant flutter in her stomach. So different from the almost kiss flutter. And yet, not completely apart from it.

"What? Do you think that's dorky?"

"Not at all. I just…" *Think I might be falling for you and have no idea what to do with that.*

Audrey folded her arms. "Just?"

She scrambled for something—anything—other that the words that almost came tumbling out. "I'm just thinking how lucky we are to have you on our team."

"Mm-hmm." Audrey looked not remotely convinced.

Suddenly, the cramped office felt even tinier. And hot. She resisted the urge to tug at her shirt. "We are. I'm going to go tell

Dylan all about it right now so she can thank me for getting into your good graces."

Audrey rolled her eyes but smiled. "Well, give me two seconds so I can print everything out and you can look at it together."

"Fantastic. I'll go tell her we're having an impromptu partners meeting." Because if she didn't, it was entirely possible she'd kiss Audrey right then and there.

She headed toward the barrels where she'd left Dylan a few minutes before. Removing herself from Audrey's immediate proximity helped cool her physically, but her insides continued to jump around like a pot of popcorn on an open flame. She told Dylan Audrey needed to talk with them but didn't say why. Not to punish Dylan for being obnoxious exactly, but, well, it seemed only fair.

Dylan didn't have to suffer in suspense very long. Audrey gave them both a thorough overview of the program, her ideas for how to frame the grant proposal, and assurances they had nothing to lose. By the time she was done, any weird energy was long forgotten, an almost giddy vibe in its place. They weren't a shoo-in by any means, but the mere prospect got them talking about the tasting room more than they had in months.

The conversation wrapped up, but Rowan wasn't ready for Audrey to go home or retreat to her office. "I'm going to get my walk in before it rains this afternoon. Care to join me?"

Audrey looked her up and down. "Depends. Are you offering because you'd feel bad if you didn't?"

It was hard to say if she wanted Audrey to know exactly how far from the truth that was. "Of course not."

Audrey looked to Dylan. "Be real with me. Is she just being nice? Does she secretly hate company?"

Dylan cleared her throat. "She doesn't like all company, but I'm utterly confident you are an exception."

Audrey looked at her, which prevented her from shooting eye daggers at Dylan. She opted for a smile instead. "It's true."

"Okay. Let me change my shoes."

She loved that Audrey had taken to leaving a pair of comfy, closed-toe shoes under her desk for afternoon walks. She also loved that she thought of it as Audrey's desk, even if she'd regret it later. Audrey scurried back to the office and Dylan gave her the full-on knowing look. "Don't even with that. You're nothing but trouble."

"Don't change the subject."

"From what?"

Dylan let out an indignant sigh. "When the two of you are going to give in and hook up already."

"That is absolutely not the subject." In her mind, sure. But of the conversation? Not a chance in hell.

"Come on. We always talk about the chicks we're seeing."

"Chicks?" It was bro speak, even for Dylan.

"You know what I mean."

She did. She was arguing on principle. "I like her. I'm attracted to her. And I don't think acting on it is a good idea."

Dylan shook her head. "I'm going to stop harassing you because I have work to do, but if the way she was looking at you is anything to go on, the feeling is mutual."

"Didn't you literally just tell me not to do anything that might mess up this nice little arrangement we have going?"

Dylan angled her head. "I did."

"So?"

"Maybe I think not acting on it is the bigger mistake."

Rowan groaned. She rolled her eyes. But as she headed for the side door, she couldn't stop herself from weighing the possible truth of Dylan's words.

CHAPTER SEVENTEEN

After checking on things at Ernestine's—complete with delighting over and devouring a pair of perfectly ripe peaches—they doubled back through the orchard in the direction of Rowan's house and the cidery. "Thank you for coming with me."

Audrey grinned. "I like it. I like even more that Dylan calls it your daily constitutional."

She chuckled. "It is important to keep an eye on the apples, but Dylan knows I'm a lot less cranky with hours of bottling if I get to go outside a couple of times during the day."

"To be fair, it's practically the end of the day. And you two have been working like dogs this week."

The disgorging was her least favorite task in the bottling process. While cool in principle, in reality it felt like the worst blend of fussy and chaotic. Which, of course, was exactly how Dylan would describe grafting. "I'm glad we're in the home stretch."

Audrey regarded her with curiosity. "What's your favorite part? Besides walking the orchard, I mean."

"I love the harvesting and pressing. It's hard work and messy, but seeing that initial transformation from fruit to cider gets me every time. And I swear the aroma is better than anything on the planet."

"Sounds incredible."

When Audrey didn't say more, Rowan debated asking the question that seemed to hang in the air. "Do you think you'll be here in September?"

Audrey took a deep breath. "I think so. Even if she's home, I can't imagine Ernestine being ready to be on her own by then."

"I'm not glad for that, but I'd love for you to experience it." She gave Audrey's shoulder a gentle bump. "Besides, we can always use an extra pair of hands for picking."

The teasing seemed to chase the shadows from Audrey's eyes. "I wouldn't mind being put to work."

"Is your job okay with that?"

Audrey nodded. "I'm approved to be on leave through the end of the year."

"That's great." It was, for Audrey's sake and for Ernestine's. But even as she took comfort in knowing Audrey would likely be around a few more months, a small part of her was already sad to see her go. Silly, really. Audrey might be settling into life here with apparent ease, but it wasn't really her life.

"I'm grateful, if not entirely sure what to do with myself."

"I don't know. Tending the farm, whipping our books into shape, learning to knit. You seem to be keeping busy." She added a wink to make sure Audrey knew she was mostly teasing, but also not.

Audrey smirked. "I suppose you have a point."

Because she was teetering on the edge of asking too many personal questions yet again, she cleared her throat. "I think the rain is coming in quicker than the forecast predicted. We should probably—"

As late summer storms often did, this one hit all at once. A faint rumble of thunder and the skies opened, releasing the kind of fat, pelting drops that could soak a person through almost instantly.

Audrey looked at the sky with something resembling alarm, then at Rowan. But the second she did, alarm faded and a grin spread across her face. Joyful, playful, exuberant. Without thinking, she grabbed Audrey's hand and ran in the direction of her house. Audrey kept up and they made it to her porch in a matter of seconds, though it hardly mattered. They were drenched, probably even before starting the dash for cover.

Audrey's clothes were plastered to her skin, revealing the tantalizing swell of her breasts and nipples that had gone hard even through her bra. Her hair was wet enough to give Rowan a hint of what she would look like coming out of a shower, and tiny droplets of water clung to her eyelashes. Just like the sensation of not wanting

Audrey to leave crept up on her without warning, so did the urge to kiss her. Well, not entirely without warning. She'd been thinking about kissing Audrey and wanting to kiss Audrey for the better part of three weeks. Even during that stretch of time Audrey was livid with her.

But unlike those times, this one swept through her in a giant rush, all heat and longing. Combined with the storm and Audrey's soaked clothes and dripping hair, not to mention her own drenched state, it was all too much. Her senses and her desire overrode any premise of sound judgement. She closed the distance between them, thrust her fingers into Audrey's hair, and let her mouth take the lead.

Audrey tasted of peaches and rain—fresh, verdant, bright. The heat of her mouth contrasted sharply with the slight chill on her skin. Everything about her was soft and lush and perfect and Rowan realized with only a hint of passing concern that she could utterly lose herself in this kiss, this moment. Lose herself, but maybe, also, find something she hadn't even known she was missing.

It was as though she'd been waiting her entire life to kiss Audrey Adams.

A clap of thunder brought her back to reality. To her front porch and the rain beating the roof and Jack's tail thumping against the doorframe. To their rush to get somewhere dry out of expedience more than exuberance. To the fact that Audrey hadn't technically invited a kiss.

"I'm sorry. I shouldn't have done that."

Audrey blinked a couple of times, those slow sort of blinks that are never good.

"I got caught up in the moment. It was your energy. I know that's a weak—"

Audrey's mouth crushed against hers, cutting off the half-baked explanation. It may have been less spontaneous, but it packed a hell of a lot more punch. Audrey's hands moved up and around Rowan's neck, her teeth nipped suggestively at Rowan's bottom lip. Any internal lecture she may have started giving herself about being too impulsive vanished. She brought her hands to Audrey's hips, pausing only a second before wrapping her arms around Audrey's waist and pulling their bodies together.

A jumble of half-formed thoughts whizzed through her mind: that this was a mistake, that Audrey tasted even better than she imagined, that she'd always wanted to make out in the rain but never had. But above everything else, like the pulsing bass of a dance song whose lyrics and tune hardly mattered, was desire. She'd tried and tried to convince herself that wanting Audrey was some passing thing, an alchemy of her beauty and proximity and that trace of damsel in distress she had going on. Now, with Audrey's tongue teasing, challenging hers, she knew better.

Audrey broke the kiss and pulled away, her eyes dark with what Rowan desperately hoped was desire. "Are you still sorry?"

She had no idea how to answer, and not just because Audrey had melted her brain. It seemed like the sort of trick question where anything she said would get her into trouble.

"Cat got your tongue?"

That was putting it mildly. "Something like that."

"Let me rephrase." Audrey lifted her chin in delicious challenge. "Do you want me?"

Okay, that definitely had to be a trick question. It was direct, though, and she couldn't bring herself to say anything but the truth. "Yes."

Audrey smiled. "That's a start."

Start to what? "Okay."

"Here's the thing. I want you."

Those three words—without any added context or connotation— sent her already thudding pulse racing. And her libido, well, it was revving at a level she didn't know existed until today.

Audrey angled her head. "Do you want to go to bed with me?"

She nodded. Words. She needed words. "Yes."

Audrey let out a breath that made it clear she'd been holding it. "Good."

"But..." She had a thousand reasons why it wasn't a good idea but couldn't bring herself to articulate any of them.

"I know. We're working together, we're barely in friend territory. I could go on."

She really hoped it was Audrey's turn to have a but.

"But I can't stop thinking about you." Audrey shrugged. "It's driving me crazy and making it really difficult to get any work done. And things between us are already messy and complicated, so what's one more layer piled on really?"

"Uh."

"I know." Audrey stuck both hands out in exasperation. "I know."

It felt sort of like she'd stumbled into some alternate reality. Not only one where Audrey wanted her, but one where Audrey could admit it was dicey and didn't care. A tiny, rational part of her mind screamed to slow things down, talk some sense into both of them. It was very easily and very quickly drowned out by the part that had been attracted to Audrey from the moment they met, that had been wanting her almost as long. "So?"

"So, I think you should take me inside and we see what we can do to get this out of our systems."

If, deep down, she knew that one time with Audrey would do absolutely nothing to get anything out of her system, she also knew better than to say so. "Okay."

Another nod. "Okay."

The simple answer struck her, especially since Audrey had essentially carried the conversation. Command and consent all rolled into one. And Audrey would likely kick her ass if she used the word submission, but it felt like a little bit of that, too. It was sexy as fuck.

She opened the door and took Audrey's hand. Despite the desire coursing through her veins, despite the edge of urgency that crackled in the air, she didn't rush. Through the living room and up the stairs, down the short hall to her room. The overcast sky cast an almost eerie light through the windows. The rain continued to pelt the metal roof, the sound softer and yet somehow more pronounced than on the porch. When was the last time she'd made love to a woman in the middle of the afternoon?

"I like your space."

It could have been a pleasantry, but she got the sense that Audrey meant it. It maybe shouldn't have mattered, but it did. "Thanks."

Audrey's smile was coy as she came in for another kiss. Perhaps because she paired it with undoing the buttons of Rowan's shirt in rapid succession. She didn't waste time shoving it from Rowan's shoulders. Or tugging Rowan's undershirt free from the waistband of her pants. In fact, the only time Audrey broke the kiss was the two seconds it took her to tug the shirt over Rowan's head.

She kicked off her shoes and Audrey did the same. Audrey's mouth returned to hers—hot, hungry, and aggressive—and her fingers went to work on Rowan's belt. Okay, maybe she'd been wrong about the submission part. There was nothing submissive about this. Not that she was complaining.

Not to be outdone—or to be the only naked one—she grasped at the waist of Audrey's skirt. She found the zipper at the side, complete with one of those impossibly small hooks. Fortunately for her sex addled brain, it released with a pinch. Even wet, the fabric slinked down Audrey's legs, tickling the tops of Rowan's bare feet.

She had a passing thought of asking Audrey if she wanted a towel, if she wanted to get under the covers and warm up first, but Audrey nudged her onto the bed and that was the end of that.

Audrey stood over Rowan, who lay sprawled across the bed in sexy invitation. She took a moment to appreciate Rowan's muscular body. Not angular, exactly, but so different from the softness of her own lines and curves. When her brain started to process what was about to happen—what she'd initiated—she shut it off and climbed in. Into bed. On top of Rowan.

Rowan's skin against hers managed to turn off every thought, leaving only sensation. She straddled Rowan's thighs and sat up, delighting in the feel of Rowan's skin and the patch of hair against hers. She gyrated a couple of times for her pleasure as much as Rowan's, then looked into Rowan's eyes. "Yes?"

"Yes."

She'd been seeking consent, but Rowan's expression conveyed a hell of a lot more. Between that look and the subtle thrust of Rowan's hips, it wouldn't take much for her to come. She willed her body to slow, to wait.

Rowan's hands settled on the curves below her waist, where hip met ass. She managed to guide Audrey's movements without dictating them, setting a rhythm that brought them into sync. Audrey's head fell back. "Fuck."

"Oh, I'm planning on it. But I'm enjoying this an awful lot."

The hint of cockiness should have bugged her, but it didn't. It made her want to see exactly what Rowan had in mind. What Rowan had to offer. She couldn't remember the last time she wanted someone that much and knew deep in her core she wouldn't be disappointed. "In that case…"

She planted a hand on either side of Rowan's head, leaning forward just enough to brush her nipples up Rowan's chest, grazing hers in the process. She rocked back and forth, creating just the right amount of friction along her clit.

Rowan's expressions intensified, her blue eyes darkening to a shade Audrey hadn't seen before. "But I can only take being teased for so long."

"What are you going—"

The rest of the question vanished when Rowan took hold of her wrists. With what seemed like little more than a twist of her body, she managed to reverse their positions, pinning Audrey's hands over her head in the process. Audrey gasped.

"Too much?"

Too much, perhaps, for her poor short-circuited brain to process. But somehow just the right amount and also not nearly enough. "No."

Rowan smiled that slightly smug smile again. "Good."

It was Rowan's turn to move against her. But instead of straddling her thighs, Rowan settled between them. She released Audrey's wrists and braced herself over Audrey. She used the new leverage to press her pelvis to Audrey's.

Audrey let out a moan before she could think about what sounds she should make, what sounds would sound the sexiest. She spread her legs wider. The quiver in her abdomen grew. And just like with the sounds, the orgasm flashed through her before she could stop it. Hot and fast, like steam erupting from a kettle hitting the boil.

Rowan stilled and searched her face. "Was that—did you?"

It struck her suddenly that maybe coming so quickly was rude. Or selfish. Or desperate. The flush of coming gave way to embarrassment. She bit her lip and nodded.

Rowan grinned. "That's hot."

Something resembling a giggle escaped her. Rowan didn't seem to notice. She was already kissing her way down Audrey's torso.

"I'll go easy, but tell me if it's too much."

Realization dawned a fraction of a second before Rowan's tongue pressed into her. Just like before, it was at once too much and not enough. Unlike the thrust of her hips, though, Rowan kept her mouth slow—not quite soft but light enough to tease her back to arousal. "I—"

Rowan sucked her clit gently and the half-formed words gave way to a groan. The sound seemed to encourage Rowan, who gripped her thighs and interspersed the sucking with laps of her tongue. Like she knew Audrey's body better than Audrey knew herself.

Her pulse thudded and her vision blurred. She fisted her hands in the sheets, grasping for purchase, for something to keep her tethered to this moment. Seeking release again but also trying to keep it at bay.

The second orgasm bore little resemblance to the first. There was no flash and there was nothing fast about it. The sensation started in her center but radiated to every finger and toe, every muscle and hair follicle. But unlike ripples in water, it didn't dissipate. Her body arched and it reverberated back through her, over and over until she collapsed onto the mattress too limp to move. "Fuck."

Rowan crawled up her body and kissed her. "Good fuck, I hope."

"Uh-huh. I'd use more words but you melted my brain."

"Hmm. I guess I'll let it cool off a bit before asking if I can do that again."

Audrey shook her head, in response to Rowan's question but also in a state of wonder at how easy, how playful sex could be. "Not before I get a turn with you."

"Well, that sounds amazing, too, so I won't argue."

"Good. Because I want you. And then I'm going to need to have you inside me."

Rowan kissed her again. "I can get behind this plan."

If playfulness had been a surprise, discovering she could be brazen was a revelation. She wasn't sure what to do with it, but it hardly seemed to matter. Because Rowan—magically, wondrously—did.

CHAPTER EIGHTEEN

Audrey stared at the ceiling, allowing her focus to soften and her vision to blur in the rapidly fading light. It struck her how she could make everything go sort of misty around the edges. She hadn't realized she could do that. Such a fucking metaphor, it was all she could do not to laugh.

"Are you okay?" Rowan's voice held worry, which was sweet.

She turned her head, but it took a few seconds to reengage her occipital lobe and bring Rowan's face into focus. The look of concern on her face matched her voice. "I am."

"Are you sure?"

She laughed, as much at herself as Rowan. "I'm sure. Do I not seem okay?"

"You seem…" Rowan closed one eye, then the other, and it was hard to tell if she was fumbling for the right word or choosing it carefully. She opened both and frowned. "Not here."

"Are you worried that I'm not thinking about what we just did or that I'm thinking too much?"

Rowan nodded. "Yes."

Both were fair concerns, all things considered. And she liked that Rowan seemed to get her cerebral tendencies but not be annoyed by them. "I'm thinking about how I'm not overthinking and how it's kind of nice."

"Huh."

"I know." An anomaly for her—on so many levels.

"I don't want you to regret anything."

Did she? Time would tell. But if that wound up being the case, it wouldn't be fair to hang it on Rowan. No, she'd gone into this with clear intentions and no illusions. If anything, she'd been the one to nudge Rowan into it. "I don't." The follow-up question threatened to lodge in her throat. "Do you?"

"I don't."

Ostensibly the answer she wanted, but the brevity of Rowan's reply left her wanting more. She rolled onto her side. "Are you just saying that?"

Rowan's gaze shifted from Audrey's eyes to her mouth and back. Then she kissed her long and slow. "No."

For some reason, the terse answer didn't bother her this time. Her need for reassurance did, but that was another matter entirely. "Okay, good."

"I'd love to make you dinner and then come back to bed and show you exactly how much I'm not just saying that. Assuming you don't have somewhere to be, of course."

It shouldn't be possible to be turned on again, but she was. And maybe she was imagining it, but Rowan's comment about having somewhere to be felt like her own way of needing a touch of reassurance. Funny how that made such a difference. She trailed a finger between Rowan's breasts. "Let me guess. You've got a special box of mac and cheese for when the ladies come over."

Rowan's mouth fell open. "I should be offended by that."

"But you aren't because you've already admitted you're a terrible cook."

"I'm a lazy cook. It's not the same thing." Rowan's haughty expression made it clear she didn't really take offense.

"Okay, then. What's for dinner?"

"Shit."

She laughed then. "Didn't expect me to say yes?"

"I offered before thinking about what I have in the house and then overplayed my hand."

Like before, the playfulness struck her. Completely out of character for her. Kind of like impulsively going to bed with someone. It made her wonder about what might be in or out of Rowan's character. "How about we rustle up something together and I promise to keep my expectations super low?"

"Now that's just insulting. I mean, yes please, but insulting."

Another laugh escaped. And since she was so busy surprising herself, she figured why the hell stop there. "Don't worry. You're good enough in bed to get away with being a lousy cook."

"I'm not lousy. I'm willfully ignorant. And I make killer scrambled eggs."

She poked Rowan in the ribs. "You should have stuck with lousy. I'd give you credit for trying."

"Now she tells me." Rowan planted a kiss on her mouth and climbed from the bed.

Audrey sighed. If she'd thought Rowan was gorgeous before seeing her naked. This? This was swoon-worthy. She laughed at the idea of being a swooning female and sat up. Only to realize her clothes sat in a sopping wet pile on the floor. "Crap."

"Want to borrow some sweats and I can put those in the dryer?"

"That would be great. Thank you."

A few minutes later, her clothes tumbled in a small room off the kitchen and Rowan poked around for what she might have on hand, humming as she opened various cabinets.

"I don't mind eggs for dinner."

"Aha." She pulled a box of linguine from one of the shelves.

"Is there a jar of sauce lurking in there, too, or do we need to wing it?"

"I can do you one better." She headed to the freezer. "There's this old Italian woman at the farmer's market who sells sauce. Marinara with sausage or pesto?"

"Pesto sounds delicious." As did the image of Rowan poking around a farmer's market and chatting up an Italian grandma.

"Coming right up."

Since the rain brought a cool front with it, Rowan got a fire going in the wood stove to chase away the chilled, damp air. They sat on the sofa cross-legged with bowls of pasta and *Gentlemen Prefer Blondes*. They washed the dishes, standing hip to hip at the sink like they'd done it a thousand times before. To be fair, they had done it at least a dozen times. At Ernestine's, though. And always only as friends. The shift—going to bed together—managed to change everything and nothing at the same time.

Rowan finished drying the pasta pot, then handed her the towel. She wiped her hands before hanging it to dry on the oven door. And for all the times they'd eaten together in the last couple of months, all the times she'd done that exact action, it only hit her in that moment that she'd never shared the simple domestic chore with any of her previous girlfriends.

Restaurants? Sure. Takeout? Plenty. And yes, there'd been a few occasions where things felt serious enough and her work schedule had enough give for her to prepare a meal for another woman. But that had been more about creating a special evening, creating a certain mood. Never was it this chummy, casual affair with whatever was on hand and a dog waiting patiently for something to be dropped. Never—ever—was it this fun.

Rowan flicked off the light over the sink. "Penny for your thoughts."

She might have been more inclined to share if the revelation didn't leave her with a sad, hollow sensation in her chest. "You don't want to know."

"The sex or dinner? Which are you rethinking?" Rowan seemed to be joking but not.

"Neither."

"The staying over, then? I promise I'll get up super early with you and help with the animals, if that's what you're worrying about."

"It's not but I'm not going to turn down the offer of help. It's mucking day."

Rowan shook her head. "Every day is mucking day."

Technically true, though there was the daily maintenance mucking and there was the weekly dear God how did they get manure there mucking. And tomorrow was the latter. "I wasn't rethinking that, either. The staying over, I mean."

"Oh." Rowan looked relieved but like she was trying not to show it, and it was seriously endearing.

"My thoughts were random, and I was hoping to get back into your bed if the invitation stands." Who was this woman and where had she come from?

Rowan came to where Audrey stood and threaded her arms around her. "It definitely still stands."

"Then we should probably get to it. I hear dawn comes pretty early around these parts."

"That's what the neighbor's rooster tells me."

God, this was fun. "Well, then, lead the way."

"One sec." Rowan released her and went to the back door. Jack shuffled to his feet and loped out, only to lope back in about thirty seconds later.

Audrey cringed. "I feel bad for Matilda."

"Doesn't she sleep on her bed in the barn at least half the time?"

"Yes, but she's used to having the option and she has opinions about it." She was almost catlike in that way. "And the goats and sheep are used to being tucked into the barn for the night."

Rowan pressed her lips together.

"You think I'm being silly."

"Nope. I think you're being adorable."

Heat rose in her cheeks. Had anyone ever—literally ever—called her adorable? It struck her as the sort of word she'd remember yet couldn't conjure a single memory from her adult life. Or her childhood. "I think you're being indulgent."

Rowan shook her head. "I want you to stay, but I want you to be happy and relaxed. What if we walk over together and check on her. And everyone else while we're at it."

"It's almost eleven."

"And the rain has cleared and it's a gorgeous night." Rowan's expression turned serious. "Unless you don't want to stay. That's really okay, too."

Rowan's concern for what she wanted sent a ripple of warmth through her. "I do want to stay. And, not to be weird, I'd rather stay here than spend the night at Ernestine's, even though that might be more logical."

Understanding passed through Rowan's eyes. "Not weird at all. Let's go check on all the creatures great and small so we can come back here and I can take you to bed."

Was it really as simple as that? Apparently, it was.

At Ferdinand's first crow, Audrey mumbled and burrowed deeper into the crook of Rowan's shoulder. At his second, she let out an unhappy groan. By the time he let the third one rip, Rowan was pretty sure Audrey mumbled something about a fucking rooster and Rowan didn't try to stop herself from laughing.

"You're really not used to it yet?"

Audrey lifted her head and looked around, one eye still closed. "Oh, I'm used to it. I just find it extra offensive when I'm not in bed alone."

"Ah." She kissed Audrey's temple. "I'll give you that."

"For the record, it's not nearly as loud here."

"Are you taking back feeling bad about him waking me up?"

As if part of the conversation, Ferdinand crowed again.

"No, because it's still plenty obnoxious." Audrey made a show of wiggling under the covers.

"I really would have pegged you for a morning person."

Audrey propped on her elbows this time. "There's morning and there's dawn. Let's not conflate the two."

God, she was beautiful first thing. "That's a very city girl thing to say."

"I resemble that remark."

She wanted to say that Audrey was settling into country girl pretty damn well but didn't want to overplay her hand. "Well, city girl, the day's not getting any younger and the chickens will be wanting their breakfast."

"Fine." Audrey let out another groan of protest, but it had a playful edge.

"Would coffee help?" Because offering was the nice thing to do, not because she wanted to cozy up with Audrey for a few more minutes.

"Yes, but I'll make it at home while I start the chores. I have a system."

"I bet you do."

Audrey sat up, putting her sex-tossed hair and glorious breasts on full display. "I resemble that remark, too."

"We have to get up now or I might never let you out of this bed." Honesty was the best policy, right?

"Would you mind grabbing my clothes?"

"Oh. Yes. Of course." She made a feeble gesture in Audrey's direction. "You, uh, distracted me."

She got out of bed and pulled on her robe. The sound of Audrey's laughter followed her downstairs. She gathered Audrey's things from the dryer, slightly guilty that she hadn't the night before and now they were all wrinkled, and headed back to the bedroom.

"Thank you." Audrey pulled on her skirt and top and finger combed her hair. "I feel like I should make a walk of shame joke."

The phrase gave Rowan pause. "Do you feel shame?"

Audrey seemed to really consider before answering, making Rowan wonder once again if she regretted sleeping together. "No."

The answer—simple and decisive—caught her off guard. "Good. Shame is dumb."

Audrey smiled.

"I mean, I get why people feel it. Especially women. Society is so messed up sometimes. I'm glad you don't, at least when it comes to this. Us." Christ. When had she gotten on the awkward train?

Audrey continued to smile. "Agreed. In this instance, I was poking fun at myself. Especially since we went to my house last night after deciding I would stay over and I was so focused on having sex with you again I didn't bother to get clean clothes."

"Well, I'll admit to distracting you. I'm not really sorry for that, though." She'd had a hard time keeping her hands off Audrey. And when Audrey giggled about it? Well, that did her in.

Audrey's smile turned into a flirtatious smirk. "You shouldn't be sorry."

Rowan couldn't decide if she wanted to pull Audrey into her arms and squeeze her or drag her back to bed and rip off the clothes she'd just managed to put on. The desire to do both was unusual for her and left her a little off-balance. "Do you want some help with the animals this morning? I don't have to be at work right away."

Audrey waved her off. "No, no. You go on. You promised to help with mucking this afternoon and I'm going to hold you to it. I'll take care of everyone and find my way there. I shouldn't be too much later than usual."

She wanted to remind Audrey again that she didn't punch a clock at the cidery, but they'd had the conversation enough times she worried Audrey might smack her. So she walked Audrey to the door, where they shared a sweet if slightly awkward kiss good-bye.

"Could you maybe not tell Dylan about this? I know you're friends, but I—" Audrey abruptly stopped and shook her head. "You know what? Never mind. That's not fair of me."

The abrupt shift didn't help her off-kilter state. "I don't want to make you uncomfortable."

"Just let me know if you're going to do it right away or later so I can plan my embarrassment accordingly."

"I don't want you to be embarrassed either."

Audrey squeezed her eyes shut and cringed. "I'm not embarrassed that we slept together. Just that someone I work with is going to know that I had sex last night and with whom. If you hadn't noticed, I have a tendency to be strait-laced."

She laughed, then, and had another wave of that squishy mixed with sexy feeling. "I promise I'll keep it vague and I'm pretty sure Dylan will act like an adult, at least with you."

"Thank you. I'm going to leave before I get even more ridiculous."

"You're not ridiculous. I'm pretty sure you're being adorable again."

Audrey shook her head. "I'm glad you think so. I'll see you soon."

She resisted saying she liked Audrey like this. Just as she resisted kissing Audrey again or asking if she had plans for later. Not because she didn't want to but because she got the sense Audrey needed some time to settle. "I'll see you soon."

She watched Audrey longer than she should have, enjoying the subtle sway of her hips in the floral-print skirt. When she finally closed the door, she simply leaned against it. Her own way of settling, maybe.

As tempting as it was to indulge in a mental replay of the night before, she summoned the events that led up to it instead. The thunderstorm. The kiss that was even better than she imagined. And Audrey's assertion that acting on the attraction would get it out of their systems.

Ha.

She'd known better then and now, in this moment, the reality of her situation came into sharp relief. What she felt for Audrey had nothing to do with a passing attraction. No, she had it pretty bad. And sex had only intensified it.

She was pretty sure Audrey didn't feel the same. Still, she'd stayed the night. And she didn't seem to have regrets, even with the prospect of Dylan knowing what had happened. But was that the end of it? Was Audrey's curiosity—her desire—satisfied?

She guessed she'd have to wait and see. In the meantime, she needed to get herself showered and ready for work. And try not to think too long or too hard about her beautiful neighbor and the chance they'd get to spend the night together again.

CHAPTER NINETEEN

Audrey checked her reflection in the mirror on the back of the door. Jeans and a flannel. She was wearing jeans and a flannel shirt on a date. Sort of date. A day with Rowan at least. One she hoped ended in Rowan's bed. More of a date than she'd had in a long ass time.

She headed downstairs, chuckling at the idea of what her three-months-ago-self would have to say about what her today-self had planned.

She'd barely finished tying her boots when Rowan's truck rumbled in the driveway. Outside, she offered Rowan a wave and climbed into the passenger side, sliding across the bench seat to steal a kiss. "Where are we going again?"

Rowan grabbed her arm before she could slide back and pulled her close. "Nowhere until you kiss me for real."

The second one packed enough of a wallop that she wished the only place they were headed was Rowan's house and Rowan's bed. The heat of Rowan's mouth was a perfect foil to the chill in the air. The softness of her lips giving way to the firmness, the insistence of the kiss itself. It was the kind of kiss that invoked an involuntary whimper of protest when Rowan eased away. The kind of kiss that left Audrey rooted where she was, a little too dazed to do anything at all.

"Better." Rowan grinned. "We're going to an old farm on the far side of Cayuga Lake to forage crab apples."

She did that slow blink that came with trying to get her bearings. "Crab apples."

"Yes, little red things about yea big." Rowan made a circle with her finger and her thumb. "Great for jelly. Even better for cider."

That snapped her out of it and she gave Rowan's arm a smack. "I know what they are, jerk."

Rowan shrugged. "You didn't seem sure."

"That's because you melted my brain with your mouth."

"Oh." Rowan wiggled her eyebrows with almost comical panache. "I could do that again."

She scooted back to her side. "Maybe later. If you play your cards right."

Rowan hung her head. "It was the crab apple comment, wasn't it? You're punishing me."

Audrey folded her arms. "Yep."

The thing was, she wasn't. Rowan's teasing didn't get on her nerves. Like, ever. If anything, it got her to loosen up, too. She wouldn't be winning any awards for being happy-go-lucky, but it was a marked change for her. One she hadn't expected or would have even said she wanted, but one she kind of liked.

"Heartbreaker."

"Hey, I said maybe later. You just have to get back in my good graces."

Rowan's smile was slow, sly, and sexy as fuck. "I think I might be able to pull that off."

"I'll hold you to it." God, this was fun.

Rowan pulled out of Ernestine's driveway and headed south. Autumn color was beginning to kiss the tips of maple leaves. Green remained the predominant color, but every now and then, a single bush or tree was aflame in shades of red, yellow, and orange.

"Why do some trees turn sooner than others?" She'd wondered it more than she meant to say it.

"Are you asking for real?" Rowan glanced her way, the curiosity on her face tinged with doubt.

"Do you know the answer for real?"

"I did spend four years studying trees, if you recall."

"Right, right." She nodded slowly. "Tell me everything."

Rowan chuckled and returned her gaze to the road. "I know better than to do that. You'd be bored to tears. But I've worked on my abbreviated version."

"I might surprise you, but lay it on me."

Rowan cleared her throat and Audrey got this flash of her in a bow tie and a sweater vest lecturing in front of a chalkboard. Probably the last thing in the world Rowan would do—or wear—but it made her smile nonetheless. "Leaves change color when they stop producing chlorophyll, which they do in response to less light."

"Mm-hmm. That makes sense. I have vague recollections of that from high school biology."

"That shift is triggered in different species of trees at different times. But even in the same kind of tree, things like a north-facing location can make one start the process, or rather stop the process, sooner than others."

"Huh."

"You don't believe me?"

"Of course I believe you. You literally have a degree in trees. Why do you always think I'm dubious?"

That got her a raised brow.

"Okay, I'm a little suspicious by nature, but mostly of people and situations I don't know yet. I know you. I trust you."

Rowan's features softened and she smiled. "I'm glad."

"I like you, too." More than like, if she was being entirely honest.

"I like you back."

She sat with that for a moment, let herself enjoy it. Rowan continued to drive and she realized the road they were on was about to take them through Kenota. "Hey, can we—"

Before she could get the question out, Rowan pulled into the parking lot of Bake My Day.

"You already planned to stop."

Rowan winked. "I am trying to get back into your good graces, after all."

"Well played, Marshall. Well played."

"I do my best."

Despite having coffee and breakfast at home, she ordered a cup and a cherry Danish. Rowan went with a bear claw and they piled back into Rowan's truck with enough sugar and caffeine to jump-start any adventure. "I can't believe I haven't gained twenty pounds with how much I've been eating."

Rowan looked her up and down. "You could gain fifty pounds and still be gorgeous."

She'd had her share of body image struggles through the years, being a bit thicker in the middle and not having the luscious hips to balance it out. She didn't obsess about it, but she wasn't the most self-confident either. The simplicity of Rowan's assertion hit home. "Thanks."

"My guess is you're doing way more manual labor than you've ever done before."

"Understatement of the century."

"Burns a lot of calories. And it's good for you. I like the freckles you've developed, too."

She laughed. "I was thinking more about my biceps, but if you want to find my freckles endearing, I'm not about to stop you."

"I find all of you endearing."

Maybe Rowan meant it as a joke. Or maybe it was one of those throw-away lines, meant to flatter but without a lot of meaning behind it. But she sounded sincere. And Audrey's heart tripped in her chest with such fervor she struggled to breathe.

Rowan gave her a smile before starting the engine and pulling back onto the road. She didn't seem to need a response and Audrey was glad because she wasn't at all sure what to say.

Rowan dumped her basket into the crate she'd forklifted into the back of her truck. Not as easy as having the bins scattered among the trees, but not a bad system for foraging. She leaned against the side of the truck and watched Audrey balance on the tripod ladder, holding her basket in one hand and reaching for a small cluster of apples with the other.

She'd invited Audrey to join her mostly for fun—wanting to spend the day together and thinking Audrey would get a kick out of the experience. But as with everything it seemed, Audrey took to it with a combination of eagerness and energy that made her a quick study and as diligent a laborer as she ever hired.

Now that they'd slept together, Rowan's appreciation of that hit a new level. The respect and the attraction that she'd mostly managed to keep separate swirled together into something that could quickly turn into feelings if she wasn't careful. Feelings that would leave her high and dry when Audrey went back to her real life.

She shook her head. That wouldn't be for a while yet. No point borrowing trouble. Especially on such a glorious early fall day.

Audrey made her way down the ladder, bending over to pick up the few that had escaped her grasp. She picked up her now full basket and turned to Rowan. "You could have told me it was break time."

Rowan lifted her chin. "It's break time."

Audrey positioned the basket against her hip and came over to the truck, tipping its contents into the crate. "Hey, it's more than half full already."

Rowan snaked out an arm, wrapping it around Audrey's middle and pulling her close. "Yeah, I should bring a helper more often."

Audrey didn't wiggle away, but she got on her tiptoes and continued to peer into the back of the truck. "You should give me a raise, too."

Audrey dropped back onto her heels and looked at Rowan in a way that made it impossible not to kiss her. So she did. "I'm prepared to double your salary."

Audrey smirked. "You can't double zero."

She looked to the sky and let out a sigh. "You and your math. Don't you know it's the thought that counts?"

"I didn't know that." Audrey's expression turned grave. "I'm just a cold, hard accountant."

"There's nothing cold about you, except maybe your nose right now." Rowan kissed it to prove her point. "Yep. Chilly."

Audrey's shoulders dropped and her whole body relaxed into Rowan's. Such a subtle shift, but it did things to Rowan. Her libido, sure, but it was more than that. Despite her argument with herself a moment before, Audrey managed to stir up all sorts of feelings. At the strangest times, too. Protective feelings. Feelings that crept uncomfortably close to how she'd describe being in love. It somehow managed to be reassuring and terrifying at the same time.

"You look sad. Does that mean break time is over?"

She'd lost track of how long they'd been standing there. But even with Audrey's tendency toward the impatient, it was probably longer than she'd meant. "Yep, yep. Back to work."

Audrey stepped out of her embrace and planted her fists on her hips. "The tree I was on is mostly picked, the ripe ones at least. How's yours?"

"Needs the ladder." See? This was fine. No need to get all caught up in emotions.

"On it." Audrey hustled over to where she'd left the ladder and dragged it to the next tree. "Why isn't Dylan here?"

"Engagement party."

"Ah. I guess that's a good excuse."

"It's her sister. They're close, but I think she might almost rather be here."

Audrey laughed. "You people with your siblings. You don't know how lucky you are."

She thought of hers. They couldn't be more different in some ways, but she loved them. "I do. Or at least I try, even when they get on my nerves."

They picked until the crate was full, leaving close to half the fruit to continue ripening for another day or another forager. Audrey snapped a few pictures with her phone, both of the trees and the haul. "I'm very impressed with us."

"I am, too. You might be a better picker than Dylan."

"Really?" Audrey seemed delighted by the prospect.

"To be fair, she spends a fair amount of time soaking up the aromas and appreciating the terroir, aka, daydreaming about the cider."

Audrey squared her shoulders. "You don't have to worry about me daydreaming."

So much for not getting caught up in emotions. "You could, you know."

"Could what?" The genuine confusion in Audrey's voice slayed her.

"Daydream."

"Oh."

The surprise got her even more than arguing would have. "It's good for the soul and it recharges your batteries. I could even argue it helps you be even more productive in the long run."

Audrey smirked. "That's a pretty hard sell."

She shrugged, not wanting to press her luck. "I'm just saying you might enjoy it. And if it's anything like picking apples, you might be better at it than you think."

The smirk gave way to a real smile. "I'll keep that in mind."

"Good. Now, I think we're done here. Shall we head home?"

"Okay." Audrey continued to smile but seemed almost reluctant to go.

"We'll get to start our own harvest in a week or two, if you haven't gotten your fill today." It was so easy to imagine harvesting alongside Audrey, doing the work but also kissing her between the rows of trees.

"I'd like that."

"Excellent. You're hired."

They piled into the truck and Audrey peered out the back window as she fastened her seat belt. "Do we get to turn these into cider today?"

She couldn't help but smile at the enthusiasm. "Not today. I'm hoping to get two more crates that size, then we'll do a press."

"More foraging?" Audrey's eyes lit up.

"Not technically foraging, since the trees are part of an orchard and I know the owner."

"Hmm."

"His wife used to make jelly for their shop, but they got divorced. And there's not a lot of demand for crab apples in the u-pick market, so he doesn't have a use for them."

"Aw, that's sad."

"Well, from what I gather, he was having an affair and she took her half of their money and moved to Costa Rica."

Audrey shook her head. "Possibly still sad but maybe also for the best."

The matter-of-fact assessment made her chuckle. "Something like that."

"So, now what?"

She debated with herself for only a moment before sharing the trajectory of her thoughts. "I was hoping I could convince you to come home with me for a nice shower and an early dinner."

"Early dinner, huh? What'cha making?"

"I happen to have a very fancy frozen pizza on hand, and I'd be willing to share it with you."

"Mmm."

Whether Audrey meant it or was merely humoring her, she couldn't say. But she seemed game, so Rowan wasn't about to complain. "Of course, if we got distracted, it would make an outstanding late dinner, too."

"Very convenient."

"I like to be prepared, you know, for whatever unfolds."

Audrey smirked. "Like a Girl Scout."

Rowan straightened her shoulders and puffed out her chest. "I'll have you know I spent thirteen years in the Girl Scouts."

"I would have pegged you for 4-H, but that's adorable."

"We were much too suburban for that." Or, maybe more accurately, her hometown liked to think of itself that way.

"Right, right. Let me guess, you were a champion cookie seller."

"I know you find me infinitely charming, but I'm actually quite shy. I mostly relied on my parents to sell them to their work friends."

"I wouldn't say infinitely." Audrey winked. "But that story makes you more charming rather than less."

"Even for a chronic over-achiever like you?"

Audrey shook her head. "Being an over-achiever was my cover for being almost cripplingly shy. If I was good enough at the things I chose to do, my parents didn't hassle me as much about being outgoing or having friends."

Audrey said it with an air of pride, but it made Rowan sad for the little girl who was a loner because it felt safe more than satisfying. "Aw."

"Don't worry. Ernestine brought me out of my shell and made me socially competent if not gregarious. And she somehow managed to make it fun."

She'd fancied what it would have been like to have Ernestine in her life during her formative years. She was glad Audrey got the benefit of Ernestine's guiding hand. "She really is a force of nature, isn't she?"

Another laugh. "That's one way of putting it."

Rowan drove and conversation lulled. It felt like a mixture of comfortable silence and the kind of happy tired that comes with a day of fresh air. Along with some reminiscing about some of her own choice moments with Ernestine. The persistent worry about Ernestine's prognosis remained, but she did her best to focus on good memories. She hoped Audrey did, too.

The combination of a rapidly setting sun and sitting still hit her and she was grateful to be heading home. Dinner was sounding better by the minute, along with a hot shower. The prospect of sharing both with Audrey? Well, from where she was sitting, that was icing on the cake.

CHAPTER TWENTY

Neither of them said as much, but Audrey was pretty certain accepting Rowan's invitation for dinner was basically agreeing to stay the night. She hadn't necessarily expected it to happen again. Hoped, sure. But not expected.

The thing was, she'd never slept with someone she'd been friends with first. Well, except for in college, but that was sort of how college worked. Definitely not since becoming an adult.

There was also the matter of them working together. Though, really, that almost fell into the category of friends helping each other out. A stretch, perhaps, but it made her feel better about sleeping together.

Such was the swirl of her thoughts while Rowan lifted the crate of apples from the back of her truck with the tractor. She watched the whole process in the side mirror, impressed by the ever-growing list of things the old Kubota could do. Of course, Rowan's skill impressed, too. The late afternoon sun slanted across her face, making the look of relaxed concentration all the more appealing.

See? Why couldn't she simply keep her focus on that? On enjoying the chemistry and the company and not analyzing it to death. She sighed. Because analyzing things to death was her nature. And, in a lot of ways, her profession. She'd honed the tendency throughout the years rather than learning to keep it in check and, in moments like this, she paid the price for it.

Enough. She was being ridiculous. There was not a single thing wrong with indulging her libido with an attractive, available woman.

If anything, doing it while she was here—with all this extra time on her hands—made it all the more logical. She'd work it out of her system and probably not have to deal with the urge to date or hook up or anything for at least a year. Even with the leave, she should be on track for partner by then and could shift her focus to finding a suitable partner and settling down with enough of a window to have kids if that's what they mutually decided to do.

Rowan and the tractor puttered out of view, so she shifted her focus to her own reflection, only to find herself scowling. What was that about? She'd given herself a free pass to have fun with Rowan and not worry about the consequences. She literally had nothing to worry about. Well, besides Ernestine of course. But worrying about Ernestine was a constant these days.

She looked away from the mirror altogether and at the building in front of her. A rather nondescript thing, really, especially from the back. She tried to envision what it would be like when the tasting room opened. Picnic tables at the front, maybe, under the trees, where customers could spill out and soak up the brief but glorious summer. They could bring in food trucks, do live music on the patio.

It wasn't hard to imagine. Even if it likely wouldn't be finished before she left. Which was okay. It wasn't her dream.

For some reason, that realization moved over her like a cloud, threatening to shadow her mood. Because she wanted to see it? Because her own dreams felt a bit staid by comparison? Because she'd be sad to leave? Maybe it was that. For all the work she was doing, this felt like somewhat of an extended vacation. That had to be it. Everyone was sad when vacation ended.

Rowan climbed back in the truck and she blew out a breath, relieved to have her thoughts—all of them—interrupted. She really got on her own nerves sometimes.

"You okay?" Rowan asked.

She nodded. "Just tired I think. And not looking forward to evening chores."

Rowan gave her knee a gentle squeeze. "I'll help and we'll be done in no time. And then you get that pizza I've been promising. I know you're excited for that."

"Well, I'm always excited for help." The funny thing was, she was excited. For the help, sure. Not for the pizza, obviously. She lived in New York and had a deep respect for good pizza. But the prospect of another night with Rowan? Definitely. Especially if she could shut off her brain for a hot minute.

"Teamwork makes the dream work."

She laughed because it was cheesy but smiled because she was coming around to appreciating how true it was.

Chores did go quickly and the pizza wasn't half bad, considering. Rowan asked if she might like a shower before bed and she surprised herself by not only saying yes, but asking Rowan to join her.

It started innocently enough—gloriously hot water, poking fun at Rowan's shampoo, conditioner, and body wash in one. "You realize this is marketed specifically to lazy men, right?"

Rowan shrugged. "Yeah, but it works and I like the way it smells."

She shook her head disapprovingly but didn't protest when Rowan soaped up her hands and lathered it over her skin. A bit masculine for her, but it did smell fresh and clean and kind of woodsy. She was glad she'd decided to tie her hair up because washing her hair with it definitely wouldn't go well, but otherwise it got the job done.

Rowan's hands continued to roam long after the suds were rinsed away. Audrey joined in, enjoying Rowan's broad shoulders and the way her nipples went hard at the slightest touch. She brought her mouth to Rowan's neck, licking away droplets of water before kissing and sucking her way up to Rowan's ear.

Rowan's hand slicked down her torso. "I want you, but I'd really like to get you into bed where I have access to all of you."

Her clit throbbed, though it was hard to tell whether it had more to do with Rowan's hand hovering teasingly close or the promise of her words. "Bed. Bed is good."

Rowan nodded even as her hand slipped between Audrey's legs. Audrey shifted to give her better access, then bucked when Rowan's fingers slid over her and into wetness that had nothing to do with being in the shower. "Fuck, you feel good."

She wanted to be sexy, to be brazen. To tell Rowan all the things she wanted and craved. But all she could manage was, "Uh-huh."

Rowan plunged into her. "Maybe bed can wait."

She lifted one leg, setting it on the edge of the tub, and grasped Rowan's shoulders to keep her balance. "Yes."

Despite the teasing and the flirting and the otherwise playful vibe they had going, Rowan fucked her hard and fast. She came in a rush, but it was the kind of orgasm that only made her want more. Which she didn't actually realize was a thing until that exact moment. Rowan eased her fingers away and nipped the spot between neck and shoulder. "Now bed."

Without waiting for an answer, Rowan turned off the water and pulled back the curtain. Audrey accepted the towel offered and rubbed at her skin in a bit of a daze. The woozy feeling was new to her, like being drunk but not. Rowan's expression was smug but still full of wanting. It was a really, really good look for her.

Rowan took the towel back and hung it on a hook on the back of the door. Silly, maybe, but she appreciated the tiny dash of practical mixed in with the sexy abandon. Or maybe it was simply how intentional Rowan was. At work, at play. Definitely when having sex. The attention to detail managed to calm Audrey and rile her up at the same time.

Rowan's bedroom was dark, with only a pool of moonlight on the bed. But as her eyes adjusted, it proved the perfect soft glow. Enough to make out the lines of Rowan's body and the intensity in her eyes. She licked her lips. "Do you like strap-on sex?"

It was only when she saw the whites of Rowan's eyes that she realized she'd asked the question aloud. Fuck.

"You don't have to answer that."

The surprised expression faded and a playful one took its place. Well, playful and hot. "Are you saying you don't want me to answer?"

Embarrassment faded as her desire ratcheted. Better to know either way. And maybe she'd like Rowan's answer. "No. I'm saying you don't have to answer."

"I see." Rowan shifted toward her. "And if my answer is yes?"

Rowan wanted her to ask for it. Knowing that made her want it even more. "I'd ask you as nicely as I could to fuck me halfway to next week."

Even with the dim light, Rowan visibly swallowed. "Nicely, huh?"

She glanced down, imagining a cock standing erect from the apex of Rowan's thighs, before looking into Rowan's eyes. "Pretty please?"

Rowan's hands came to either side of Audrey's neck and she pulled Audrey into a kiss. But instead of lingering, she let go and strode with purpose in the direction of her closet. She looked at Audrey over her shoulder. "For the record, you wouldn't have had to say please."

She smirked even though Rowan probably couldn't see it. "Then I'm banking that pretty please for future use. Specific request to be determined."

Rowan's laugh was easy and sexy and stirred things in Audrey that went way beyond being turned on. "Noted. I'll be right back."

Rowan left and Audrey's foot tapped in anticipation. It was anticipation—not big-F feelings—that had her all revved up. Right? Right. She wanted Rowan to fuck her and that's exactly what was about to happen.

❖

Rowan fumbled with the harness because apparently Audrey saying please was enough to get her turned on to the point of jittery. After a few deep breaths and some finagling, she returned to the room, cock in place and wetness threatening to run down her leg.

She'd lost track of the number of times she fantasized about making love to Audrey. Actually having sex with her only intensified things. Knowing the way Audrey felt under her, knowing the way she tasted and the sounds she made—it made her want more and more and more. It didn't seem to matter how much time they spent together, Audrey managed to surprise her at every turn. She was starting to get the feeling Audrey was surprising herself a fair amount, too.

She wasn't sure what to make of it, but she planned to enjoy every minute. Including tonight.

Audrey stood exactly where Rowan had left her. "You could have gotten into bed."

"Huh?" Audrey looked her way, clearly startled.

"I said you could have gotten into bed. It's a little chilly in here."

"Oh. I'm fine. Warm. More than warm." Audrey smiled, chasing away any worries Rowan might have about where her mind had gone.

"Well, even if that's not entirely true, I'm sure it will be shortly."

She went to Audrey and kissed her, letting desire take center stage in her mind. Distracted or not, Audrey was on the same page now. Her hand slid across the leather strap at Rowan's hip before grasping the cock with enough firmness to make her already hard clit stand at attention. "This suits you," Audrey said.

It was a simple compliment but had Rowan's pulse thudding. "I'm glad you asked for it."

"You like me asking for what I want?"

Was that a trick question? She could think of little that turned her on more. "Oh, yeah."

"In that case." Without another word, Audrey turned, bending over the bed and putting her gorgeous backside on perfect display.

"Oh."

Audrey tossed a playful look over her shoulder. "Pretty please?"

Audrey was teasing her, of course, but the way she said please sent Rowan's arousal to an entirely new plane. She licked her lips and swallowed, fighting for some semblance of self-control. "I feel like I should say again the please wasn't necessary, but I'm enjoying it a little too much for that to be honest."

Audrey wiggled her butt slightly. "How about you show me?"

She caressed the swell of Audrey's ass with both hands, across the dip of her lower back, around her hips, and back. God, she was beautiful. Rowan kept her left hand on Audrey's hip to steady them both but slid the fingers of her right between Audrey's perfectly parted thighs.

Rowan let out a groan. Audrey's clit was hard and, if it was even possible, her wetness rivaled Rowan's. She eased two fingers into Audrey, as much for her own pleasure as Audrey's. Somehow, Audrey seemed to clench and open for her at the same time. "You feel so good."

Audrey let out a hum and thrust her hips back slightly— invitation laced with insistence. Rowan slipped her fingers out and used them to lube the head of the cock. She positioned it, then eased just the tip in so Audrey could adjust to the sensation.

"Mm-hmm." Audrey didn't waste time with acclimation. She shifted her hips again, taking in more than half the length of the shaft.

Rowan stood stock-still as Audrey rocked forward and back, taking Rowan deeper and making these ridiculously perfect little noises. "Fuck."

Audrey looked back at her. "Is this okay?"

Rowan chuckled. "I was going to ask you that but there's no blood flow left for my neurons to fire."

"I'm good." Audrey pumped her hips. "So good."

Confident that Audrey was telling the truth, she started a slow thrust with her own hips. It took only seconds for them to settle into a rhythm. Each time Audrey took the cock in, the base of it pushed against her clit. So good wasn't the half of it.

She placed a hand on each of Audrey's hips, not intending to control the pace but wanting to feel as much of Audrey as humanly possible. It was the only downside of this position really—not getting to feel more of Audrey, not getting to watch her face. But even that tiny complaint vanished as Audrey rocked against her. Her noises were soon accompanied by a chorus of yeses, perfectly interspersed with Rowan's name. She seriously loved the way Audrey said her name.

Audrey's pace intensified. Rowan held on, almost in awe. "That's it. I've got you."

The sound Audrey made when she came was primal, feminine, and sexy as fuck. And it was for her. No almost in the awe this time.

Audrey looked over her shoulder, breathing hard. "I'm not done with you, but you've left me weak in the knees."

Rowan pulled out as gently as she could. "Get comfortable. I will happily take you any way I can get you. And I'm in no rush."

Audrey crawled onto and up the bed, flipping onto her back and offering what Rowan could only describe as a come fuck me smile. "Oh, I'm ready."

Rowan would have stood by her word but was grateful she didn't need to. She joined Audrey in bed, settling into the welcoming vee of Audrey's perfectly spread legs. She re-situated the cock and Audrey pulled her knees up in invitation.

She started more slowly this time, not sure what Audrey would find pleasurable at this point. Her worry faded when Audrey's legs came around her waist and pulled her closer. It vanished entirely with the flurry of dirty talk Audrey whispered in her ear.

She didn't always get off from strap-on sex, but the telltale signs of an orgasm started low in her belly. She held the sensations at bay, focusing on stroking Audrey's clit with her thumb in time with the thrust of her hips. The combination seemed to push Audrey to a different plane. Her head rocked side to side, and she mumbled incoherent strings of expletives, interspersed with more yeses and Rowan's name. She reached over her head and grasped the headboard, hips rising to meet Rowan's over and over and over.

Just when she hit the point of no return, Audrey came. She called Rowan's name as her body bucked. Rowan would swear she could feel Audrey's pussy clenching around her. Real or imagined, it sent her tumbling over the edge. The orgasm tore through her like a tornado, sucking the air from her lungs and making every muscle of her body go taut. She struggled to stay upright, to stay aware enough of Audrey not to crush her.

She managed but barely and only long enough to ease out of Audrey and collapse next to her. "Oh, my God."

Audrey rolled to her side and brought her hand to Rowan's chest, giving it a few pats. "Are you okay? Was that a good oh, my God?"

Laughing took every drop of energy she had left but she did it anyway. "Yes. Good. Very good."

Audrey pressed a kiss to her temple before resting her head on Rowan's shoulder. "Oh, good."

"You? You okay? I got a little carried away there at the end."

Audrey flopped onto her back. "I'm fucking fantastic."

"Good." She liked to think she had stamina, but damn. Audrey left her about as wrung out as a tired kitchen towel.

She stretched out her arm and Audrey settled into the crook of her shoulder like they'd done it a thousand times and not only once before. She stroked Audrey's hair and allowed her body to settle and her mind to drift in that way it did after amazing sex.

Audrey's breathing evened out and she started to snore. Softly at first, in that charming, feminine way of the movies. But it didn't take long for the sound to swell. Funny thing was, she still found it charming. Rowan stared out the window and started to drift. Before she fell asleep entirely, Audrey let out a snort—the kind that came with being startled awake. Only she didn't wake. She mumbled for a few seconds and resumed snoring. Rowan gave her a squeeze and chuckled, wondering if she knew she sounded like a freight train.

Maybe it was new. It was silly, but she liked the idea of Audrey sleeping extra soundly with her. Or after a day of fresh air and good sex. Or both.

Whatever it was, there was a solidness to it. It made Audrey feel extra real in her arms. Maybe a small part of her had started to crave permanence as much as realness, but she'd take what she could get. For now.

Chapter Twenty-one

Audrey planted her fists on her hips and turned a slow circle. She'd visited at this time of year but had paid more attention to Ernestine's apple pie than the orchard. "Do you pick them one at a time?"

Rowan smiled. "Fortunately, no."

She nodded slowly, imagining how long that would take. "That's good."

"I do that with the newer trees on my property because the trunks and branches are still fragile, but these beauties can take a good shake."

It couldn't be accurate, but she had this image of grabbing onto a branch and jumping up and down. "A shake?"

To her horror—but also amusement, strangely—Rowan did exactly that. Well, minus the jumping. She grabbed a branch and gave it a gentle push and pull. Leaves rustled, but no apples fell to the ground.

"Are you making fun of me because I don't know how it works?"

Rowan released the branch and came over to where Audrey stood. She put a hand on either of Audrey's cheeks. "I promise I'm not." She punctuated the statement with a quick but firm kiss.

Audrey smirked. "Are you saying that to stay on my good side so I'll have sex with you later?"

Rowan nodded even as she said, "No."

"You're terrible." She grabbed for Rowan's midsection and gave it a squeeze.

"Gah." Rowan jumped back and doubled over.

"Oh, God. Are you okay? Did I hurt you?"

Rowan took a deep breath and blew it out slowly. "You didn't hurt me."

Understanding took root. "You're ticklish."

Another nod. "Definitely not."

"Oh, that's fascinating. And cute." She looked up at the sky before returning her gaze to Rowan. "And really good to know."

Rowan lifted a finger. "I feel like I should remind you that with great power comes great responsibility."

"Uh-huh." She took a step toward Rowan.

Rowan took a step back. "And that maybe you want to stay on my good side so I'll have sex with you later?"

Having the phrase flipped back on her made her giggle. An honest to God giggle. When was the last time she'd done that? "I promise I'll go easy on you."

Rowan narrowed her eyes. "I'm not sure your definition of go easy and mine are the same."

She bit her lip and wiggled her eyebrows. "Scared?"

"Maybe."

She shifted her posture, going for full coquettish. "But you're so strong."

Rowan angled her head, a look of resignation taking over. "But I wouldn't want to have to hold you down."

And just like that, the playful flirtation took on an edge of something more intense. Her breath caught and every muscle in her core tightened. If she couldn't remember her last giggle, she sure as hell couldn't remember the last time she'd been that immediately aroused. "Maybe I want to be held down."

It was fun to watch Rowan's expression change, her eyes go dark. "Do you?"

Still playful, but they weren't playing anymore. "I'm not a full-on sub or anything but…" She searched for words that felt sexy but honest. "Sometimes it's nice to have someone take matters into their own hands."

Rowan nodded slowly. "I see."

"It's just..." Why was she being shy all of a sudden? "It's hard to shut off my brain sometimes."

Rowan folded her arms. "Your brain has an off switch? Fascinating."

"Okay, now you're definitely making fun."

"Oh, I'm really not. I promise. I'd love nothing more than to get you to let go, be completely in the moment."

The thing with wanting that was just how difficult it was. Finding a person who wanted to be on the other side, that she trusted enough. Well, the word unicorn seemed fitting. "I'll keep that in mind."

Rowan's features softened but the desire in her eyes remained sharp. "I hope you do."

Because it kind of shocked her how quickly Rowan could distract her from the task at hand, she cleared her throat. "Now, where were we?"

"I think you were asking me to tie you up." Humor now danced with desire, but Rowan managed not to crack a smile.

"We'll see."

Surprise replaced both laughter and lust in Rowan's eyes. Clearly not the answer she was expecting.

Audrey tried for a perfectly innocent smile. "But for now, we have apples to pick."

Rowan took a deep breath and blew it out slowly. "Apples. Right."

They employed a bit more of the shaking method, collected the first drops from the ground. Apparently, the day's outing was more about checking ripeness than true harvesting. The real deal would happen any day but involved big nets and crates like the one they took foraging, and the tractor. Today, mostly, they meandered.

Despite the rather insistent throb between her legs, Audrey asked lots of questions about timing and whether or not Rowan worried about the fruit being damaged. The whole process fascinated her. The start-to-finish of it, maybe, even if she'd started experiencing the cycle somewhere in the middle. So different from anything she did in her work.

"How did you decide this was what you wanted to do with your life? Does it run in the family?"

A shadow passed through Rowan's eyes, making her regret the question. The second one, at least. "It definitely does not."

For some reason, she'd assumed Rowan was close with her family. But maybe not. As much as she wanted to ask, it wasn't any of her business. "Okay. So, how did it happen?"

"When I was a kid, I wanted to be a farmer."

Definitely not where she thought that was going. "That's adorable."

"It's adorable when you're sprouting seeds in Dixie cups and convincing your mom to plant berry bushes in the backyard."

She didn't have to stretch her imagination far to picture it. "Please tell me there are photos of you in overalls digging in the dirt."

Rowan smiled. "I was more jeans and T-shirts, but I know there are a couple of me holding up vegetables like trophies."

"That sounds equally adorable, but you should show me so I can be sure."

"Only if I get to see you with your first calculator."

"Ha ha."

"Abacus?"

There were definitely pictures of her as a kid, but most of them were perfectly posed and professionally shot. "Sorry to disappoint, but I was more of an all-around serious kid until college."

"All-around serious?"

"Classic overachiever. Constantly trying to win my parents' approval. You know the drill." She so rarely talked about her parents, it surprised her how easily the assessment slipped out.

"Yeah." There was an almost wistful quality to Rowan's answer.

"You, too?"

"Nah. I was pretty average. My parents were thrilled when I set my sights on Cornell. And then they realized I meant the ag school."

"It's still an Ivy, no?" She'd gone to Colgate, a solid school in the top fifty if not the top twenty-five—a decision that landed her a nice scholarship and not just admission.

"Eh."

She chuckled at the assessment. "Confused or disappointed?"

"Definitely confused. They couldn't—still can't—understand why I'd throw everything I have into a risky venture that requires manual labor when I could have a nice stable desk job."

"As someone with a stable desk job, let me assure you—" Rowan's hands went up defensively. "I didn't mean—"

She put a hand on Rowan's arm. "Don't apologize. I'm just saying I'm not close with my parents at all, so I get them not getting you. Whatever that looks like."

"Is that why you and Ernestine are so close?"

"Sort of. They're not bad people, but I don't think they really wanted to be parents. Just figured that was the thing to do. They loved to travel and that meant I spent a lot of summers with Ernestine."

Rowan frowned. "I'm sorry."

"Don't be. I had a lot more fun with Ernestine than I would have had with them."

"She does have a way, doesn't she?"

Audrey let herself indulge in some of her favorite childhood memories. "She took me to my first Pride parade when I was eleven."

"Wait." Rowan stopped walking. "Is Ernestine gay? I always wondered. And part of me definitely wanted her to be, but she never said anything."

She shook her head, slightly gratified to have intimacies with Ernestine that Rowan didn't. "Not to overshare, but I think she's ace. Like, she'd never use that term, but we had so many talks when I was little about it being okay to love who you love but also okay to love yourself and love being alone."

Rowan chuckled.

"What?"

"I'm remembering her giving me that exact advice when I broke up with my girlfriend a couple of years ago. I thought she was just trying to make me feel better."

"I'm sure she was trying to make you feel better. She's better at that than anyone. But also maybe sharing her life philosophy."

"I respect that. It's not me, but I respect it."

She had a flash of wondering what Rowan was instead. A casual dater? A serial monogamist? Not that it was any of her business. "I think for her, it's a mixture of preference and second wave feminism."

"Ha. For sure." Rowan nodded slowly. "What about you?"

She could pretend not to understand the question, but it wouldn't change the fact that Rowan asked it. She could decline to answer, but that seemed unnecessarily standoffish. It wasn't a revelation or anything. Just a rather sad admission. "I'm not sure."

They'd started walking again, but only gone about four steps. Rowan stopped once again. "There's something you're not sure about? I might need to sit down."

"You're so funny." She let her voice drip with sarcasm. "I'm pretty sure we established I didn't know a single thing about tending plants or animals until a couple of months ago."

She expected Rowan to back down, to agree and maybe tease her a little. But Rowan shook her head. "No, I don't mean knowing how to do everything. I mean knowing your mind. You seem to unwaveringly know your mind about everything."

It was hard to take that as anything but a dig. "Ouch."

"Come on, you know I don't mean it like that."

Whether Rowan did or Audrey knew was up for debate, but Rowan seemed genuine. And the last thing she wanted to do right now was fight. "Okay, fine. I have really strong opinions about a lot of things. My love life doesn't happen to be one of them."

"Does that mean you're open to all sorts of things or you haven't found it yet?"

"Yes?" She let out a laugh that sounded more nervous than anything else. "I mean, my focus has been on my career. I'd like a relationship I think. I'm definitely not ace. But it doesn't have any kind of shape in my mind."

"I think that's okay, especially at this point in your life. There's no rush."

"Not the opinion of all my straight friends. I swear we hit thirty and people's clocks started ticking. Some of the most ambitious women I know became obsessed with getting married and having babies and buying houses on Long Island." She blew out a breath. "Sorry, that came out way more bitter than I meant it to."

Rowan smiled. "That's okay, too."

"Maybe I need more queer friends."

"Maybe." Rowan hesitated. "Or maybe, I don't know, the pace and pressure of being in the city spills into every aspect of life."

Even with noticing—enjoying—the break from the daily grind, she hadn't really thought of it that way. And to be honest, with her life in the city feeling farther and farther away, she didn't want to. "Can we go back to talking about you?"

"Sure. I swear I didn't mean to pry."

"You didn't." It was her own thoughts she wanted to get away from.

"Well, if it's any consolation, I'm pretty sure I want to fall madly in love and get married and have the house and the dogs and maybe the kids but have no idea how to make that happen."

Rowan's deadpan delivery broke the tension settling into her chest and she laughed. "It does. Thanks."

She had more than enough on her plate right now. Thinking about what her happily ever after might look like did not need to be one of them. Even if images of a life here popped into her brain way more readily than any future visions of herself in the city.

Rowan polished off the last bite of her lasagna and let out a contented sigh. Without any real discussion, she and Audrey settled into—back into?—a routine of having dinner together. Audrey would cook at Ernestine's; Rowan would show up with a bottle of cider or wine based on what they were having. Only now, they'd finish eating and tuck all the animals in for the night before heading over to Rowan's.

An odd routine in a way, but Ernestine's kitchen was way better equipped than hers. And she could appreciate Audrey's discomfort at having sex in her aunt's house, especially when said aunt knew them both but remained stuck in a rehab facility and had no idea they'd started sleeping together. She hoped it was that, at least, and not some veiled attempt to keep things somehow less personal between them.

"I hope I didn't overstep before. This afternoon. Out in the orchard."

Audrey's expression hovered somewhere between a smile and a smirk. "When you were questioning my relationship with my parents or prodding me about my life choices?"

She cringed. "I could swear again I didn't mean to, but I'm not sure you believe me anymore."

Audrey laughed. "I'm not complaining. What's funny is that I don't normally bare my soul to people I hardly know."

"I'd say we've gotten to know each other quite a bit in a short time." More than the last two women she dated, if she was keeping score.

"Maybe I should have said it like that. I don't open up very quickly. Usually."

"I blame my sister. She's a social worker and has this innate way of getting perfect strangers to open up. I think she's rubbing off on me." She shrugged. "And I still think an all-night goat birthing is a hell of a bonding experience. Put us on the fast track."

Audrey smiled and it was easy to imagine her remembering that night. "There is that."

"I guess I wanted to own that I seem to ask a lot of personal questions. You can tell me to back off if you want." Even though she really liked asking. And liked Audrey's willingness to answer even more.

"I will. It's been weird but nice in a way. Like therapy. And I have all this time to think about things."

It wasn't her place to say that sounded like a good thing, especially since her whole point was being less intrusive. But as Audrey sat there with a glass of wine and a wistful smile on her face, at least a dozen new questions swirled in her mind. What gave Audrey joy? Was she happy in New York? Did she want to stay there forever? "I'm glad."

"Besides, I got a few proddy questions in myself."

"True." She raised her glass. "Here's to deep talks and good dinners."

Audrey smiled. "I can drink to that."

They clinked glasses and fell into a comfortable silence. Well, as comfortable as she could be thinking about taking Audrey to bed soon. It was hard to be around Audrey in any capacity without wanting to take her to bed. Knowing she would soon gave the wanting an edge of urgency.

It was probably safer territory—the wanting—than some of the other places her mind had started going in the last couple of weeks. Places that involved Audrey deciding not to go back to the city at all.

"You're thinking about sex, aren't you? I can tell."

"Guilty." Sex was definitely part of it, so it wasn't a lie.

"I love that you want me." Audrey got up from the table and came in for a kiss. "I love the simplicity of it. Especially when everything else feels so damn complicated."

Rowan nodded, deflated but trying not to look it. Her life was pretty damn complicated, too. Connecting with Audrey was an unexpected surprise and a really nice diversion. Having a fondness for Audrey—feelings, even—didn't make that any less true.

"Dishes, animals, and your place?"

See? A perfectly simple and simply perfect proposition. "I'll wash if you dry."

CHAPTER TWENTY-TWO

Rowan spent the morning in the orchard, gathering the modest crop of Baldwins that marked the first official harvest from the rows they'd planted four years prior. By the time she made it inside, Dylan was off to meet with a local restaurant owner about a paired dinner event and the cidery was quiet. So quiet she wondered if Audrey had opted not to come in after all.

"Rowan, is that you?"

Apparently not. "Yep."

"Oh, good." Audrey's voice grew louder. "I wanted to talk to you about something."

"Okay. Is it good or bad?" She was kidding. Sort of. Wanting to talk was the sort of phrase that could go a lot of ways.

A moment later, Audrey stood in front of her, looking both excited and nervous. "Okay, don't laugh, but I've been doing some research."

"Why would I laugh at that?" Rowan hesitated. "Wait. What have you been researching? I should ask that before I decide whether or not I'm going to laugh."

Audrey gave her an exasperated look. "See? That's why I said it. You have to agree not to laugh first."

"Fine, fine. I promise. What is it? The suspense is killing me."

Audrey took a deep breath. "So, when I submitted the grant, I had to include some ball park figures for how you'd use the money."

"You did?" Why wouldn't Audrey have included that in their conversations?

"You're not locked into anything if you get it. I think they just wanted evidence of a thoughtful plan."

"And you did that?"

"Well, you and Dylan told me what you wanted. I just expanded on it and attached some estimates."

"Okay." She wasn't bothered by the prospect. Surprised, maybe. Definitely not laughing.

"One of the things I looked into was the type of furniture you might want."

"Yeah." She'd made a point of paying attention when she visited other cider houses and wineries but hadn't gotten further than that.

"I sort of fell down a rabbit hole. I found a local guy that does tables out of used barrels and reclaimed barn wood, but then I couldn't imagine how many you'd need so I found this interior design software and started playing with it…"

Audrey didn't continue but Rowan was starting to get the idea. And since Audrey was clutching a folder to her chest, she had a feeling she was about to get a whole lot more than an idea. "You designed the tasting room."

"I mean, sort of. I worked up a few concepts. Looked into seating." Audrey shrugged. "You know."

She knew in theory at least. In reality, she and Dylan hadn't gotten past the bar Dylan's brother built for them. In part because of finances but also because neither of them had a lick of skill or interest when it came to interior design. "Is that what you have there?"

Audrey nodded. "I can show them to you and Dylan together, but I worried I might be overstepping or getting ahead of myself, so I figured I'd run it by you first in case you want to gently put me in my place and tell me to focus on the numbers like we agreed."

Audrey was clearly excited but also hesitant. The combination was so unlike her, and yet adorable. It made Rowan want to kiss her. She resisted, but only because she didn't want Audrey to think she was uninterested in her ideas. "You absolutely didn't overstep and I'm sure Dylan will want to see, but I think you should show them to me first so I don't have to wait."

Audrey smiled. "Really?"

"I figured we'd have to hire someone if we wanted anything more than a random scattering of tables and chairs. If you've come up with something even remotely decent, we're going to be ecstatic."

Audrey opened the folder. "So, it's not a fancy rendering or anything, but it shows the flow and where things will go. Behind it are pictures of the furniture I was thinking."

Rowan flipped through pages before returning her focus to the one on top. The bar was there, of course. But so were little circles and rectangles to denote tables and chairs. And other shapes along the wall that she realized were places for displays of cider. The tasting area and the retail space worked together rather than simply dividing the space in two.

She looked through the pages again. Lots of wood that looked rustic but modern at the same time. Shelving made to look like stacked apple crates. Or maybe made from apple crates. And the last page. Audrey had put the Forbidden Fruit logo onto tote bags, T-shirts, and glassware.

"I didn't know if you were considering branded merchandise, but I think you should. People love that kind of thing and they're basically paying to advertise you."

She looked at Audrey, down at the images, and back at Audrey.

"You don't have to take any of my suggestions. I'm a numbers girl, not a marketer. And I don't have a creative bone in my body."

"This is amazing."

"Rowan, you don't have to say that. I promise my ego isn't hanging in the balance. I just didn't want you to laugh."

"I'm not stroking your ego and I'm not just saying it. It's everything we need to get the tasting room up and running."

Audrey smirked. "Well, aside from the money."

Yes, the money was a big part of why they hadn't gone there yet, but so was the rest of it. Knowing what to do and how to do it. Understanding that ambiance would be a huge part of doing it right but having no idea what that should look like. "Yeah, but even if we don't get the grant, we can do this. More slowly, maybe, but we can do it. You made it real."

Audrey beamed. "I'm glad you like it."

She more than liked it. She loved it. Dylan would, too. "Thank you. I don't think you know what a gift this is."

Audrey folded her arms and jutted her hip slightly. "I think you're more excited about this than everything I've done with your books and I can't decide if I should be offended."

"I love what you've done with our books. This"—she waved the pages up and down—"this is a surprise. A wonderful, unexpected surprise."

Audrey's eyes narrowed. "Mm-hmm."

"Did you do this as my accountant or as my girlfriend?"

Audrey smiled. "Are those things mutually exclusive?"

She was pretty sure stickler CPA Audrey would say they absolutely were, but she liked the idea of girlfriend Audrey embracing a certain gray area. Not to mention Audrey embracing the term girlfriend in the first place. "I don't know. I'll have to ask my accountant."

"Ha ha." Audrey was rocking the put-upon vibe, but Rowan could tell it was a front.

"Maybe I could get a few minutes alone on her calendar around lunchtime."

Either Audrey feigned shock really well or she'd managed to shock her at least a little. "Are you trying to schedule a nooner?"

"Well..." She didn't continue, letting insinuation do the heavy lifting.

"There is no way Dylan wouldn't know that's what we were up to."

"If she did, she'd be jealous as hell. But she's not here, so..."

Audrey looked around. "Well, maybe a kiss."

This increasingly playful side of Audrey had the very real potential to do her in. "Just one."

To ensure she didn't get carried away, she didn't bother setting the folder down. She slid her free hand to the back of Audrey's neck, letting her fingers slide into the thick waves Audrey had left down for the day. And, honest to God, she had every intention of keeping the kiss brief. But then Audrey sighed and let out a barely audible hum of pleasure and she was a goner.

She angled her head to take the kiss deeper. And when Audrey parted her lips in invitation, she couldn't resist. It wasn't even lunchtime, but she had half a mind to call it a day. To take Audrey's hand and drag her across the street and spend the entire afternoon making love. The sheer intensity of her desire should have given her pause, but she was too busy enjoying the movement of Audrey's mouth under hers to care.

"Okay, okay. That's enough. Do I need to remind you two that this is a place of business?"

Audrey leapt back at the sound of Dylan's voice. Rowan merely turned her head to offer a withering stare. Audrey cleared her throat. "Sorry."

"Don't apologize. She's not really bothered. She just feels compelled to give me a hard time."

"That's not true." Dylan shook her head. "Audrey is enough of a friend at this point that I feel obligated to give her a hard time, too."

Audrey let out a sound somewhere between a giggle and a snort, which made Rowan want to kiss her all over again. "I'll have you know that was a kiss of gratitude on behalf of both of us." When Dylan raised a brow, Rowan let out a huff. "That came out wrong."

Audrey's smirk returned. "What she's trying to say is that I came up with some design ideas for the tasting room and she thought you'd be excited about it, too."

"Yeah, that."

Dylan's expression changed to genuine excitement. "Really?"

Audrey beamed. "Really."

"Well, before I stumbled upon you two making out between the fermentation tanks, I was coming to tell you I brought lunch."

"Lunch?" As much as she'd rather have an hour alone with Audrey, she wasn't going to turn down lunch. Especially if it came from where Dylan had her meeting. "Is it from Fig? Please say it's from Fig."

"What's Fig?" Audrey asked.

"Just one of the best restaurants in the area. It's where Dylan was this morning."

Dylan angled her head in the direction of the break room. "Nick and Drew hooked me up since I brought them some of our new bottles to try."

"This day is getting better and better. Come on. Let's stuff ourselves while you tell Dylan about your brilliant ideas." She grabbed Audrey's hand before thinking better of it, but Audrey didn't seem to mind. Dylan popped a bottle of the perry they'd finished bottling only a few days before and they spent the better part of two hours tasting and talking. She'd be working past dusk to make up for it, but as far as she was concerned, that freedom was one of the reasons she worked for herself.

As the conversation flowed, she couldn't help but feel like they were part of a team. She and Dylan, of course, but Audrey, too. It was like she'd always been there. Like she belonged. And she found herself wondering if Audrey felt the same.

Audrey offered her usual hellos to the crew at the nurses' station before hanging a right and heading down the hallway that led to Ernestine's room. It had become as much a part of her routine as feeding the chickens or watering the garden. Or spending the night with Rowan.

Rowan.

Without meaning to, she'd become more involved with Rowan than with any other woman since college. A fact that only struck her when Rowan made a joking reference about being her girlfriend. She hadn't argued because there wasn't really another way to describe what they'd become. Which in turn managed to make her uncomfortable with both her current relationship and utter lack of serious relationships otherwise.

Not that she never had relationships. It was just that scheduling dates and sleepovers proved a hell of a lot more complicated when one person lived in, say, Brooklyn and both people worked until seven or later most nights. Which meant Audrey had already spent more time with Rowan than her last three girlfriends combined.

What did that say about her priorities? And maybe more importantly, what was she going to do about it?

"Hello, dear." Ernestine's greeting pulled her from the thought spiral and rooted her back in the moment.

"How's my favorite aunt today?"

Ernestine offered an uneven shrug. "About the same."

"Well, you look fantastic." Which wasn't a lie. Ernestine's color was good and she'd gotten a haircut that week, making her look more herself than she had in a while.

Ernestine chuckled softly. "You look good. Farm life suits you."

"It's the freckles." She tapped her fingers on her cheeks. "Who knew I'd be susceptible to freckles?"

"You look happy."

It seemed funny that Ernestine would say that when her thoughts had been laced with worry. But even as she fretted over the significance of Rowan in her life, she couldn't argue that Rowan made her happy. That being on the farm made her happy. "I am."

Rather than answering, Ernestine merely smiled. Well, not merely smiled. There was something expectant in it. Like she knew Audrey was holding something back. Which, to be fair, she was.

"Bert and Ernie are total hams." She set her purse on the dresser and settled in the chair next to Ernestine's wheelchair. "I officially have more tomatoes than I know what to do with."

A nod. More smiling.

"And Rowan and Dylan loved the plan I put together for the tasting room. I think they were more excited about it than all the accounting I've been doing, so maybe I have a future in interior design."

Still with the smiling.

"And Rowan and I are seeing each other. Have been seeing each other." Audrey coughed. "It's weird but also not weird at all and really nice and easy and I don't know what's going to happen in the long run, but I'm trying not to worry too much about that right now because it makes my head hurt."

She stopped talking because she ran out of oxygen more than anything else. And surely Ernestine would have something to say about that, right? Only she didn't. She closed her eyes and let out a sigh. But the smile remained.

"I didn't tell you at first because I thought it was a one-time thing. But it happened again and again after that and we're spending all this time together, so of course it can't just be about sex. Not that I want it to be only about sex, I figured that would be less complicated."

"I'm glad."

When Ernestine didn't elaborate, Audrey's mind raced in several directions. Glad that she and Rowan were seeing each other? Glad that, if they were, it wasn't just sex?

"I always thought you two were perfect for each other."

All the races came to a screeching halt. "You did?"

"It's why I never introduced you."

Suddenly everything and somehow also nothing made sense.

"Perfect but from different worlds. Too attached to those worlds, too stubborn to change."

It made her feel better to think Ernestine imagined the match implausible as opposed to being against it on principle. But the consolation was short-lived as the reality of her assessment sank in. She and Rowan were from different worlds. The overlap that brought them together was a temporary proximity. "You're right."

"But things change. People change."

She nodded even as warning bells clanged in her mind.

Ernestine leaned in and gave Audrey's hand a gentle squeeze. "It's all right, dear. Everything will work out."

She clung to Ernestine's words because she didn't see any alternative. Short of ending things with Rowan immediately—a prospect that made her queasy—she'd made this bed and now she had to lie in it. Things would fall apart at some point and it would probably hurt like hell, but there was no point in hastening her misery. "I'm not sure I believe you, but I'll take it."

"You'll see." Ernestine patted the hand she'd just squeezed. "You'll see."

Since she had no desire to discuss her impending heartbreak— or confront her newfound desire to put off dealing with things—she shifted the conversation to safer topics. Things like the goats and the weather. Of course, talk of the weather led to talk of the orchard and when Rowan would be harvesting the bulk of the apples. "She thinks the major haul will happen next week. She's recruited everyone she knows to come and help."

Ernestine's features softened and she got this faraway look in her eyes. "I'll miss the harvest."

She didn't seem frustrated by this reality and not really sad, either. Wistful, maybe. It had Audrey's throat constricting and tears threatening. When did she start wearing her heart on her sleeve? "I'll take pictures and we can look at them together. And I'll sneak in some pie."

"I'd rather you sneak in some cider." Ernestine punctuated the comment with the semblance of a wink.

The shift back to Ernestine's usual playful demeanor helped Audrey refocus. If Ernestine could keep her chin up, she had no excuses to do anything less. "I'll see what I can do."

She stuck around long enough to accompany Ernestine to physical therapy, wanting to see her progress but also not ready to be left alone with her own thoughts. But as Ernestine paced the length of the room with her walker and worked on lifting her arms over her head, all she could think about was Ernestine's simple assessment that she and Rowan were perfect for each other. With it, thoughts of all those previous relationships, the ones that never amounted to much more than a string of pleasant dates and decent sex. And the painful realization that she'd never—not once—even thought the phrase perfect for each other.

CHAPTER TWENTY-THREE

Audrey set the plate of grilled chicken on the table and sat. She picked up the glass of wine next to her plate and took a long sip. The kind of sip that said she had something on her mind. Rowan eyed her and debated asking or waiting for Audrey to come out with it.

"Thank you. This looks amazing." It never hurt to open with a compliment, right?

"Thank you for pouring wine." Audrey took another sip and let out a sigh. "I told Ernestine we were, you know, involved."

Rowan slathered butter on an ear of corn so sweet it didn't technically need it. "You did?"

"I didn't mean to, really. She was giving me this look like I was holding out on her and I don't know if she suspected it, but it came tumbling out."

"I've been the victim of that look." About her business plan, her love life, and her fertilizing techniques. Among other things.

"You're not upset?"

Upset that Audrey told the most important person in her life that they were involved? The truth of the matter was she was more inclined to do a happy dance. But something told her that wasn't the answer Audrey wanted. "Not at all. She's close to both of us. It's actually felt a little strange keeping it a secret."

Audrey frowned.

"Not that we've been actively lying or anything. Just weirdly omitting, you know?" She cleared her throat. "I think it's great."

Audrey tapped her index finger on the table. "You don't even know how she responded."

It hadn't occurred to her Ernestine might not take it well. The possibility landed in her gut with a thud. Was she overly protective of Audrey? Or, what if she thought they were selfishly fooling around while she was slogging through her recovery? That didn't seem like Ernestine, but then again Ernestine didn't seem to think all that highly of romantic entanglements in the first place. "Was it not good?"

"She was fine, but after that keeping it a secret comment, I thought you deserved to squirm a little."

"I didn't mean it in a bad way." Even if part of her wanted anyone and everyone to know Audrey was her girlfriend.

"Mm-hmm."

"I mean it. It didn't bother me, I'm used to Ernestine prodding me about the women I date."

"Oh, really?"

Why was she digging such a hole? "Not the specific women, exactly. Just whether or not I was dating."

"Ah. I suppose I've gotten my share of that, too."

"I'm kind of surprised she never tried to set us up." The second she said it, about a thousand reasons why Ernestine wouldn't flooded her mind. If the look on Audrey's face was any indication, at least a few of them were valid. Why would Ernestine want her super successful niece hooking up with a fledgling entrepreneur who had more dreams than savings?

"She said she knew better than to play matchmaker with people who lived so far apart."

A perfectly valid reason, but it seemed like there was more to it. But Audrey didn't elaborate. Probably for the best. As good as things were, she had her moments of wondering what was next. And then putting aside that wondering because the possibilities might be nice, but the more probable subset left her cold.

"Do you have plans for Thanksgiving?" Audrey asked.

The abrupt shift left Rowan almost as confused as the question itself. "Is that a trick question?"

"Why would that be a trick question?"

Audrey seemed genuinely confused, too, so Rowan gave her the benefit of the doubt. "Requisite family dinner. All the family. Much chaos. Even more food."

"Aw." Audrey smiled. "That's nice."

Rowan loved her family. Really, she did. She just loved them more in small doses—both in terms of number and time. In spite of that—or maybe because of it?—she suddenly found herself wanting Audrey to join her. "You're more than welcome to come. They can be overwhelming, but they mean well. I'm sure they'd be happy to give someone new the third degree."

"Um."

As counterintuitive as it might be, the idea grew on her. "No pressure, obviously. I'm sure you'll want to visit Ernestine, but we tend to eat on the later side."

Audrey stabbed a salt potato with her fork but set it down without taking a bite. "I was actually thinking I'd see if I could spring her for the day so she could have Thanksgiving at home."

"Oh. Wow. That's a fantastic idea. Can you do that?"

Audrey shook her head. "I don't know. I mean, she's there of her own free will, so I'd think she could come and go."

"Do you think she'd be up for it?"

"She tires easily, but she doesn't need round-the-clock care like she did. I'm worried about the stairs more than anything. I confess I've wondered if she'd deign to be carried into the house."

Rowan laughed before she could stop herself.

"Exactly."

"What if we built a ramp?"

Audrey's whole face lit up. "Could we?"

"A temporary one at least. I'm sure we could find some plans. It's only three steps."

"She'll probably grumble, but it might be worth looking into making it more permanent. Like the lift chair I've been researching for the main stairs."

"Grumble?" Ernestine was a practical woman but stubborn as a mule. Even if she accepted there were some things she wouldn't be able to do anymore, Rowan imagined she had a line she would refuse to cross. A line that had geriatric written across it in big bold letters.

"I know. But if it's the compromise that gets her home sooner, maybe she'll go for it?"

She blew out a breath. "Maybe. Because she might hate the prospect of being difficult even more that the prospect of being infirm."

Audrey glared. "Let's not get in the habit of using that word, okay?"

She laughed. "Fair enough. So, build a ramp and spring her for the day."

"Yes. I thought it might also be a way to test the waters of her being at home."

"Yep, yep. It will help you and her get a handle on what kind of assistance she'll need to transition back."

"Exactly." Audrey drummed her hands on the table. "Because as much as I might like to, I can't stay here forever."

If a small part of her wanted to ask why not, she shoved it aside. It wasn't her place to question Audrey's life choices. "Well, count me in for both. Just don't ask me to make a pie."

Audrey laughed and the sound made Rowan want to gather her up and kiss her senseless. And, well, more than kiss her, too. "I'll put you in charge of drinks."

"See? That I can do. Though, to be honest, I could probably bring pie. Bake My Day has a whole holiday menu and the caramel apple crumb pie is to die for." It was one hundred percent what she'd be bringing to her parents' house.

"No, no. I'll cook. I know most of Ernestine's recipes and I want her to feel like it's a real, almost normal, Thanksgiving."

The prospect of a holiday meal with Audrey and Ernestine made it easy to set aside her worries about everything else. The harvest would be pretty much done by then and the pace of life would slow a bit. And whatever her long-term intentions or plans, Audrey seemed set on being around. She'd worry about the rest when the time came.

❖

Audrey rarely wanted to extricate herself from bed, especially now that most mornings included waking up with Rowan. On this particular morning, that desire to burrow for a few more minutes was exacerbated by a distinct chill in the air. To be honest, it wasn't a chill. It was fucking freezing.

"Why is it so cold?" She pulled the covers over her face and snuggled harder against Rowan.

"Because it was so nice last night I forgot to close the windows."

She groaned her displeasure.

"What if I get a hot shower running for you?"

The prospect of a hot shower appealed, especially if it included Rowan and the possibility of coaxing her back to bed. But that wouldn't happen today. Today was what Rowan referred to as the big haul—she'd invited people to come and help and they'd do most of the picking in Ernestine's orchard and have a big party after. She'd been looking forward to it, actually. But it still didn't make her want to get up. "No."

She hadn't bothered to keep the poutiness from her voice and Rowan tutted and kissed her. The top of her head, her shoulder, and her neck before settling on her lips. "What's wrong, love?"

The sweetness made her smile. The pet name did, too, even though they'd both steered very clear of using the word between I and you. "I'm fine. I just want to stay in bed all day."

Rowan gave her a squeeze. "You can. I wanted you to experience today, but I never want you to feel like I'm putting you to work."

"You love putting me to work. Fortunately, I like it." In a lot of ways, they put each other to work. But it also wasn't like that at all. She'd never had the experience of working with someone the ways she and Rowan worked together. At the cidery, at the farm. She'd always imagined getting sick of a person. But even as she tried, she couldn't imagine getting sick of Rowan. Was it because she knew the arrangement had an end point? Maybe. Though a little voice somewhere deep in her mind—or was it her heart?—told her that wouldn't make a lick of difference.

Rowan propped on her elbow and frowned. "You know what I mean."

She slid her arm into the open space under Rowan's side and used the gained leverage to pull Rowan on top of her. "I'm just being lazy. And also a sex hound."

"Sex hound?"

"Yeah." That was a phrase, wasn't it? She hadn't had a lot of occasion to use sex lingo. Until now.

Rowan shifted her weight and grabbed Audrey's wrists, pinning them lightly over her head. "You're adorable."

"Are you making fun of me?" Not that she'd necessarily mind.

"Not even a little." Rowan kissed her.

"Because if you are, I might have to tickle you in retaliation."

"I said I wasn't." Rowan's assertion was as quick as it was adamant.

"Okay, okay. I believe you." Though now, she kind of wanted to make Rowan laugh and squirm. "Let's get this show on the road."

Rowan kissed her like she might be willing to stay in bed all day. "We could skip breakfast."

She gave in to a single poke at Rowan's side. "Tempting, but you're not cute when you're hangry."

Rowan sighed. "Truth."

They climbed out of bed together. Rowan made coffee while Audrey threw together egg sandwiches, then she headed home for morning chores while Rowan went across the street to get everything ready for the harvest. It sort of made her feel like the farm version of a fifties housewife, which should have been weird but wasn't.

By the time she took care of the animals and made her way into the orchard, at least a dozen people milled around. Since Rowan was already on the tractor, Dylan did introductions. She knew better than to think she'd remember all their names, but the group included one of Rowan's siblings, college friends, and the woman Dylan was dating. Even Jamal, the intern who'd been at the cidery for the summer, came.

There were bushel baskets and crates, tarps and bungees and elaborate ways of coaxing ripe apples to fall. Since everything would be pressed in the next few days, there was no need to be delicate about it. They moved from row to row, collecting the windfalls and picking clean every tree Rowan deemed ready.

It was hard work but fun. A lot of fun. Part of it was how communal it felt, how nice Dylan's and Rowan's friends were. Part of it was how sexy Rowan looked in a Carhartt jacket and Forbidden Fruit ball cap, riding the tractor around.

Rowan and Dylan had packed coolers with water and soda and sandwiches. Since it was such a gorgeous day, pretty much everyone plopped themselves right on the ground for lunch or when they wanted a break. They moved quickly, but it didn't feel rushed.

Like so many moments of the last few months, it was unlike anything she'd ever experienced. When she said as much to Rowan, Rowan promised that she'd proven herself and would be summoned from the far corners of the globe for any and all future haul days. Though it was hard to think about leaving, and even harder to think about Ernestine recovering enough to stay on the farm alone, she let herself imagine being here, with Rowan, next year. And the year after that. And, maybe, just a little, for a lifetime of harvests.

CHAPTER TWENTY-FOUR

Rowan called it just as the sun started to set and, as if by magic, someone arrived with a massive amount of takeout from the barbecue joint up the road. Pans of chicken and ribs, mac and cheese, coleslaw, and cornbread covered the bar in the tasting room. Coolers of beer appeared and cider flowed.

A few people ate and headed out, clapping Rowan and Dylan on the shoulder and joking about getting their payment in cases of cider. Most lingered, though, and the next thing she knew, she was cuddled next to Rowan in front of a bonfire, a log at her back and a wool blanket over her legs. The exhaustion of the day mellowed into relaxed perfection.

When a bag of marshmallows made its way around the circle and Dylan handed her a telescoping fork, she pressed her lips together and looked to Rowan. "Will you show me?"

Rowan kissed her before asking, "Show you what?"

"How to do this." She waved the fork back and forth.

"Have you," Rowan paused, "never had a s'more?"

"My roommate in college would do them in the microwave sometimes. I tried one but ended up just eating the chocolate."

Rowan shook her head in what appeared to be a combination of disappointment and disbelief. "That doesn't count."

"Of all the things I've been clueless about, you're most bothered that I'm a s'more virgin?"

Rowan lifted a shoulder. "The rest made sense. This? This makes me feel sorry for you."

"A little dramatic, don't you think?"

Rowan tutted as she threaded a marshmallow onto each of the forks and extend the tines in the direction of the fire. "Watch and learn."

And learn she did. About the pitfalls of the quick char, the importance of rotation, and the delicate balance between toasty shell and gooey insides. By the time Rowan sandwiched them between the graham crackers with a small square of chocolate, she was ready to do some tutting of her own and call Rowan a diva. But then she took a bite. Rather than a sickly-sweet pile of goo, the marshmallow had the toasty outside Rowan promised, complete with that deep, burnt sugar flavor she associated with a good crème brûlée. It changed everything. "Oh."

Rowan smiled. "Exactly."

She devoured the rest, licked her fingers, and seriously considered a second. "I'll never be the same."

"You have a little chocolate—" Instead of telling her where, Rowan kissed her, making a point of running her tongue along Audrey's bottom lip. "There. I got it."

A little speechless and a lot turned on, all Audrey could to was nod.

Rowan threw more wood on the fire and Dylan pulled out a guitar. Brianna, the woman who'd come with Dylan, started belting out Tegan and Sara songs—well but not so well Audrey hesitated to sing along. It felt cliché but at the same time magical, like scenes she'd seen in movies or read in books or fantasized about in her younger years.

Rowan settled back next to her, tucking under the wool blanket and scooting close. She leaned in and kissed Audrey's neck, right below her ear. "Having fun?"

Fun seemed like a hopelessly insufficient word, but she nodded.

Rowan reached into the pocket of her coat and pulled out a small flask, unscrewing the cap before holding it up for Audrey. "It's applejack, not whiskey. It'll warm your insides, not set them on fire."

She took it from Rowan's outstretched hand and brought it to her lips. As promised, the liquid went down easy, leaving her with a subtle warmth that radiated from her chest out. "Wow. Did you make that?"

Rowan tipped her head toward Dylan. "She did."

"Of course." Audrey passed the flask back. "How bad are you going to tease me if I admit that's the first thing I've ever drunk from a flask."

"Well, it can't compete with never having a s'more, but really?"

"You can't be that surprised. We've discussed what a nerd I am. I went to a couple of parties in college, where I nursed a single cheap beer all night so no one would think I was too much of a stick in the mud to drink."

Rowan grinned. "You're adorable."

The warmth coursing through her now had nothing to do with alcohol. "You probably wouldn't have thought so then."

"Maybe not. But I'd have thought you were hot so I still would have tried to talk you up."

She imagined Rowan at twenty—more swagger but less finesse. Still a huge improvement over the guys she had to fend off. Or the baby butch who made her pulse race but was only looking to fulfill her girlfriend's request for a threesome.

"Are you deciding how you would have shut me down?"

She licked her lips and the taste of apple on them made her smile. "What makes you think I would have turned you down?"

"I see. And what if I tried to talk you up now?"

"I'm already planning to go home with you. You don't have to impress me."

Rowan lifted her chin. "Maybe I want to impress you."

She angled her head and tried for playful exasperation. "And why would you do that?"

"Maybe I know a good thing when I see it. And maybe I know better than to take it for granted."

By all accounts, it was a line. She should have rolled her eyes and given Rowan a gentle elbow to the ribs and told her to cut it out. But her insides, warmed by the drink, were all melty with the feelings she mostly tried to keep boxed up. "Well, this good thing is counting the minutes until your guests leave."

"Why is that?"

Rowan wanted her to say it. While she might have chafed at that not long ago, Rowan had unlocked some kind of inner sex kitten in her. "Because I want you to take me home and take me to bed. Because if I'm not naked and under you, with your fingers inside me, very, very soon, I might die with wanting you."

Rowan's smile faltered and she swallowed, clearly surprised by such an explicit answer. "We can't have that."

Audrey shook her head.

"Let's get out of here."

Rowan climbed the steps of her front porch and tried to summon a time when she'd been this tired while simultaneously buzzing with anticipation. And failed. Even after the sixteen-hour day, with Audrey practically pressed against her back, she all but vibrated with pent up wanting.

Sexual wanting, sure. But this was more. This was the deep resonance of how perfectly Audrey fit into her life. Of knowing that if Audrey would only give it a chance, they could build a life together. And of finally allowing herself to hope Audrey might feel it, too.

Audrey slipped out of her jacket and hung it on the coat tree just inside the front door. "I can't remember the last time I felt this good."

She smiled. "How drunk are you?"

Audrey reached over and gave her arm a swat. "I'm not drunk at all. I'm relaxed."

"Oh, I see. Pardon me."

Audrey did a slow turn, arms extended. "Happy."

The playful banter should have put her at ease, but it left her as edgy as that first afternoon she and Audrey went tumbling into bed together. "I like you happy."

Audrey took a deep breath and let it out. "I like me happy, too."

"Would you like a shower? A glass of water? Anything?" Maybe a ring and a few decades of til death do us part?

"I think I'm good. Unless the smell of campfire on my hair will bother you."

Since it seemed like a genuine question more than a rhetorical one, she shook her head. "I don't mind."

Audrey's eyes narrowed. "You secretly like it, don't you?"

"Ever since I was eleven and kissed Emily Schuster the last night of Girl Scout camp."

"Do you have to be so fucking charming?"

Unlike the previous question, this one seemed to be in jest. So she answered with a quip of her own, even if the core of it held true. "I have to make sure you won't get bored with me."

"Impossible."

She took more from the certainty in Audrey's voice than perhaps she should, but the ship of reining those thoughts in had sailed. "I might have to hold you to that."

Audrey smirked, but with a gleam in her eye. "Take me to bed?"

Rowan smiled in return. "I thought you'd never ask."

She took Audrey's hand and, like so many times now, led her up the stairs, each step a promise of what was to come. But unlike so many of those times, she regarded Audrey with as much love as longing. Could Audrey sense it? Did she feel the same?

After following Rowan upstairs, Audrey stood in the center of the bedroom and licked her lips. Despite knowing exactly what was about to happen, the intensity of Rowan's gaze made her blush. She'd been honest downstairs. She wasn't drunk. But something had softened her edges.

Unlike most of their nights together, marked by an urgency that had her tugging at Rowan's clothes and trying to see how quickly they went tumbling into the bed naked, there was no rush now. Rowan threaded her fingers into Audrey's hair and kissed her with the kind of patience that made her insides melt like a thick beeswax candle that's been left burning for hours. Despite her own tendencies—to seek, to push, to give herself over to the kinds of sensations that made thinking impossible—she was transfixed by this softer, gentler touch.

Rowan gathered the hem of Audrey's sweater and lifted it over her head. Audrey instinctively reached to do the same, but Rowan caught her wrists. "Will you let me do it my way tonight?"

She opened her mouth to argue, or maybe to ask what Rowan meant by that. But just as Rowan's kiss had checked her impatience a moment before, the intensity in her eyes did so now. Even as not knowing exactly what Rowan had in mind gave her a hitch of anxiety, she wanted whatever Rowan had to offer. And perhaps more thrilling, for that moment at least, she trusted Rowan completely. She pressed her lips together and nodded.

Rowan's smile—a little surprised, confident, and full of wanting—was a reward on its own. But Rowan no doubt had a hell of a lot more in store. Now that she'd given herself over, she couldn't wait to find out what it would be.

She'd put on a front-clasping bra that morning and Rowan unhooked it with a single flick of her finger and thumb. She smiled. "Smooth."

Rowan quirked a brow. "I try."

Rowan slid it from her shoulders, kissing where each strap had been. Then across each of her clavicles and the hollow of her throat. When Rowan's mouth made its way down to Audrey's nipples, she arched forward instinctively.

"Patience."

She'd always considered herself a patient person. Efficient, but patient. But Rowan managed to stir things in her she'd never felt before. Until now, she'd chalked it up to an intensity of wanting, fueled by a sexual spark she hadn't known existed. Tonight, though. Tonight was different.

It felt as though Rowan was inviting her to places she'd never been before. Places that made her heart trip with longing and tremble with uncertainty. But even as her brain warned of potential danger, she wanted nothing more than to go, to follow wherever Rowan led. Through the haze of arousal, her heart finally admitted what her body seemed to have known all along. Things were different with Rowan. She was different with Rowan.

Rather than fighting that revelation, she embraced it. She ran her fingers along Rowan's torso with new appreciation. Opened herself fully for whatever Rowan had to offer. Slow kisses that threatened to set her insides on fire. Touches that promised as much as they pleased. And when Rowan slipped inside her, it felt inexplicably like home.

Rowan made love to her with the same unhurried patience. Each time she came, Rowan shifted her attentions. But she never let up. Over and over, until one orgasm merely spilled into the next and her body felt like a vessel into which Rowan poured a seemingly infinite amount of ecstasy.

When she thought another orgasm might literally kill her, she implored Rowan for a moment to catch her breath. She used the reprieve to turn the tables, to try to return even a fraction of the pleasure Rowan had given her.

When exhaustion finally claimed them both, Rowan tugged the blankets up and pulled her close. And in the few minutes before she gave herself over to sleep, she let herself bask—without questions or caveats—in the fact that she was utterly and completely in love with Rowan Marshall.

CHAPTER TWENTY-FIVE

Since Rowan and Dylan were off doing a delivery for the morning, Audrey opted to stay home and work on the books for Woolly Bear Wear. Gretchen had finally pulled the trigger on opening her online shop and she already had more orders than she knew what to do with. Helping her set everything up—from pricing and postage rates to tracking the cost of her yarn purchases—would have been a stretch a few months ago. But working with Forbidden Fruit's finances had taught her plenty, and starting from scratch for such a modest operation had been more fun than she ever would have anticipated.

If she let herself think about it, the reality was that the small business aspect proved significantly more satisfying than her real work. That though, of course, came with figuring she'd earn less than half of her salary doing it. But the thing was, at least in a brain like hers, one thing led to another and she couldn't help but calculate that her cost of living in a place like she was now would be less than half, too.

She sighed. Maybe someday. She'd never planned to stay Big Four for her whole career. It might be nice to have a concrete alternative to think about, plan for.

Even if she didn't end up in Ernestine's backyard, she'd developed a real fondness for the Finger Lakes. Though, even as she told herself that, she struggled to imagine herself anywhere but where she was right now. If she decided to do it at all.

Silly. She was getting ahead of herself. That kind of move would be years down the road. Years during which anything could happen. Like Rowan moving on and falling in love with someone else.

She'd gone deep enough into what-if territory that yanking herself back gave her a case of mental whiplash. She rubbed her neck, as though that might ease the jarring sensation, and gave herself the sort of don't borrow trouble talk she typically reserved for her friends. And because she was, above all else, a mature and rational adult, she put it out of her mind. Mostly.

By the time she had lunch and walked down to the cidery, Rowan and Dylan were in the production area, moving a huge batch of something from one of the fermentation tanks to barrels for aging. "That was fast," she said in lieu of a greeting.

Rowan turned briefly. "It's the wild crab from the apples we foraged."

"It is?" She hurried over to take a look, even though she knew it all looked the same at this point.

"First batch we pressed this year, so it's the first one ready to start the aging process."

There was something mesmerizing about the golden liquid flowing through the clear tubes from one container to another. A couple of small jars, filled with the same liquid, sat on a nearby table. "Is that it? Can I try it?"

Rowan looked to Dylan, who grinned. "You're welcome to, but you'll probably be disappointed."

"I still want to." She picked up one of the jars. "Can I drink it right out of here?"

Rowan tipped her head. "If you don't mind sharing my cooties."

"Pretty sure that ship has sailed." She brought the jar to her lips and took a small sip. The liquid had a frothy fizz to it and managed to be both harshly acidic and unnervingly sweet. Not terrible, exactly, but nothing like the finished ciders of theirs she'd had. "Oof."

"And that's why we age it," Rowan said.

"And do a second fermentation to adjust the residual sugars."

"Yeah, yeah. I'm sure it'll be amazing." She waved a hand. "Still. I picked these apples. I want to keep an eye on them, follow their journey. It'll make me appreciate it all the more when I pop open a bottle next spring."

"We'll be sure to keep a couple of bottles with your name on them," Dylan said.

"See that you do. In the meantime, I'm going to go keep the trains running." She offered a playful salute and headed to the office.

Between seeing what she'd started to think of as her cider making its way through the process and the progress she'd made on Woolly Bear, Audrey sat down at her desk in the tiny office almost giddy. She turned on the computer and let her mind wander while it booted. Maybe she and Rowan could go buy the supplies for Ernestine's ramp tonight. Maybe they could go out to dinner instead of cooking. She wouldn't say she was tired of cooking, but the prospect of a date night appealed. Especially since they'd both been working so hard the last few weeks.

Dinner out and a trip to a home improvement store. How domestic was that? More than she could have fathomed a few months ago, that's for sure. Way more than she would have thought she wanted. And yet, somehow, deeply satisfying.

There she went with that word again. It was like her subconscious was trying to tell her something.

She eyed the stack of receipts and invoices in the inbox but decided to start with email. Not that she was responsible for the cidery email account, but she'd gotten in the habit of taking a first pass and pulling the ones that would come to her anyway. Easier for her, and Rowan and Dylan seemed happy to have fewer to deal with at the end of the day.

When she saw Upstate Agricultural Development Coalition in the from line, her heart leapt into her throat. Funny how no emails at her real job had that effect on her—good or bad. She clicked on it and skimmed the contents before going back and reading the whole thing thoroughly. Then she did it again. On the third pass, the contents remained the same: good news that wasn't entirely unexpected but a total surprise at the same time.

She'd gotten the grant. Well, not her. Her proposal. Rowan and Dylan—Forbidden Fruit—had gotten the grant.

❖

Rowan walked into the office as Audrey abruptly stood, sending the old, wheeled chair rolling into the wall. "Am I interrupting?"

Audrey beamed. "I was just coming to find you."

"Well, that's convenient. What can I do for you?"

"I need a bottle of your finest champagne." Audrey winked, then added, "Style cider, please."

"Are we celebrating or just day drinking? Or are you looking to get the taste of that half-baked wild crab out of your mouth?"

Audrey straightened her shoulders and lifted her chin. "We are celebrating."

As far as she was concerned, a celebratory bottle of cider didn't need a reason, but it was clear Audrey had something on her mind. "Do I get to know the occasion?"

"We are toasting the newest recipient of the Upstate Agricultural Development Grant."

It took a second for the name to register and another for meaning to follow. "For real?"

"It's a rolling thing, so they review applications as they come in and they liked ours." Audrey coughed. "Yours."

"Ours. How much did we get?" She'd sort of put it out of her mind so she wouldn't be disappointed if it didn't pan out.

"Twenty thousand dollars. Ten up front and another ten when you demonstrate you've added at least one additional person to your payroll."

"You're serious."

"I'm serious."

It wasn't technically a life-changing amount of money, but it might as well have been. It literally meant they could open the tasting room as soon as they could outfit it and have it inspected. And, of course, hire people to staff it. "Audrey, I—"

"What's going on?" Dylan filled the doorway of the office, making the tiny space feel even smaller. "Why does Rowan look like she just found out she's going to be a mom?"

She offered an eye roll and decided she'd give Dylan a hard time about the choice of phrase later. Now, however, was for celebrating, and she didn't want to keep Dylan in the dark. "We got the grant. Well, Audrey got us the grant."

Dylan's eyes went wide. "No shit."

Audrey smiled. "You two run the business. I just filled out some forms."

Rowan shook her head. "Yeah, but we didn't even know there were forms to be filled out, so you get to take a lot of the credit."

"Agreed. This calls for a celebration," Dylan said.

Rowan laughed. "Audrey said the same thing."

"Good thing we keep bubbly on hand." Dylan didn't wait to head in the direction of the coolers.

Rowan and Audrey followed, but they'd barely gotten out of the office before a phone that wasn't hers rang. Audrey pulled hers from her pocket and frowned. "I need to take this."

She stepped away and tapped the screen. Rowan wondered briefly if it might be the grant people calling to iron out logistics already. Hopefully not calling to say there'd been a mistake. She tried to read Audrey's face, but Audrey stepped out of view before she had the chance. No need to be intrusive. Audrey would share if it had to do with her.

She returned her attention to Dylan and the celebration at hand. They abandoned cleanup momentarily and headed to the space that would become the tasting room. Thanks to Audrey's scouting and sketches, she could readily imagine how it would look. It wasn't a stretch from there to imagine people—laughing and talking, drinking cider, eating locally sourced cheeses and other snacks. And now, thanks to Audrey, it would be a reality so much sooner.

Dylan shook her head and turned in a slow circle. "Dude, this is really happening."

Rowan nodded. "It's really happening."

Audrey appeared and Rowan felt this urge to sweep her off her feet and spin her around. And kiss her. Kiss her now and kiss her always.

Her flash of happily ever after came to an abrupt halt. Audrey plodded more than walked, her movements strangely slow and an almost vacant expression on her face. The sort of look that would inspire a jab about who died. It only took a fraction of a second for the reality of that possibility to hit her. She crossed the room in a flash. "What is it? What's wrong?"

"Ernestine's gone." Audrey's delivery was calm and her eyes dry, though Rowan attributed it to shock more than taking the news well.

"Oh, honey." She moved to pull Audrey into her arms, but Audrey didn't give her the chance. She practically fell into Rowan's embrace.

"She was napping. They think she had another stroke."

Of all the ways to go, she could think of a lot worse. She wondered if that was the sort of thing Audrey would take comfort in. "I'm so sorry."

Audrey took a step back. Her chest rose and fell with what Rowan imagined was a fortifying breath. "When I visited yesterday, she gave my hand an extra squeeze and told me to take care of myself." She looked into Rowan's eyes. "And you. She told me to take care of you."

Rowan's heart flipped like a tumbleweed in her chest. "She said the same thing to me a few days ago."

"Do you think she knew?"

She believed in that sort of thing, of some people knowing or being ready or something similar. She liked to think of it as a gift from the universe. If anyone deserved that sort of gift, it was Ernestine. "Maybe."

Audrey nodded, though she seemed a million miles away. "I'm going to go."

"Go where, sweetheart?"

She looked confused then, though it was hard to tell if it had more to do with the question or the term of endearment. "Home."

Rowan's heart tripped. Because in that moment, she didn't know if Audrey meant home to Ernestine's house or home to New York City. She had to mean Ernestine's, right? At least for now. "Do you want me to go with you?"

Audrey's features softened and she almost smiled. It did more to chase away the panic than anything she could have said. "No, I'm okay. I'd like to be alone for a little while."

Even as she told herself it was a logical request, it stung. "Okay. I'm going to check on you later. Is that all right?"

Another nod, almost mechanical, told Rowan her mind was already elsewhere. She walked Audrey to the side door but resisted escorting her any farther. Giving Audrey what she wanted, giving her space, was more important that her protector tendencies.

She headed back toward the soon-to-be tasting room, realizing they hadn't even gotten to the celebratory bottle of cider. Dylan took one look at her and frowned. "What's wrong?"

"Ernestine passed away. Audrey just got the news."

"Oh, no."

"Yeah." Since it was Dylan, she didn't need to say more.

Dylan crossed the room and yanked her into a hug that was harder and tighter and longer than their friendship typically bore. It held her together and threated to tear her apart at the same time. She eased away and sniffed, willing herself not to cry.

"How's Audrey?"

Not really knowing was almost as bad as not being able to help. She shrugged. "Okay, I think? She asked to be alone."

Dylan nodded. "I can't believe she's gone."

"Yeah." Dylan didn't spend nearly as much time with Ernestine as she did, but they'd been friendly. Mostly, Dylan joked that they brought out the spitfire in each other, but in a good way.

"What does that mean? What do you think is going to happen?"

"With what? The land? Christ, Dylan. I don't know."

Dylan shook her head. "I meant with Audrey."

"Oh." She'd barely started to process Ernestine's passing. She hadn't even scratched the surface of anything else. "I don't know."

"Do you love her?"

She flinched. "Does that really feel like an appropriate question right now?"

Dylan lifted a shoulder. "I'm not sure, but your guard is down, so I thought you might answer without filtering."

She sighed. "Yeah. I do."

"Well, whatever happens next, it's good to know that."

She nodded, letting the truth of saying it out loud settle into her bones.

"Why don't you get out of here? Walk the orchard, check on Audrey. I've got things here."

"I'm not going to leave you with this mess. At least let me help clean up."

"It'll keep, Rowan."

She knew perfectly well it wouldn't. Of all the processes that went into making cider, very few could be paused halfway through. "I'm fine. Audrey needs some space and I'll have plenty of time to be alone with my thoughts."

Dylan seemed to consider. "All right."

They resumed their positions and Dylan flipped the valve on the siphon. Rowan focused her attention on ensuring the flow of liquid went where it was supposed to. A somber mood settled over her and she sank into it. She'd have to deal with the questions and the unknowns, all the what nexts, soon enough. For now, she simply let herself feel sad.

CHAPTER TWENTY-SIX

The morning of the funeral brought with it the first frost. It blanketed every leaf, every blade of grass, in sparkling white. An end of sorts in its own way but bathed in beauty.

Audrey had declined Rowan's offer of company the night before, so she moved through her morning routine alone. She opted for tea instead of coffee, sipping it at the kitchen table with a piece of toast the way she had on so many visits throughout the years. The way Ernestine probably did herself thousands of times. The way she wouldn't ever again.

No more holiday dinners. No more afternoon jaunts to wineries where Ernestine made it clear she could drink just about anyone under the table. Audrey allowed herself a few minutes down the rabbit hole of things that would no longer be before straightening her shoulders and heading out to tend the animals, then upstairs to shower and dress. Ernestine wouldn't wallow, so neither would she.

Rowan knocked on her door at nine on the dot. Audrey had never seen her so dressed up—black suit and a button-down in Ernestine's favorite shade of lilac. "You look nice."

Rowan smiled. "I wore this the day we met with the bank to finalize the loan for the cidery. I came by the land after, to imagine what it would become. That was the day I met Ernestine for the first time."

"Aw."

"She looked me up and down and I'm pretty sure decided by the looks of me that I wouldn't last a season."

Even as she teetered on the verge of tears, she laughed. "That sounds like Ernestine."

"I was dressed like a farmer the next time I saw her and I couldn't help myself. I assured her I only wore suits for weddings, funerals, and meetings at the bank."

"I love that."

"She told me she figured we could be friends then."

She'd known, at least intellectually, but it hit her in that moment how much Ernestine meant to Rowan. And how much Rowan meant to Ernestine. "I'm sorry I ever doubted how close the two of you were."

Rowan visibly swallowed but quickly shook her head. "You were being protective. I would have done the same."

She tried to summon a vision of Rowan yelling and swearing and came up empty. "Would you really, though?"

That got her to chuckle. "Okay, maybe I wouldn't have done the exact same, but I would have felt the same if I thought someone was taking advantage."

"I'll take it."

Rowan cleared her throat. "Did I interrupt anything? We don't need to leave for a few minutes yet."

"No, I'm ready. And I'd just as soon be early."

"Yeah."

Because Ernestine had lived there most of her life and had chosen to be interred at Mount Hope Cemetery, the funeral was held in Rochester. The gathering was a large and varied group. Her parents didn't make the trip, of course, but dozens of Ernestine's former students and colleagues did. As did folks from neighboring farms and even Ernestine's vet. Dylan came, which was sweet. And Rowan never left her side.

The service passed in a haze of laughter and tears. Though she'd been unwilling to face the idea of Ernestine's death before it happened, Ernestine had given it plenty of thought, even before her stroke. The service was a brief but eclectic mix of prayers and readings—religious and not—under the umbrella of her loosely held Unitarian Universalist faith. The minister's words included notes from Ernestine—if the cemetery was good enough for Susan B. Anthony and Frederick Douglass, it was good enough for her—and reflections on a full life well lived.

She'd hesitated about holding a luncheon, but was glad she did. Seeing people celebrate Ernestine's remarkable eighty-six years on the planet, but also connect and catch up with each other, gave her joy. She was pretty sure it would have given Ernestine joy, too.

By the time the last of Ernestine's friends left, Audrey was exhausted. Still sad, of course. But also, somehow, light.

Rowan, who she'd lost sight of in all the thank-yous and good-byes, appeared at her side. "How are you holding up?"

She took a deep breath. "You know, I'm okay."

"I know Ernestine had a lot of it sorted out ahead of time, but you did an amazing job today. She'd be pleased."

"I know it's a weird thing to say about someone's funeral, but I wish she could have been here."

Rowan's arm came around her shoulders. "It's not weird at all."

"She touched so many people."

Rowan nodded. "Even more than I imagined."

As much as that gave her joy, the truth of it sat heavy in her chest. "Not to be self-absorbed, but I can't help thinking about how wan my life feels in comparison."

She didn't expect Rowan to be jerky, but the gentleness of her smile had Audrey choking back tears again. "Teachers are a unique breed, for sure. But besides that, you haven't even lived half your life yet. The best is still to come."

Was that true? She hoped the part about having more than half her life left was, but what about the best parts? How were the next thirty-some years going to be different from the first? She had no idea.

"And let's be honest. Few of us can aspire to Ernestine's level of coolness."

Like much of the day, she went from practically crying to laughing in a matter of seconds. "True."

"I'm not saying you shouldn't ask yourself those big, hard questions, but maybe go easy on yourself today. The next few days. The rest will keep."

It would. Ernestine didn't even start her life on the farm until her retirement. "Yeah."

"You ready to head home?"

"Would you..." She hesitated. "Would you stay with me at Ernestine's tonight?"

Rowan didn't hesitate at all. "Of course."

She was glad they'd driven together, glad Rowan didn't even ask before shepherding her into the passenger seat for the ride home. They fell into silence, more welcome reprieve than sadness or discomfort. She couldn't remember the last time she'd talked to so many people in one day.

Rowan dropped her off and went home long enough to change clothes. They fed the animals and she warmed up the soup she'd made with the last of the tomatoes. They ate on the sofa with an old Audrey Hepburn movie.

It was barely nine, but she fell asleep on Rowan's shoulder. Rowan guided her upstairs and waited patiently while she washed her face and brushed her teeth. When they climbed into bed, Rowan simply opened her arms. She curled into the warmth and comfort they promised and shut out everything else.

Rowan had never been to the reading of a will before. Her only frame of reference was what she'd seen in movies or on TV—warring factions of families sitting in an ornate room while a lawyer read aloud who'd be getting what. She wasn't sure who those factions would be, especially after Audrey turned out to be the only blood relative at the funeral, but when she and Audrey walked into the attorney's office and it became apparent it would just be the two of them, she almost laughed. She didn't, of course, but it helped to break the tension of such a somber process.

The attorney, a rather starchy woman who introduced herself as Ms. Brown, ushered them to a pair of narrow leather armchairs across from her desk and offered them coffee or tea. When she and Audrey both declined, she sat across from them and laced her fingers together. "I'm so sorry for your loss."

Clearly a line she used a lot, but it felt genuine. She and Audrey mumbled their thank-yous in unison.

"I had the pleasure of first meeting Ms. Adams just over a decade ago. Her previous attorney relocated to Florida, and she was not impressed with the idea of working with him remotely." She chuckled politely. "We touched base periodically through the years, and I have to say, she was one of my favorite clients."

Audrey smiled. "She had that effect on people."

Ms. Brown nodded. "I'm not surprised. Anyway, Ms. Adams's will is fairly straightforward. She essentially left everything to the two of you."

"The two of us?" The bewilderment on Audrey's face matched the confusion Rowan felt.

"Not collectively. Sorry. I meant the two of you are the only named parties in her will."

"Ah." Audrey nodded.

Rowan did, too, but her mind raced ahead. Had Ernestine put their agreement in her will? Relief vied with worry. She'd been saving but had a good five years until she anticipated needing the amount she and Ernestine had agreed to. Would Audrey give her time? Assuming, of course, everything went to Audrey.

"The ten acres that constitute the orchard are to go to you, Ms. Marshall."

Rowan felt her mouth open and close in complete surprise. She had no idea what she was expecting, but that absolutely wasn't it. She looked from Audrey to the attorney and back.

"Did you know this was going to happen?" Audrey asked.

Was she imagining it or was there betrayal in Audrey's voice? In lieu of words, she merely shook her head.

"Really? No idea?"

Audrey didn't believe her—a fact that set off warning bells—but she was still too floored to pay them much attention. "We never discussed it."

Audrey's expression turned stony. "Well, we both know that's not true."

The lawyer cleared her throat and Rowan had never been more grateful for an interruption. She physically shifted in her chair, back toward the lawyer and the explanations she wanted but feared she wasn't going to get. "Are you sure there are no stipulations or payment noted? That's what she and I discussed."

"Ms. Adams was very clear. The property was to be divided such that you would receive the land containing the orchard and Ms. Adams would receive everything else. That includes the remaining four acres, the house and barn, the contents therein, and any remaining assets."

Audrey shook her head, that sort of slow, continuous movement that comes with disbelief. Rowan tried to stifle her joy, at least for the moment. That she owned the land, yes. But even more significant was that Ernestine loved her and trusted her enough to take care of it, that she believed in what Rowan and Dylan were doing.

"Ms. Adams did make provisions for the animals. She set aside five thousand dollars to be donated to Fuzzy Muzzy Farm Sanctuary in exchange for them providing a home and care for any and all animals that survived her."

It was in that exact moment it hit her Audrey would simply leave. Naive? Absolutely. Illogical? That, too. But Rowan's heart sank and her stomach turned, almost as much as when she'd learned Ernestine passed away in the first place.

She braved a glance in Audrey's direction. Her head shake of denial had morphed into the equally slow nod of resignation. Something resembling panic settled in Rowan's chest, making it difficult for her to breathe.

"You don't need to do that now, of course. Or ever, if you choose. Ms. Adams simply didn't want the burden of finding them homes placed on you. She'd seen too many cases of pets dumped at shelters when their elderly owners died and wanted to make sure hers were looked after."

"Of course." Audrey nodded slowly.

The attorney went through the logistics of probate, how and when things would officially transfer ownership. An overview of tax implications. Audrey seemed more stilted than when they'd arrived. Sad still, but something more. Was she mad that Ernestine had left her the orchard? It was hard to imagine Audrey wanting it, but it was hard to imagine a lot of what had happened in the last few months, much less what would follow.

They rode home in silence. Only it wasn't the shared, reflective quiet after the funeral. No, Rowan got the distinct impression Audrey's silence came from stewing. As much as she didn't want to ask—didn't want to know—she needed to. In Ernestine's driveway, she put Audrey's car in park. "You seem really upset. Do you want to talk about it?"

"What's there to talk about? You got what you wanted all along and I got everything else."

Even as the rational part of her mind knew Audrey was reeling with grief, she flinched at the accusation. "Audrey."

Audrey lifted her chin, showing no signs of backing down. "It's true, isn't it? You got your land. It's what you were angling for from the beginning. Sure, you'll miss Ernestine. But she wasn't your family. She was mine."

"She felt like family. That might not mean anything to you, but it means something to me. You feel like family, too." It was the closest she'd come to saying I love you, to admitting she wanted Audrey in her life in all the big ways and for a very long time. Not how she wanted to express that, but none of this was going how she wanted.

Unfortunately—or maybe fortunately—the underlying meaning didn't seem to register with Audrey. She merely shook her head. "You like having me around. I'm an easy neighbor and fun to fuck."

Audrey was insulting herself as much as Rowan, but it registered in Rowan's gut like a sucker punch.

"I'm sorry," Audrey said.

"Uh." The abrupt shift might have helped, but the lack of context left her reeling almost as much as the attack.

"I'm being a bitch. Just like before." Audrey closed her eyes and shook her head. "Don't listen to me."

"I know you're hurting. I'm not saying it's great to lash out, but I get it."

Audrey looked at her but continued shaking her head. "I know you think you do, and I appreciate you trying to be nice, but you really, really don't."

Every instinct told her to shift into self-protection mode. But those same instincts told her she was on the verge of losing Audrey completely. "Try me."

"I really don't want to talk about it right now."

She also knew better than to force it. "Okay."

"I really am sorry. I just need to be alone for a while."

She handed Audrey her keys. "Well, you know where to find me."

Audrey nodded but got out of the car without another word and disappeared into the house.

CHAPTER TWENTY-SEVEN

S he apologized, right? For flying off the handle at the lawyer's office?"

Rowan sighed. Audrey had apologized. Tersely. And she'd repeated that apology in a text later that night. But since? Radio silence. And it had been three days. "Yes, but shouldn't she think more of me at this point? Even if she's grieving, it bordered on cruel."

Dylan nodded. "Fool me once, eh?"

Was that what had happened? Should she have learned her lesson the first time Audrey assumed the worst of her? Even with the simultaneously crushing and hollowed out feeling in her chest, she couldn't bring herself to see it that way. Too much had happened. Too much goodness and honesty and intimacy. But what if it had been one-sided? What if Audrey played along, but kept a wall around her heart the whole time? Not knowing what was real at this point had to be the worst of it. "I don't know."

"Do you want to know what I really think?"

"Are you going to tell me whether I want you to or not?"

Dylan shrugged. "Probably."

"Well, go on then."

"I don't think Audrey resents Ernestine leaving you the orchard."

"No?" It sure as hell felt like that.

"I think that, on top of the grief of losing Ernestine, she has to deal with the fact that you got something you really wanted, and she got something she doesn't know what to do with."

"Huh."

"She's attached to the house, the animals. But she can't keep that without turning her life inside out, so it's as much a burden as a gift. If she sells, it would be like losing Ernestine all over again. If she doesn't, she—what?—abandons her career and her life in the city and moves here permanently?"

"Yeah." Though it had been so easy to imagine Audrey building a life here, along with a different sort of career. A more satisfying one. But more satisfying to her, not necessarily to Audrey.

"If she resents anything, it's that she's stuck in that position and you're not."

Perhaps it was self-centered, but she hadn't really considered Audrey being in that sort of catch-22. One that had nothing to do with Rowan being gifted the orchard. It was a small solace that Audrey would likely feel that if she'd inherited everything. "I didn't think about that."

"Because you've secretly, or not so secretly, been wishing for her to stay."

She'd spent so much time and energy at the beginning reminding herself that Audrey's presence would be temporary. And yet, the closer they got, the less she thought about it. Ironic considering how much higher the stakes were now than at the beginning. Talk about head in the sand.

"You don't have to admit it. It's written all over your face."

She didn't doubt it. "If it's so obvious, how come Audrey can't see it?"

"I'm pretty sure she wants to think about it even less than you do."

"Yeah."

"Have you asked her if she's considering staying? Or telling her that you want her to?"

The mere thought put a lump in her throat. "I couldn't put that kind of pressure on her."

"But how can she make an informed decision without knowing how you feel?"

Maybe Dylan had a point. Too bad that point involved baring her soul with the very real possibility of having it kicked to the curb. "But what if she stays for me and regrets it? Talk about resentment."

"I'm not saying she should stay for you. I'm saying she deserves to know you're in love with her as part of her decision-making process."

She didn't even flinch at Dylan's use of the L-word. "I don't think whether I'm in love with her should be the point."

Dylan let out an exasperated groan. "You are so fucking stubborn."

Was she? Sometimes. When it came to relationships, though, she tended to be pretty honest. Of course, no woman had ensnared her heart the way Audrey had. Which meant few had the capacity to utterly gut her. "I'm no more stubborn than she is."

Dylan gave her a look that hovered somewhere between amusement and pity. "And that's why you're perfect for each other."

Rowan let out a grumble. "You're no help. You know that, right?"

"I could pass her a note for you. Ask if she likes you and have her circle yes or no."

She scrubbed her hands over her face. "I'm going for a walk."

"Maybe walk yourself over to Audrey's house and tell her how you feel."

More grumbling, this time with a few swear words. She put on her jacket, yanked a knit hat onto her head, and strode out into the cold and rapidly fading afternoon. And even though she told herself she wouldn't, her legs carried her into the orchard that was now hers and in the direction of the house that now belonged to Audrey.

My dearest Audrey,

If you're reading this, it means I've moved on from the physical realm. (I've always wondered if people really begin letters to their surviving loved ones like this and here I am, so apparently they do.) I'm sure that you're sad and feeling perhaps a little lost. Chin up, darling girl. I've lived a full and happy life and any time beyond this moment of putting pen to paper has been a gift.

You'll know by now that I've left Rowan her apple trees and the rest of the farm to you. If I know you, you're sloshing around in a crisis of conscience. I'm here to tell you—this whole letter is to tell you—to stop it at once.

The farm was my dream. It's never been yours and it doesn't need to be. If you discover it gives you joy, by all means keep it, make it your home. If not, sell it without a moment of hesitation and use the proceeds to forge your own path.

I'm not one for deathbed promises, but I hope with all the breath I have in me that you listen to your heart and follow wherever it leads. I know you tend to trust your mind in all matters of importance, but it will only take you so far. Be good, be brave, and know how very much you are loved.

Yours,
Ernestine

Audrey looked up from the piece of paper, wiping tears from her cheeks but not as quickly as they fell. She'd read the letter several dozen times by now, but each time brought a fresh wave of tears. Because like always, Ernestine knew her better than she knew herself. But unlike all the other big moments in her life, Ernestine wasn't there to see her through.

She read the letter once again. It had been written before Ernestine's stroke, at a time when Audrey's visits to the farm were mostly long weekends and holidays. Long before she'd come to understand what living on the farm entailed—what it demanded and what it offered. When Ernestine had every reason to believe she'd feel sad about it but sell and not look back.

Things were so different now. Now it was a crisis, not of conscience, but of character. Of who she was and what she did with her life. Because unlike some vague outline on a distant horizon, this decision had to be made now. Soon, at least. And it would determine everything that came after. Everything.

The knock on the back door nearly sent her out of her skin. She didn't deserve to hope it was Rowan, not after the harsh words and weak apologies. But she hoped it was Rowan nonetheless.

When she opened the door and found Rowan standing there, looking about as miserable as she felt, a new wave of guilt and questions washed through her. "Hi."

"I wasn't sure you'd want to see me, but I was out walking and couldn't seem to help myself."

She lifted her shoulders and let them fall. "If anyone deserves to play the avoiding game, I'd say it's the other way around. Come on in."

Rowan did and proceeded to pace the length of the kitchen a few times. "I'm sorry Ernestine's will added another layer of stress to losing her. Obviously, that isn't the case for me and I'm sorry for that, too."

Audrey leaned back against the counter and allowed her shoulders to slump once again. "Thanks."

"I didn't come here to tell you what to do, but I think you should stay. And I wanted you to know that."

She searched Rowan's face for meaning—for words she hadn't said and feelings she hadn't expressed—and got nothing. For some reason, that got her hackles up. "I appreciate the sentiment, but it's a bit quixotic, don't you think? I don't have a job here."

"You could open a private practice. You said so yourself."

Basic tax services, consulting for small businesses and startups. It wasn't her expertise by any stretch of the imagination. Still, it was more expertise than a lot of rural communities had access to. "I only meant that one could. That the community would benefit from that."

"And why not you?"

"Because I wasn't serious about it." She wasn't. She had no desire to take on the risk or headache of working for herself. Even if, in quiet moments in the garden or her daily conversations with the goats, she'd let her guard down and allowed herself to imagine what a life here might look like.

"But you could be. I don't know the New York City version of you, but I know how you were when you got here and I'm pretty sure you're happier now."

Was she? Maybe. But she attributed it to being on sort of a retreat from her regular life, not a permanent change. "It's more complicated than that."

"I know. But you also have to remember you have prospects here, and people who would support you. It wouldn't be much, but the cidery could start paying you. And I bet Gretchen would too, now that she's got her shop up and running. It's not enough, but it would be a start."

Normally, this sort of rational argument would be right up her alley. She was all about weighing the pros and cons, the costs and benefits. But for some reason, it left her flat. Not to mention beholden to people she cared about. "It's easy to give turn-your-life upside-down advice when it's not your life that would get turned upside down."

"I know that, too. But you've managed to make a really nice life here and maybe that's worth taking into account."

Something about phrasing—logical and almost sterile—reminded her of her parents. "Maybe a successful and stable career is worth taking into account, too."

"I'm not saying it isn't. I'm—"

"You're what, Rowan? Slinging platitudes about life when it's not your life on the line. Thanks, but no thanks."

She didn't usher Rowan to the door, but she turned toward the sink and stared out the window overlooking the flower garden. Rowan sighed. Audrey waited. Though whether she waited for Rowan to leave or to make another case was hard to know. All she knew was that her heart ached and Rowan was making it worse instead of better.

The door opened and closed and she was left standing in the kitchen alone. She shook her head, willing her breath to steady and her pulse to slow. Though anger seemed somehow preferable to the other emotions threatening to swallow her whole.

Where did Rowan get off, anyway? She didn't get to come in and act like she knew best. Especially when her ideas of what was best meant Audrey uprooting everything and changing the course of her life.

It wasn't like Rowan was chomping at the bit to change. If anything, her oh-so-helpful suggestions meant she got to plod merrily along and not have to change anything. Like consider moving to the city.

The very idea registered as ludicrous. Rowan was as tied to the land as Ernestine had been, if not more. She could almost see Harriet navigating the subway before she could imagine Rowan doing it.

She let out a snort of indignation, but with it came visions of herself, briefcase in hand, pressed into a packed A train heading to midtown. Swept up in a sea of people heading to one of a million office spaces that, deep down, all looked the same. Different clients, but every day sort of the same. Easy dinner, a book or a couple hours of mindless television.

When did it start to feel like a drudge? And when did she start resorting to fights to avoid showing her real emotions? Since Rowan, that's when. Because Rowan stirred things in her she'd never felt before. Didn't know how to feel. Wasn't sure she wanted to feel.

It sure as hell didn't help that Rowan didn't seem to share those feelings. Yes, Rowan had asked her to stay. But she hadn't uttered a peep about wanting Audrey to stay. About wanting her, period. About being in love. Surely, if there was a time to make that sort of declaration, today had been it.

She tried to imagine a scenario where Rowan had said that. Would it have changed her mind? Given her clarity? Probably, but even if Rowan had and she had given in to the warm and fuzzy moment, it was hard to imagine the doubt and the questions not creeping back in.

So, maybe it was for the best. She was left to slog through on her own, just like always. Well, not like always. Usually she had Ernestine to be her sounding board and cheerleader.

She picked up the letter and read it again. Once again, the tears started, though for a slightly different reason this time. Without meaning to, Ernestine had created more questions than she'd answered. And for the first time in her life, Audrey had absolutely no idea what to do.

CHAPTER TWENTY-EIGHT

S o, for real, how long are you going to mope?"
Rowan scowled. "I'm not moping."

"No?" Dylan didn't say anything more.

"Okay, fine. I'm moping."

"I'm not saying you aren't entitled. If I was head over heels for some woman and she left me for some stuffy corporate life in the city, I'd mope, too."

Her first instinct was to argue the "some woman" descriptor, but she knew Dylan didn't mean it in a dismissive way. Or, she did, but she meant it in her universally dismissive way of referring to serious relationships. Ones involving sacrifice and compromise and forever.

Forever.

That was the worst part of it. She'd somehow let herself imagine she and Audrey were meant to be. That the universe had thrown them together in some unlikely circumstances and they'd managed to forge the kind of relationship that could withstand anything.

Even now, she struggled to pinpoint exactly how she'd gotten it so wrong. "I thought she was different."

Dylan's look was sympathetic, but she shook her head. "You thought she'd changed."

The distinction was small but significant, and the reality hit her right in the ribs. Because she never would have fallen for the Audrey who showed up a few months ago, no matter how strong the attraction. No, it was everything that happened after. The way

Audrey softened, the way she opened up. The way she discovered joy in little things and the fact that she wasn't afraid to put her ideas and opinions out there. She thought she'd fallen for the Audrey that blossomed before her eyes, but it turned out to be nothing more than smoke and mirrors.

She'd lost sight of who Audrey was and fell in love with who she wanted her to be.

Rowan let out a groan and Dylan's expression crossed the line into pity. That got her attention. She did not need—or want—to be pitied. "Okay, enough about my moping. We have work to do. What's on the docket?"

"Well…"

When Dylan didn't continue, Rowan scowled. "What? I said I was ready to get to work."

"We have pressing to do, but the new tables are being delivered today, so we need to be prepared to stop whenever that happens."

"Oh." It should have been—should be—welcome news. It meant they were one step closer to opening the tasting room to the public. But there'd be no way she could enjoy it without thinking about Audrey. Because not only had she been the one to secure the grant that made it possible, she'd also scouted options and selected literally every piece.

"Since the floors got finished early, I thought we'd go ahead and get everything placed where we want it."

"Yeah."

"You're not having second thoughts, are you? About getting the tasting room up and running?"

"What? No. Of course not." Even though the idea of seeing it sent her thoughts down some fairly dark paths.

"Are you sure you don't want to talk?"

She let out a sigh that, unfortunately, sounded a lot more like a growl. "There's nothing to talk about. I'm pissed and disappointed that she left, but it's her life. I'm not going to resent or regret the things she helped make possible while she was here."

Dylan offered a decisive nod. "That's the spirit."

If it felt a little bit like coddling, she let it slide. "So, what can we do that doesn't mind interruption?"

Dylan cast a glance behind her. "We can get the tanks ready."

Her lip curled. Sanitizing the tanks was important and, really, not that awful a job. She just seemed to be incapable of doing it without getting herself soaking wet. "All right."

"We could hang the art in the tasting room instead."

Yet another of Audrey's ideas. They'd collected a smattering of vintage art and apple-themed paraphernalia to make the space feel more like a relaxed bar and less like a walled off corner of a warehouse. Brilliant, but also a touch tainted now. "Yeah, I think I'd rather scrub tanks."

Dylan grinned. "I knew you'd say that."

"You simply wanted to remind me there are even less pleasant tasks?"

"Not everyone considers interior decorating unpleasant."

She went for a bland look. "You're really pressing your luck today."

Dylan shrugged. "I usually do."

They'd no sooner donned their galoshes when a truck rumbled outside. Rowan didn't waste a second kicking hers back off. "I can get them started if you want to press on here."

"So noble."

She shrugged, her mood slightly improved by the back and forth. "I try."

"But not a chance. I'm right behind you."

She made her way to what would become the main entrance to the cidery. Outside, two guys had already started unloading high-top tables and stools. One of them was the owner of the company, the one she and Audrey had met with. They exchanged greetings and she propped the door open to give them easy access.

She didn't want to, but she pulled out the map Audrey had made to make sure everything went where it was supposed to. Not that it was overly elaborate, but they'd decided to let the communal bar-type tables anchor the room and scatter the mix of high and low tables around them. She and Dylan helped, unloading and placing the dozens of stools and chairs. The whole thing only took a couple of hours and by the time they were done, her heart ached with how much better it was than anything she could have imagined.

Audrey may not have turned out to be the woman of her dreams, but she had a damn good eye for furniture and design. Not only had she helped make the tasting room possible, she'd made sure it had the right feel. It would be the perfect space to welcome customers and give them the Forbidden Fruit experience. That's what mattered at this point. Even if she had to keep reminding herself to believe it.

❖

Audrey didn't know what exactly she expected to happen when she returned to the city. Two solid days of being restless and irritable wasn't it though. Neither was insomnia. Or embarking on a borderline laughable cycle of opening and closing her windows because she wanted fresh air but couldn't handle how much louder it made the sirens and traffic.

She chalked it up to anxiety about discussing her return to work. Plus grief. And general malaise from the whole Rowan situation. It had a different edge, though, even to her stress levels over the last week. Like the mere fact of being in the city amped her up even more.

She tried to talk herself out of it even as she berated herself for it. She'd simply gotten used to a different flavor of ambient noise. Different smells. Different light.

This was the conversation she had with herself while drinking a too sweet cosmo and half-listening to her work friends fill her in on what she'd missed. She didn't zone out entirely; she wasn't that rude. Ella had slept with a partner after three months of flirting and was deciding whether to take a job in another division so she could keep seeing him. Margaret's admin adopted a baby with his partner and was on paternity leave.

"So, are you back, back?" Ella asked.

"Not until the first of the year. I need to clean out my aunt's house, get it ready to sell."

They offered sympathetic nods. "Sounds awful," Margaret said.

Ella tutted and gave her hand a squeeze. "I'm sorry she didn't pull through."

"Thank you. She was ready, but it doesn't make it any easier."

More sympathetic nods.

See? These were nice women. She'd known them both for more than five years now. And she had way more in common with them than with Gretchen and the rest of the knitting group. Even if the things that caused them stress, that gave them joy, felt foreign to her at the moment. Even if she dithered about what stories to tell them because she wanted to protect those memories from…well, she wasn't sure from what, but she wanted to protect them all the same.

"How long are you here? You're welcome to come out to Massapequa for Thanksgiving. Laurie's family is next-level dysfunctional, but her mom makes a killer turkey." Margaret's question pulled her back to the moment.

"Only a few days. I'm meeting with Vera tomorrow and taking care of a few things, then heading back."

Ella winced. "Are you sure you want to be alone on the holiday, especially after, you know?"

She'd gone back and forth and settled on wallowing. Well, wallowing and making the exact meal Ernestine would have made as sort of a tribute to her. Which sounded a little more morose than she cared to admit. "I only got someone to tend the animals through Tuesday."

That, of course, opened the floodgates of questions about farm life. She talked about the baby goats but left out how they'd come into the world. Described the beauty of the orchard but didn't mention the cider maker who now owned it.

By the time they exchanged hugs on the sidewalk in front of the bar and wished each other good night, she was exhausted. Even though the whole evening barely clocked in at two hours. Back at her apartment, she made herself eat the pho she'd picked up and took two Benadryl so she'd get a decent amount of sleep before her meeting with Vera. She managed to pass out by eleven and woke up groggy but sort of rested. Even if she kind of missed waking up to Ferdinand.

After a nice long shower—her apartment had the water pressure of Ernestine's beat by a mile—she stood in front of her closet and sighed. "I want to say I missed all of you, but I'm not sure I did."

She settled on a fitted dress in deep plum with a charcoal jacket and her go-to Manolo pumps. She slid her feet into the shoes. "Okay, maybe I missed you."

Though, even as she did, her thoughts wandered to her polka dot muck boots and the smell of fresh hay. The persistent nudges from Ernie and Bert when they wanted attention. The press of their little hooves when they climbed in her lap. Did it make any sense to miss them as much as she did?

She considered the subway, but went for a ride share instead, telling herself it was okay to ease back into being surrounded by that many people. The lobby of her building, like her apartment, felt familiar yet strange. She headed for the elevators like she always did, only to have her ID badge rejected by the access gates. Right.

A stop at the security desk got her through and she still managed to arrive at Vera's office twenty minutes early. She counted her breaths so she wouldn't fidget and wondered if she'd be able to rejoin her team or be assigned to a new one. She tried to conjure the client she'd been working on right before getting the news of Ernestine's stroke but couldn't. Strange. And so unlike her.

Of course, her mind had no trouble pulling up images of the tiny office at the cidery. The dated computer and desk that had seen better days. Such a far cry from her office here. But even as she made the comparison, she recalled the satisfaction of creating a new system for their financials. And the joy of practically bursting out of it to tell Rowan and Dylan they'd gotten the grant.

Once she'd started down that path, memories flooded her senses. The smell of the bonfire at the harvest party. The taste of cider direct from the press—sharp and sweet and fresher than anything she could have imagined. She did her best to shove aside thoughts of Rowan— the look in her eyes when she explained apple varieties, the feeling of being wrapped up naked under the blankets on a chilly morning— and failed. Every detail, every second, of the last five months hit her. And they all pointed in a single direction.

"She's ready for you." Vera's admin offered a perky smile and didn't comment on the fact that Audrey jumped a mile at her words.

"Thank you." Audrey walked into Vera's office with purpose. She perched on the edge of the chair, shoulders straight and hands folded neatly in her lap. "I want to tender my resignation."

Vera laughed. "It's not nice to joke about these things."

She swallowed. "I'm not joking."

Vera's smile faded. "Did I misunderstand? I thought we were meeting to discuss your return."

"We were. I'm sorry. I've changed my mind."

A line formed between Vera's eyebrows and her lips pursed in what looked like irritation. "When did this change happen?"

The absurdity of the truth might make Vera question her judgment, but she'd take that over questions about her integrity. "About sixty seconds before I walked into your office."

"I see." The irritation vanished. In its place, concern. "Audrey, you've been through a lot in the last few months. I'm not sure rash decisions are in your best interest."

"I appreciate the sentiment. And honestly, if our positions were reversed, I'd probably be saying the same."

"But?"

"But I think I've known this is my decision for a while. I'm only just now getting around to admitting it."

Vera regarded her for only a minute, but it felt to Audrey like eternity. "You mean it."

"I do."

"Can I ask what happened?"

She knew better than to say she'd fallen in love. Especially since it was entirely possible that whatever she and Rowan shared had run its course. "I'm not sure, exactly. I love the house, the animals. But even when I learned my aunt left them to me, it didn't occur to me to uproot my life to hold onto them."

"Please don't tell me coming in today made you realize how much you hate working here."

"It's not that. I promise. It's more..." How could she express what she couldn't even wrap her own head around? "I think being back in the city made me realize how much I've come to love a very different version of my life. It might be impractical or irrational, but it's in my power to live that version and I can't think of a good reason not to."

Vera nodded. "And it's a version that involves goats."

"Goats, yes. But also sunshine and quiet and doing enough manual labor in a day that you sleep well every night."

"I don't know if I've ever had that kind of sleep."

"I highly recommend it."

Vera let out a rather resigned sigh. "I know it's probably not the right thing to say at this moment, but you have a lot of talent, Audrey. I hate thinking it's going to be wasted on farming…things."

Rather than making her feel bad, Vera's halting delivery, especially at the end, made her smile. "It won't go entirely to waste. I did some consulting for a couple of small businesses nearby and I'd like to expand that. Maybe even take on personal income tax clients."

"I have this image in my head now of you doing people's taxes at a kitchen table, surrounded by vintage appliances and lace curtains on the windows."

She tipped her head and tried for the kind of playful expression that would tell Vera she wasn't too far off the mark.

Vera shook her head and tutted. "You know, I always worried you'd be seduced by greener professional pastures. It never occurred to me we might lose you to actual pastures."

She laughed, even as her body ached to be back at the farm. To be home. "You and me both."

"If it's truly what you want, then I'm happy for you."

Rather than the anxiety she would have expected with quitting her job, she felt inexplicably calm. "Thank you."

CHAPTER TWENTY-NINE

If Audrey was acting entirely rationally, she'd take a few extra days in the city. Pack her apartment, meet with a Realtor, arrange for movers. Maybe have lunch or drinks with the handful of people she considered friends. But from the minute she set foot on Seventh Avenue—officially unemployed for the first time since she was eighteen—all she wanted to do was go home.

Well, that wasn't entirely accurate. She wanted to get back to Rowan, to try to make things right. If that was even possible.

For the millionth or so time in the last week, she replayed their last conversation in her mind. She wanted to call it a fight, but that wasn't an accurate description. Rowan hadn't even seemed angry. Just disappointed. And maybe, deep down, not surprised. It was the not surprised part that haunted her. For as resolute as she was in her decision, she had zero certainty around what it would mean for her future with Rowan. If she even had a future with Rowan.

It was that uncertainty that drove her to leave the city a mere two days after her arrival. Which was funny considering she didn't even know if Rowan would want to talk to her. But again, she had to try.

She texted Gretchen to let her know she'd be home in time for evening chores, then started the fool's errand of getting out of the city in the late afternoon. It took her a full hour to cross the George Washington Bridge and another to clear the tangle of souls making their daily exodus from Manhattan. If she'd needed a sign from the universe—or even a gentle reminder—that she'd made the right decision, it would have done the trick.

As she drove farther from the city and into the Catskills, she switched from her standard jazz playlist to the hip-hop she reserved for workouts and days she wanted to drown out her own thoughts. Though, for all the anxiety she had about Rowan, about how she'd support herself, about everything that came with upending her life, the main feeling coursing through her in time with the pulsing bass was joy. The kind of joy she'd never felt in the city. The kind she'd convinced herself existed only in movies and romance novels.

She was going home.

Although she imagined an epic drive and a heroic homecoming—just like in the movies—reality looked more like a pit stop in Roscoe and a gas station hot dog to keep herself from passing out with low blood sugar. Still, pulling into Ernestine's driveway felt like a victory of sorts. Even in the dark.

Wait. No. Not Ernestine's driveway. Hers.

Even as that gave her a pang of sadness, the joy remained. Sure, it had a bittersweet edge. Discovering a home here too late to enjoy more time with Ernestine. Things she'd never learn, things they'd never share. Yet, she also knew in the deepest, surest parts of herself that Ernestine would be with her. That the gift Ernestine had given her would live on and be a tribute to her. And she'd do her best to make Ernestine proud.

As much as she wanted to go straight to Rowan's, she made a loop of the barn, feeding and checking on all the animals. The sheep and the chickens seemed mostly happy for dinner, but the goats put on a show of welcoming her home. Everyone chattered at her, and Bert and Ernie frolicked and jumped.

Despite still being in her work clothes, she stepped into the pen to rub noses and scratch ears. "Did you two get even bigger in the time I was gone?"

Both kids bleated their agreement. Ozzie snuck up behind her and offered his signature headbutt greeting. Unlike the first twenty or so times he tried it, she instinctively shifted her weight and kept her balance. "Nice try, pal."

She'd swear he laughed in response.

"I want to catch up with you, too, but I have some urgent business with our friend next door."

Harriet nodded.

Feeling oddly calmer—or maybe fortified—by the exchange, she wished them a good night and headed to Rowan's. As tempting as it was to cut through the orchard, she resisted. A sprained ankle or, worse, a run-in with a skunk, would definitely put a damper on the conversation she wanted to have.

She tried Rowan's house but got no answer. No lights on, though, so hopefully Rowan wasn't simply avoiding her. With her truck in the driveway, it basically left the cidery. Even though it was ten at night, that didn't surprise her.

She crossed the street, laughing at herself for looking both ways. After briefly considering the new main entrance, she headed for the side door she'd used for the last few months. She opened it to bright light and a wall of sound. It took her a second to place the swelling seventies vocals but, when she did, she almost laughed.

Maybe she stood a chance after all.

"Hello?"

Rowan barely heard the greeting over the heartbreak power ballad swelling around her, thinking vaguely it was strange for Dylan to announce her presence in the form of a question. Especially given that she'd left a few hours prior for a hot date. She walked toward the sound of the voice, stopping at the speaker to lower the volume of the music. "Was the date a bust?"

She rounded the row of fermentation tanks and found herself face-to-face with Audrey. She opened her mouth, but no words came out.

"I wouldn't call it a bust."

"I thought you were Dylan."

Audrey's hesitant smile faded slightly. "No."

"What are you doing here?" Not an ideal opening but probably preferable to the alternative—grabbing Audrey by the shoulders and kissing her for days.

"I was hoping we could maybe talk? If you're still working at this hour, you must be really busy, but I decided to take my chances."

No way was she going to admit that working had a lot more to do with keeping herself busy than any pressing deadline. Especially after getting caught listening to her heartbreak anthem playlist. "Give me a minute to close up."

"Are you sure?"

She'd already pushed the boundaries of work she should be doing solo and had resorted to cleaning. "Yeah. Hang on."

A few minutes later, she sat across from Audrey in the tasting room, at one of the tables Audrey had picked out. Not entirely neutral territory but better than her house. Or the one Audrey was about to sell. "So."

"So."

Audrey did that hesitant smile again, the one that made Rowan want to gather her in her arms and offer every reassurance she could think of. Too bad Audrey didn't want that from her. "I don't mean to—"

"I was wondering if you knew any decent contractors." Audrey's question cut her off and came tumbling out in a rush that didn't fit the banality of her words.

Rowan shook her head. Leave it to Audrey to decide something needed to be done at ten o'clock at night and dive right in. "Why, are your buyers looking to renovate?"

"I was thinking the house would do well with a real office, the kind with its own entrance that didn't connect to the rest of the house."

"Is that a thing?" Seemed awfully particular, but what did she know.

"It's a thing if you're planning to set up shop and don't want your clients parading through your kitchen."

"Ah." It still didn't make sense to her, but maybe Audrey already had an offer and was trying to seal the deal quickly.

"Someone told me this area could use a decent accountant. Not some national chain that set up in some abandoned storefront, mind you. Someone who knew the community, lived in it."

Meaning sank in. With it, a glimmer of hope she refused to let take root. "Are you going to be that someone?"

"I'm going to try."

She got the impression Audrey's words had to do with more than offering CPA services. Well, two could play at that game. "The problem is that we've had a handful of flash in the pan, fly-by-night operations. Folks get this romanticized notion of life upstate and then bail when it turns out to be less idyllic than their imaginations."

Audrey nodded. "Yeah. It's almost like people should have to pull weeds and muck stalls and lose one of their chickens to a fox before they get to decide to move here."

They weren't technically sparring, but Rowan tipped her head, conceding the point. "Something like that."

Audrey looked down at her hands before returning her gaze to Rowan's. "I don't have the best imagination, you know?"

She wasn't sure where Audrey was going but couldn't resist lodging her protest. "I know you don't give yourself enough credit on that front."

Audrey smiled. "Well, my second point was that I'm stubborn, so there you go."

She could feel her resolve crumbling. Though it was a struggle to pinpoint exactly what she was so resolved against in the first place. "I'm not going to argue with you on that one."

"It was too much of a leap. I love you, I love being here. But I couldn't imagine my entire life up to a few months ago not being my life anymore."

If part of her wanted to acknowledge the overall sentiment in Audrey's declaration, it was drowned out by the roar of her own pulse in her ears. I love you. Did Audrey mean it? Did she even realize she said it? As if answering her unspoken questions, Audrey's eyes got huge. That answered that. "It's okay. I know you didn't mean it like that."

"But I did mean it like that. I mean, my timing is crap and it's not how I wanted to say it, but those things don't make it any less true." Audrey blew out a breath. "I'm sorry. That's probably the last thing you want to hear from me right now."

The back and forth of her emotions was almost enough to give her whiplash. "No."

"I know. I barge in here with my big announcement about staying and lay that on you as well. It's not fair and if I really love you, I need to back off and—"

"Audrey."

Audrey pressed her lips together. "Sorry."

"I meant, no, that's not the last thing I want to hear right now."

She shouldn't take pleasure, or satisfaction, in watching the confusion play across Audrey's face. But given the roller coaster Audrey had her on, she let herself enjoy it for the briefest of moments. "I love you, too."

"What?" The declaration only seemed to intensify Audrey's bewilderment.

"I said I love you, too. Assuming that's what we're talking about, of course."

Audrey nodded slowly, the look of confusion becoming one that resembled wonder. "You love me."

"Well, I didn't want you to stick around for the hell of it. Though, I did objectively think you were happier here than you let yourself believe."

"But why didn't you say so?"

As much as she didn't want to ruin the moment, they only stood a chance if they could be honest with one another. "Something about being told I must be happy because I got what I wanted. It put a damper on things."

Audrey cringed. "I did say that, didn't I? I'm sorry. That was awful and unfair."

Having Audrey readily admit she was wrong wiped away any remaining sting. "I said some things I'm not proud of, too. I'm sorry for that."

"I guess neither of us were at our best." Audrey looked around, then right into Rowan's eyes. "You love me."

Despite the strange turns the conversation seemed to be taking, the reality of being in love with Audrey—and not some ill-advised, unrequited sort of love—swelled until it was all she could think about, all she could feel. "I do."

"And I love you. I'm in love with you. Over the moon. Completely gone. I'm 'I didn't even know this kind of love existed' in love with you." Audrey lifted her shoulders and let them fall, like the truth of it still surprised her.

"You're really back for good?" An hour ago, she'd been kicking herself for wanting that, hoping for it.

"I quit my job, so it's feeling pretty definite."

"And you're okay with that? It's what you want?"

"It's what I want even if you decide you don't want anything to do with me." Audrey took a deep breath. "But I really really hope you still want me. Still want to be with me."

"I want you. I want to be with you. I don't know where that's going to take us or what it might look like, but I really, really want to find out."

Audrey nodded again. She smiled but a pair of tears spilled over and made their way down her cheeks. "I want that, too." She sniffed. "I'm sorry. I don't know why I'm crying."

"You've had an intense couple of weeks. It's okay to have feelings."

Audrey laughed and sniffed again, then she reached out and gave Rowan's arm a swat. "Don't make fun."

"I'm not. I'm validating you. And if you'll let me, I'll wrap you up in my arms and tell you to let it all out."

Audrey wrinkled her nose. "Maybe later."

"The offer stands."

"Right now, I'm hoping you'll pull me into your arms and kiss me."

"Oh."

"I've missed your kisses rather desperately."

It wasn't the sort of squishy sentiment she ever expected from a woman like Audrey. But in that moment, she couldn't imagine anything sounding better. "I think that could be arranged."

Audrey smiled, almost shy now. It gave Rowan a whole bunch of feelings of her own. And because Audrey asked, and because she'd wanted to from the moment Audrey walked in, Rowan pulled her into her arms and kissed her.

CHAPTER THIRTY

The following June.

Rowan made a face. "Are you sure you're okay with this? You're basically going to be waiting tables."

Audrey planted her hands on her hips. "Are you worried I'm going to spill cider in people's laps?"

"No, no. Of course not. I just don't want you to feel roped into doing something that's beneath your, you know, skill level."

She took more pleasure than maybe she should watching Rowan squirm. She brought her hands together and laced her fingers, hoping for the perfect mix of exasperated and demure. "I muck goat manure. I think the ship of being uppity about my skills has sailed."

"You're right. I'm sorry. There's nothing uppity about you."

"Thank you."

"But now that you mention it, are you going to spill cider in people's laps?"

Audrey folded her arms, completing the irritated woman stance trifecta. "Given I'm the help you've got, I guess you're going to have to trust me and hope for the best."

Rowan's teasing expression faded and her features softened. "I do."

Even with the contrite face, she couldn't resist. "Trust me or hope for the best?"

Rowan grinned. "Yes."

"Good."

The tasting room technically had been open since April, but they'd settled on the summer solstice for a grand opening, complete with music and food and tables both inside and out. It would also be the christening of the four fire pits Rowan had built with the tumbled bluestone leftover from the patio build. It amazed her still how quickly everything came together, and how much of the final design matched the sketches and ideas she'd come up with months before.

The band arrived to set up. The food truck they'd contracted with pulled in. Dylan finished setting up the bar exactly how she wanted it and quizzed Audrey one more time on the varieties. It was more a running joke than a real test, but Audrey breezed through, complete with her own tasting notes.

People began to arrive even before the official start time and came in a steady stream well past the nine o'clock end. She managed a couple of short breaks, enough to snag a snack and pull Rowan into the stock room for a stolen kiss. The new staff seemed to be in their element—chatting and smiling and making customers feel welcome and comfortable.

When the last car pulled away, Rowan and Dylan pulled everyone together for a celebratory toast. Audrey felt like part of the team but also like the proud girlfriend, getting to observe Rowan's hard-earned success. She lingered as Dylan and Rowan locked up for the night so she and Rowan could walk to her place and put the animals to bed together.

They strolled hand in hand and she let her gaze flit between the starry sky and the twinkle of fireflies over the meadow surrounding the orchard. "Did you know it was a year ago to the day that I came here to take care of things after Ernestine's stroke?"

Rowan frowned. "Really?"

"Time flies when you're having fun? Or does it feel like you've been wrangling me for much longer than that?"

"Both. Neither." Rowan chuckled. "It feels like yesterday and yet I'm having a hard time imagining my life without you in it."

She'd planned to wait until morning, when they were drinking a cup of coffee on the porch before morning chores, but the moment seemed too perfect to pass by. "How would you feel about a lot more of me in it?"

Rowan's quizzical look made her smile. "More than I have already?"

They'd been spending more and more nights at her house, especially now that she was able to think of it as hers. Not that Ernestine wouldn't always be a part of it, of course. But since that transition, Rowan's house sat empty more of the time than not. And she'd started to wonder if renting it out might help finance the new tractor Rowan wanted. "Yeah, like all the time. With all your stuff."

Understanding vied with uncertainty on Rowan's face. "Are you asking me to move in with you?"

She lifted a brow. "Depends. Are you saying yes?"

"If you're asking, I'm saying yes."

"Then I guess it's settled."

Rowan narrowed her eyes. "How long have you been thinking about this?"

"Since it occurred to me that a month of rental income on your house would be more than the monthly payment on that shiny new Kubota you've been eyeing."

"You don't have to do that. We'll work it into the budget at some point no matter what."

She'd thought Rowan might say that. It was one of the reasons she knew it was the right decision. "I'm not saying that's why you should. I'm saying that's when I started thinking about it."

"Once an accountant, always an accountant."

"Something like that." They'd gotten to the driveway and the goats, unused to being out so late, bleated their enthusiasm at the return of their humans. "And I promise I'm not asking so you're officially on the hook for stall mucking."

Rowan shook her head. "I already do most of the mucking."

"Exactly. I mean, I'm not going to pretend I'm not happy about the prospect of locking that in, but it's not why I'm asking, either."

"No? Why are you asking?"

The accountant part of her brain had a thousand reasons why it was the logical, cost-effective thing to do. But none of them were really the why. She might have shied away from admitting it not that long ago, but the last year with Rowan had changed things. Had changed her. "Because I'm completely in love with you and it feels like the next step in our happily ever after."

Rowan smiled. "That's a very compelling reason."

"So, your answer is still yes?"

"Yes."

Rowan wrapped her arms around Audrey and kissed her long and slow. The kind of kiss that was full of love and also full of promise. The goats bleated and Audrey would swear they were cheering. Audrey was, too, at least on the inside. And in her mind—somewhere, somehow—Ernestine was cheering, too.

About the Author

Aurora Rey is a college dean by day and award-winning lesbian romance author the rest of the time, except when she's cooking, baking, riding the tractor, or pining for goats. She grew up in a small town in south Louisiana, daydreaming about New England. She keeps a special place in her heart for the South, especially the food and the ways women are raised to be strong, even if they're taught not to show it. After a brief dalliance with biochemistry, she completed both a BA and an MA in English.

She is the author of the Cape End Romance series and several standalone contemporary lesbian romance novels and novellas. She has been a finalist for the Lambda Literary, RITA®, and Golden Crown Literary Society awards but loves reader feedback the most. She lives in Ithaca, New York, with her dog and whatever wildlife has taken up residence in the pond.

Books Available from Bold Strokes Books

Cold Blood by Genevieve McCluer. Maybe together, Kalila and Dorenia have a chance of taking down the vampires who have eluded them all these years. And maybe, in each other, they can find a love worth living for. (978-1-63679-195-1)

Greener Pastures by Aurora Rey. When city girl and CPA Audrey Adams finds herself tending her aunt's farm, will Rowan Marshall—the charming cider maker next door—turn out to be her saving grace or the bane of her existence? (978-1-63679-116-6)

Grounded by Amanda Radley. For a second chance, Olivia and Emily will need to accept their mistakes, learn to communicate properly, and with a little help from five-year-old Henry, fall madly in love all over again. Sequel to Flight SQA016. (978-1-63679-241-5)

Journey's End by Amanda Radley. In this heartwarming conclusion to the Flight series, Olivia and Emily must finally decide what they want, what they need, and how to follow the dreams of their hearts. (978-1-63679-233-0)

Pursued: Lillian's Story by Felice Picano. Fleeing a disastrous marriage to the Lord Exchequer of England, Lillian of Ravenglass reveals an incident-filled, often bizarre, tale of great wealth and power, perfidy, and betrayal. (978-1-63679-197-5)

Secret Agent by Michelle Larkin. CIA agent Peyton North embarks on a global chase to apprehend rogue agent Zoey Blackwood, but her commitment to the mission is tested as the sparks between them ignite and their sizzling attraction approaches a point of no return. (978-1-63555-753-4)

Something Between Us by Krystina Rivers. A decade after her heart was broken under Don't Ask, Don't Tell, Kirby runs into her first love and has to decide if what's still between them is enough to heal her broken heart. (978-1-63679-135-7)

Sugar Girl by Emma L McGeown. Having traded in traditional romance for the perks of Sugar Dating, Ciara Reilly not only enjoys the no-strings-attached arrangement, she's also a hit with her clients. That is until she meets the beautiful entrepreneur Charlie Keller who makes her want to go sugar-free. (978-1-63679-156-2)

The Business of Pleasure by Ronica Black. Editor in chief Valerie Raffield is quickly becoming smitten by Lennox, the graphic artist she's hired to work remotely. But when Lennox doesn't show for their first face-to-face meeting, Valerie's heart and her business may be in jeopardy. (978-1-63679-134-0)

The Hummingbird Sanctuary by Erin Zak. The Hummingbird Sanctuary, Colorado's hottest resort destination: Come for the mountains, stay for the charm, and enjoy the drama as Olive, Eleanor, and Harriet figure out the meaning of true friendship. (978-1-63679-163-0)

The Witch Queen's Mate by Jennifer Karter. Barra and Silvi must overcome their ingrained hatred and prejudice to use Barra's magic and save both their peoples, not just from slavery, but destruction. (978-1-63679-202-6)

With a Twist by Georgia Beers. Starting over isn't easy for Amelia Martini. When the irritatingly cheerful Kirby Dupress comes into her life will Amelia be brave enough to go after the love she really wants? (978-1-63555-987-3)

Business of the Heart by Claire Forsythe. When a hopeless romantic meets a tough-as-nails cynic, they'll need to overcome the wounds of the past to discover that their hearts are the most important business of all. (978-1-63679-167-8)

Dying for You by Jenny Frame. Can Victorija Dred keep an age-old vow and fight the need to take blood from Daisy Macdougall? (978-1-63679-073-2)

Exclusive by Melissa Brayden. Skylar Ruiz lands the TV reporting job of a lifetime, but is she willing to sacrifice it all for the love of her longtime crush, anchorwoman Carolyn McNamara? (978-1-63679-112-8)

Her Duchess to Desire by Jane Walsh. An up-and-coming interior designer seeks to create a happily ever after with an intriguing duchess, proving that love never goes out of fashion. (978-1-63679-065-7)

Murder on Monte Vista by David S. Pederson. Private Detective Mason Adler's angst at turning fifty is forgotten when his "birthday present," the handsome, young Henry Bowtrickle, turns up dead, and it's up to Mason to figure out who did it, and why. (978-1-63679-124-1)

Take Her Down by Lauren Emily Whalen. Stakes are cutthroat, scheming is creative, and loyalty is ever-changing in this queer, female-driven YA retelling of Shakespeare's Julius Caesar. (978-1-63679-089-3)

The Game by Jan Gayle. Ryan Gibbs is a talented golfer, but her guilt means she may never leave her small town, even if Katherine Reese tempts her with competition and passion. (978-1-63679-126-5)

Whereabouts Unknown by Meredith Doench. While homicide detective Theodora Madsen recovers from a potentially career-ending injury, she scrambles to solve the cases of two missing sixteen-year-old girls from Ohio. (978-1-63555-647-6)

Boy at the Window by Lauren Melissa Ellzey. Daniel Kim struggles to hold onto reality while haunted by both his very-present past and his never-present parents. Jiwon Yoon may be the only one who can break Daniel free. (978-1-63679-092-3)

Deadly Secrets by VK Powell. Corporate criminals want whistleblower Jana Elliott permanently silenced, but Rafe Silva will risk everything to keep the woman she loves safe. (978-1-63679-087-9)

Enchanted Autumn by Ursula Klein. When Elizabeth comes to Salem, Massachusetts, to study the witch trials, she never expects to find love—or an actual witch...and Hazel might just turn out to be both. (978-1-63679-104-3)

Escorted by Renee Roman. When fantasy meets reality, will escort Ryan Lewis be able to walk away from a chance at forever with her new client Dani? (978-1-63679-039-8)

Her Heart's Desire by Anne Shade. Two women. One choice. Will Eve and Lynette be able to overcome their doubts and fears to embrace their deepest desire? (978-1-63679-102-9)

My Secret Valentine by Julie Cannon, Erin Dutton, & Anne Shade. Winning the heart of your secret Valentine? These award-winning authors agree, there is no better way to fall in love. (978-1-63679-071-8)

Perilous Obsession by Carsen Taite. When reporter Macy Moran becomes consumed with solving a cold case, will her quest for the truth bring her closer to Detective Beck Ramsey or will her obsession with finding a murderer rob her of a chance at true love? (978-1-63679-009-1)

Reading Her by Amanda Radley. Lauren and Allegra learn love and happiness are right where they least expect it. There's just one problem: Lauren has a secret she cannot tell anyone, and Allegra knows she's hiding something. (978-1-63679-075-6)

The Willing by Lyn Hemphill. Kitty Wilson doesn't know how, but she can bring people back from the dead as long as someone is willing to take their place and keep the universe in balance. (978-1-63679-083-1)

Three Left Turns to Nowhere by Nathan Burgoine, J. Marshall Freeman, & Jeffrey Ricker. Three strangers heading to a convention in Toronto are stranded in rural Ontario, where a small town with a subtle kind of magic leads each to discover what he's been searching for. (978-1-63679-050-3)

Watching Over Her by Ronica Black. As they face the snowstorm of the century, and the looming threat of a stalker, Riley and Zoey just might find love in the most unexpected of places. (978-1-63679-100-5)

#shedeservedit by Greg Herren. When his gay best friend, and high school football star, is murdered, Alex Wheeler is a suspect and must find the truth to clear himself. (978-1-63555-996-5)

Always by Kris Bryant. When a pushy American private investigator shows up demanding to meet the woman in Camila's artwork, instead of introducing her to her great-grandmother, Camila decides to lead her on a wild goose chase all over Italy. (978-1-63679-027-5)

Exes and O's by Joy Argento. Ali and Madison really only have one thing in common. The girl who broke their heart may be the only one who can put it back together. (978-1-63679-017-6)

One Verse Multi by Sander Santiago. Life was good: promotion, friends, falling in love, discovering that the multi-verse is on a fast track to collision—wait, what? Good thing Martin King works for a company that can fix the problem, right...um...right? (978-1-63679-069-5)

Paris Rules by Jaime Maddox. Carly Becker has been searching for the perfect woman all her life, but no one ever seems to be just right until Paige Waterford checks all her boxes, except the most important one—she's married. (978-1-63679-077-0)

Shadow Dancers by Suzie Clarke. In this third and final book in the Moon Shadow series, Rachel must find a way to become the hunter and not the hunted, and this time she will meet Ehsee Yumiko head-on. (978-1-63555-829-6)

The Kiss by C.A. Popovich. When her wife refuses their divorce and begins to stalk her, threatening her life, Kate realizes to protect her new love, Leslie, she has to let her go, even if it breaks her heart. (978-1-63679-079-4)

The Wedding Setup by Charlotte Greene. When Ryann, a big-time New York executive, goes to Colorado to help out with her best friend's wedding, she never expects to fall for the maid of honor. (978-1-63679-033-6)

Velocity by Gun Brooke. Holly and Claire work toward an uncertain future preparing for an alien space mission, and only one thing is for certain, they will have to risk their lives, and their hearts, to discover the truth. (978-1-63555-983-5)

Wildflower Words by Sam Ledel. Lida Jones treks West with her father in search of a better life on the rapidly developing American frontier, but finds home when she meets Hazel Thompson. (978-1-63679-055-8)

A Fairer Tomorrow by Kathleen Knowles. For Maddie Weeks and Gerry Stern, the Second World War brought them together, but the end of the war might rip them apart. (978-1-63555-874-6)

Holiday Hearts by Diana Day-Admire and Lyn Cole. Opposites attract during Christmastime chaos in Kansas City. (978-1-63679-128-9)

Changing Majors by Ana Hartnett Reichardt. Beyond a love, beyond a coming-out, Bailey Sullivan discovers what lies beyond the shame and self-doubt imposed on her by traditional Southern ideals. (978-1-63679-081-7)

Fresh Grave in Grand Canyon by Lee Patton. The age-old Grand Canyon becomes more and more ominous as a group of volunteers fight to survive alone in nature and uncover a murderer among them. (978-1-63679-047-3)

Highland Whirl by Anna Larner. Opposites attract in the Scottish Highlands, when feisty Alice Campbell falls for city-girl-about-town Roxanne Barns. (978-1-63555-892-0)

Humbug by Amanda Radley. With the corporate Christmas party in jeopardy, CEO Rosalind Caldwell hires Christmas Girl Ellie Pearce as her personal assistant. The only problem is, Ellie isn't a PA, has never planned a party, and develops a ridiculous crush on her totally intimidating new boss. (978-1-63555-965-1)

On the Rocks by Georgia Beers. Schoolteacher Vanessa Martini makes no apologies for her dating checklist, and newly single mom Grace Chapman ticks all Vanessa's Do Not Date boxes. Of course, they're never going to fall in love. (978-1-63555-989-7)

Song of Serenity by Brey Willows. Arguing with the Muse of music and justice is complicated, falling in love with her even more so. (978-1-63679-015-2)

The Christmas Proposal by Lisa Moreau. Stranded together in a Christmas village on a snowy mountain, Grace and Bridget face their past and question their dreams for the future. (978-1-63555-648-3)

The Infinite Summer by Morgan Lee Miller. While spending the summer with her dad in a small beach town, Remi Brenner falls for Harper Hebert and accidentally finds herself tangled up in an intense restaurant rivalry between her famous stepmom and her first love. (978-1-63555-969-9)

Wisdom by Jesse J. Thoma. When Sophia and Reggie are chosen for the governor's new community design team and tasked with tackling substance abuse and mental health issues, battle lines are drawn even as sparks fly. (978-1-63555-886-9)